REDEMPTION LAKE

Other books by Monique Miller

Secret Sisterhood

Soul Confessions

REDEMPTION LAKE

MONIQUE MILLER

www.urbanchristianonline.net

Urban Books, LLC
1199 Straight Path
West Babylon, NY 11704

ISBN-13: 978-1-60162-938-8
ISBN-10: 1-60162-938-9

First Printing November 2009
Printed in the United States of America

10 9 8 7 6 5 4 3 2 1

Distributed by Kensington Corp.
Submit Wholesale Orders to:
Kensington Publishing Corp.
C/O Penguin Group (USA) Inc.
Attention: Order Processing
405 Murray Hill Parkway
East Rutherford, NJ 07073-2316
Phone: 1-800-526-0275
Fax: 1-800-227-9604

Dedication

To my Auntie "V"
Mrs. Valeria F. Cooper
Loving wife, mother, sister and aunt . . .
Miss you much!

Acknowledgments

First I'd like to thank the Lord above again, for using me as a vessel and giving me this gift of writing to share with the world.

To my family—Thank you to my parents, Mr. William H. Miller and Ms. Gwendolyn F. Miller, for your continued love and support. Thank you to my daughter, Meliah, for continuing to act as my publicist in training. Thank you also to my sister, Penny, for your continued encouragement, support, and prayers. Much love to my sisters, Denita and Christina, as well as my brothers, B.J. and Christopher.

There are so many people I'd like to thank for your support and encouragement during the writing of this, my third novel. Thank you to my family and friends for continuing to help me spread the word about my novels. Thanks to all of my author friends, especially Jacquelin Thomas, Toschia, Sherri Lewis, Suzetta Perkins, Titus Pollard, and Rhonda McKnight.

A special thanks to the members of The New Vision Writer's Group—Durham, NC—Jacquie, Brian, Angela, Suzetta, Sandy, Cassandra, Titus, Lesley, Karen, Pansy, Tonya, Pamela, and Shatoya.

A huge thanks to my agent, Sha Shana Crichton, for seeing something special in my writing so many years ago and taking me on as a client.

To my editors, thank you, Joylynn Jossel and Kendra Norman-Bellamy, for your sharp eyes throughout so many words and pages.

Readers, thanks so very much for your feedback.

Please continue to keep it coming. I appreciate your support and encouragement. I hope you enjoy this new novel with the new characters, and yes, Phillip and Shelby are back.

Urban Books and the Urban Christian family—Thank you, Carl Weber, Kendra Norman-Bellamy, and Joylynn Jossel for working so diligently with me and other authors you've taken under your wing. Thank you also to my fellow authors in the Urban Christian family for all the networking.

Again, there are so many people, and if I've left your name off, please know it was not intentional. Thank you so very much, _____!

Your Name Here

☺

Thank you all so much for your support!
E-mail me at: *authormoniquemiller@yahoo.com*
Visit my website at: *www.authormoniquemiller.com*

Prologue

Xavier & Charlotte Knight

Charlotte sat stolid and poker faced in the dining room chair. She had no idea how much time had passed since she'd sat down at the kitchen table. She'd long since stopped hearing the ticking of the kitchen clock. Spread across the table were copies of the papers—evidence she'd been gathering for months. Evidence proving that without a shadow of a doubt, her husband, Xavier, was cheating on her—not only in cyberspace, but as close as the neighbor three houses down.

The grandfather clock in her living room chimed three times. It was three o'clock. In just a little over an hour, he'd be home. To her surprise, she was unbelievably calm. No, maybe calm wasn't the right word. She was numb. After three months of collecting information about her husband's infidelity, nothing could surprise her anymore, not even the letter she'd just received from her doctor's office confirming she tested positive for gonorrhea. It was the last straw. She was no longer in denial.

In a little over an hour she'd confront him with some of the things she knew. Just enough to let him know that this time, there would be no forgiving him for the lies he continually told her. Charlotte wouldn't let him know all that she was privy to until the time was right.

෬   ෨

Travis & Beryl Highgate

"Don't worry, baby. I promise I'll be there waiting in the parking lot before you get off, to pick you up."

"Whatever, Travis. Don't make promises you won't be able to keep. Bye." Beryl hung the phone up before her husband could respond.

Beryl was tired of hearing his sorry lies and pathetic excuses. Her patience meter had hit its breaking point months ago. Why she kept giving him chance after chance to prove himself, she didn't know. Maybe it was because of her two little boys. Maybe it was because she wanted to believe in her husband so badly. She knew he had potential; he just needed to apply himself more. She spent so much of her time coaxing him and stroking his ego, it felt like she had three sons instead of two.

She was at her wits end. She didn't want to give up on their marriage, but he was draining her. Beryl could see it each time she looked in the mirror. And especially when she compared herself to many of the pictures she took before she got married five years ago. Her glow was gone. The sparkle in her eyes had fizzled. No matter how much she tried to bring the glow back with makeup, it didn't help. The stress was weighing on her like a lead weight.

Continually Beryl chastised herself for giving Travis chance after chance to lie to her or to selectively feed her little bits of information here and there. She was tired of feeling stupid and listening to his ever-growing lame excuses. He always had an excuse or answer for everything. Especially when it came to explaining why he couldn't seem to find and/or keep a regular job. She wished her woman's intuition had knocked her upside the head when she first met him.

Beryl's instincts had poked at her on several occasions letting her know some things were amiss. Too many things weren't adding up. And the financial miscalculations were causing checks to bounce, bill collectors to call, and most recently, the lights to be turned off.

After getting poked one time too many, Beryl finally had to admit, enough was enough.

☙ ❧

Nina and George Jones

"Pastor Jones, here is the report you asked me to pull. Do you need anything else?" Pastor Jones's secretary, Jennifer, asked.

"No, Jennifer; that will be all for now."

"Okay, sir." She turned to leave.

"Jennifer, if anyone calls, please take a message. I don't want to be disturbed for the next couple of hours."

"Okay, Pastor. What about Mrs. Jones?"

A sharp pain surged through George Jones's head. Wearily, he took a deep breath before answering. "If Nina calls, just let her know I'm taking care of some important business and can't be disturbed. I'll call her when I'm done."

Once his secretary left the office and closed the door, George flipped through the pages of the bank statements she had compiled for him. Seven months of statements had been neatly put together and categorized by date. They were some of the bank statements for the church.

He then pulled the keys out of his pocket and unlocked his file desk drawer. There he stored personal bank statements as well as credit card statements and various other pieces of billing information. He shook his head in dismay. The devil was attacking his and wife's lives in the three areas that meant the most. Satan was making blows against their marriage financially, spiritually, and sexually.

Nina had a problem with gambling, a crisis that was ruining their credit and affecting the church he founded and was currently pastoring. An end had to be put to the craziness.

George opened his Rolodex and pulled out a business card given to him by a friend. It was for an exclusive, secluded Christian couples' retreat in the mountains. Their marriage needed not only professional aid, but spiritual help also. Being the pastor of over two thousand members in the heart of Greenville, NC, he didn't want to risk anyone finding out about his marital problems. Especially not those in his circle of bishops and pastors.

Pastor George Jones picked up the telephone and called the number listed on the card. He and his wife needed to be present on the first available date. He hoped and prayed their marriage would make it until then.

Chapter 1

Phillip Tomlinson

Sunday: 3:00 P.M.

"Ready or not, Redemption Lake, here we come." Shelby ran her finger down the lines on the map representing the highway to trace the route they were taking.

"I've even got you calling it Redemption Lake." Phillip kept his eyes on the road as he joked.

Shelby nodded in agreement. "You're right. After a while, I won't remember it's really called Lake Turner."

Phillip smiled to himself, a grin covering his entire face.

Noticing, Shelby asked, "What's the big grin all about?"

"I'm just remembering when we first came up here five years ago. We didn't know what to expect. Just as I'm sure all the couples who are coming this week don't really know what to expect either."

"I know what you mean. A week long marriage retreat wasn't something I'd ever heard of anyone going to. All I knew was I was full of hope that the retreat would at least help us to strengthen our marriage," Shelby said.

"Me too. Little did either one of us know how God was planning to completely change our lives for the better; especially mine." Phillip continued to smile with fond memories. He had found his redemption at Lake Turner by accepting Jesus Christ as his Lord and Savior. And it had happened just outside of the same cabin they were about to drive to.

As if reading his thoughts, Shelby said, "Maybe it was because I'd been praying so long for you to get saved."

"You're probably right."

"Especially all those times I invited you to attend church with me, and you sat on the couch watching sports." Shelby laughed as she mimicked Phillip's voice. "'Say a prayer for me.'"

"It only took what, seven years of prayers for them to finally come true?"

"What matters is that the Lord heard my cry, and he answered me," Shelby said.

Phillip nodded his head.

Shelby laid her head on the headrest. "I still remember our time at this retreat like it was yesterday. I had such a wonderful time. Mostly because you got saved here, but also because of the wonderful couples we met that week."

"I am glad you suggested we come up a day early. It'll be nice to get in a little rest and relaxation before all the couples get here." He stopped speaking and sighed.

"What's wrong?"

It was uncanny sometimes how his wife could read him like a book. "I've been praying, and I don't know what to expect this time."

"What do you mean?" Shelby asked.

"I know God called me to do His work. And our history of marital problems a few years back is part of His plan for our coming back to this lake today."

Shelby nodded her head. "That's pretty deep. I hadn't thought about it like that. But I guess you're right. They say when someone goes through a storm, often the trials and tribulations aren't for them, but for someone else's life who will one day need to be touched; someone who will be helped by the testimony of that similar storm. A testimony that will tell how God brought them out."

"Bingo. I wish it were just that simple. But the true fact is that there are three couples' whose lives will be affected by this weekend. Three couples who will be looking for sound advice, guidance, and answers from me. That's a huge responsibility."

"It is," Shelby agreed. "And you'll do just fine. We've both been assisting with the couple's ministry at church, and I truly feel your education and background in marriage counseling has more than equipped you."

"I know, honey, but the couples in church know us. They trust us already." Phillip shook his head. "These people don't know us from Adam."

"They don't have to, honey. Trust in the Lord. He is worth more than someone already knowing you and your degrees put together. Don't forget that," Shelby encouraged.

"I haven't. Why do you think I've been praying so hard?"

"In a day or so, you have to start living on faith. Don't doubt the power God has put in you. As long as you let God lead you, this week will turn out fine."

Phillip shook his head. He agreed with his wife but didn't feel fully optimistic. From what he read in the couples' applications, there were some emotionally bruised husbands and wives about to seek his counsel. He didn't want to let any of them down, and he really didn't want to let down God.

"Okay, take this exit," Shelby said. "The directions say

to bear right off the exit then go 1.7 miles. We should start seeing signs for the lake."

Phillip drove as Shelby directed.

"Help me look for the little sign that says, THE LAKESIDE B&B," Phillip said.

"I hope they've made a bigger sign than when we were here five years ago," Shelby said. "How many times did we pass the little dirt road leading to the cabin that night?"

"Three I think."

"Well, at least it's daylight this time," Shelby said.

"The daylight is a plus. Man, it was pitch black out that night. I was barely able to see the little path with the headlights, especially with the thickness of the forest."

"If we hadn't seen the cabin when we had, we would have driven right into the lake."

"Don't remind me. Another ten more feet and you're right; we would have."

"I felt like I was on my way to Camp Crystal Lake, and Jason, from *Friday the 13th*, was going to jump out at any moment."

"I never told you, but I had been thinking along those same lines." Phillip chuckled.

"But when we stepped into the cabin and saw how warm and inviting it was, my fears soared right out of the window. Not to mention the warm greeting Reverend and Mrs. Nelson gave us."

"They are one of the sweetest couples I've ever met," Phillip said.

"They are. Too bad we won't get a chance to see them this time."

"Maybe we can come back up one weekend with the kids and spend some time with them."

"The reverend said he was going to leave the key under the mat, right?" Shelby asked.

"Yeah, he emailed me a detailed list complete with emergency numbers and their cell phone numbers, just in case."

"Hopefully all will go well, and we won't have to bother them. I'm sure they need a rest. They've been doing this retreat for over ten years."

Navigating the car with ease, Phillip said, "I was surprised when he asked me to fill in for him this week."

"See, even Reverend Nelson feels you are capable in conducting the retreat."

Phillip nodded his head, acknowledging what Shelby was saying.

"There it is." Shelby widened her eyes as she pointed to the sign for the B&B. "They did update their sign."

"I'd say."

The new sign was billboard sized.

Shelby laughed. "Hopefully none of the couples will arrive late at night like we did. But if they do, they'd have to be blind to miss that one."

"Blind as a bat," Phillip added.

Phillip lifted the welcome mat on the front porch of the log cabin. Just as noted in his email, the key was there.

He opened the front door, allowing Shelby to enter first. Once Phillip stepped inside, his memories were heightened as he heard the tick of the grandfather clock that sat next to the fireplace. And his nostrils were filled with the aroma of many years of long put out fires. Also noticeable was the smell of oak and pine from the various pieces of rustic furniture the Nelsons had decorated the house with.

Shelby took a deep whiff of air. "Smell that pine. The smell brings back so many memories."

"In a way it feels like we never left." Shelby turned

and gave Phillip a loving hug, and he embraced her in return with a tight squeeze.

"I love you so much, sweetheart," he said.

"I love you too."

After looking around the cabin and checking each room to make sure everything was in order, Phillip said, "Let's get the bags out of the car."

They retrieved their luggage as well as what felt like hundreds of bags of groceries that Shelby had packed that morning.

Once all was unloaded, Phillip rummaged through a couple of the grocery bags on the kitchen cabinet. Picking up a bag of cheese doodles and a bag of pretzels, he said, "Uh, honey, did you forget something?"

"Like what?" Shelby asked.

"Like the real food. What are we going to do, snack the whole trip?" He held up a container of dip. "And what are we supposed to eat for breakfast?"

"Now, Phillip, baby, you should know me better than that. I've got it all under control. You worry about the counseling and ministering of the couples, and I'll take care of everything else." Shelby smiled.

"I know you are the hostess extraordinaire. But baby, the closest convenience store is at least ten miles away. And the closest grocery store is probably twenty miles away. Our schedule will be pretty tight. We won't have time to run to a restaurant every day for food," Phillip said.

Shelby pointed to the bags on the floor. "What do you think is in all these bags?"

Upon opening each one, Phillip's eyes widened as he gazed at the rest of the food. The bags held juices, eggs, bread, breakfast meats, cheese, milk, coffee creamers, jams, jellies, condiments, fresh vegetables, and fruits.

Then she led him to the deep freezer, and when Phillip opened it, he saw that it was filled with boxes of frozen entrees.

Shelby looked at Phillip and said, "Do you think we have enough food, or do I need to make a quick run to the store before our guests arrive?"

Phillip shook his head, finally understanding. "No baby, you've got this under control."

"You should know I have your back."

"What's the deal with all that food in the freezer?"

"You are not the only one who has been in contact with the Nelsons. I spoke with Mrs. Nelson, and she helped me coordinate ordering the meals for the week. Mrs. Nelson is so wonderful and so detailed that she gave me a sketch of where everything is kept in the kitchen. I told her what kinds of meals I was planning and what ingredients I'd need, and it looks like everything I need is accounted for. Plus she gave me a secret weapon."

"A secret weapon?" Phillip's eyebrows rose with curiosity.

"Yep. I won't have to slave over meals all week," Shelby said.

"What kind of secret weapon?" Phillip asked.

"Don't worry about that." Shelby grinned.

"You are something else," Phillip said.

"I know. Now don't concern yourself with trivial things like the food. And except in the matter of counseling, I'll take care of everything."

"Everything?"

"Yes, everything," she reiterated.

Phillip looked toward the fireplace. His wife followed his eyes.

"Okay, maybe not everything," Shelby said.

The previous winter, Shelby had tried to light the fire in

their fireplace and had ended up almost burning down their house. It took months for the smell of smoke to finally dissipate.

"You can take care of a fire if we need one." Shelby tapped the tip of Phillip's nose with her index finger. "But I assure you if you need anything else, I'll take care of it."

"I will probably need your help during some of the sessions," Phillip said.

Shelby pulled his head down and kissed his forehead and lips. "I've got you, baby."

Phillip sighed with more relief. "Now let's unpack the rest of our stuff and get this place ready for tomorrow. I want to relax a little tonight."

"You got that right. I didn't come up here a day early just to look in the freezer," Shelby said as she winked her eye.

"I believe that's everything." Phillip looked down the checklist that the reverend had sent him.

"I'd say we're ready for tomorrow."

Shelby assisted Phillip in putting the welcome packets together, which held each couple's agendas, notepads, pens, nametags, and a set of keys for their respective bedroom.

After setting the packets up on the bar separating the kitchen from the dining room, Shelby asked, "Did you call the kids?"

"No, not yet."

Shelby pulled out her cell phone and pressed the number two for her speed dial. "I'll check on them and let Mom know we got here okay."

As Shelby proceeded to call and check on their children, Phillip's mind drifted back to the upcoming retreat. While Shelby was filled with hopeful anticipation, he was feeling differently. He'd actually read the couples' applications, and from what he had seen it was probably going to take a miracle to help some of them.

He shook his head thinking if God could form the earth in less than seven days, surely the Lord could turn the lives of the couples around in that timeframe also.

Chapter 2

Phillip Tomlinson

Sunday: 8:30 P.M.

Phillip held Shelby in his arms as they cuddled on the floor in front of the couch. Before them sat an unlit fireplace. "This is nice. I'm glad we came a day early."

"That's what I was thinking," Shelby said. She nuzzled her face under her husband's neck.

"I wonder how the couples are faring as they prepare for their trip here," Phillip said.

"What do you mean?"

"From what I've read in their profiles, they all have some pretty heavy problems. When we first came, we'd been having problems too, but we'd pretty much resolved them."

"I see what you mean. There's no way I could have imagined taking this three-hour trip with you while we were at the height of our troubles," Shelby said.

"I know you couldn't. You had a hard enough time riding with me across town from the hospital to our house. You wouldn't look at me and barely spoke to me. And when I touched you to try and help you get out of the truck, you acted as if I'd poured hot coals on you."

Shelby pulled her body away a couple of inches. "Don't remind me. That whole time in our marriage was a nightmare for me."

"Sorry, I don't want to rehash everything, but it's in my spirit. If we are going to help the couples, we can't forget what we went through. They're all going through some pretty tough times right now. For some of them, this may be their last hope."

Phillip thought about their retreat days. Even though their marriage was already on its way back to being mended, the other two couples who'd attended were ready to throw in the towel.

"Can you believe we're actually going to be the one's helping three new couples get their lives back on track? They'll be looking to us; well, mainly you, for guidance," Shelby said.

"Don't discount your contribution in helping these families. They'll want my spiritual and professional guidance, but actions speak louder than words. They'll be watching both of us, trying to see how we relate to each other. I think that's why this retreat is set up the way it is—with a married couple counseling other married couples."

"I guess you're right. I know I wouldn't have wanted to hear any advice on what I should and shouldn't be doing from some single person with just a little book knowledge and no marital experience."

"So we agree. Your being here is just as important as my being here," Phillip said.

"Agreed," Shelby said.

Phillip's stomach growled.

"Sounds like somebody's hungry," Shelby said.

"Actually, I'm not."

"Are you still fasting?"

"No, I was officially off my fast as of sundown. When

the Lord put it in my spirit to fast, I wasn't sure why, but now I understand. I needed to fast and pray about this upcoming week. Working with these couples won't be a walk in the park. To them, their worlds are coming to an end, and I have to help them understand that with God, anything is possible. They can overcome the hurdles which the enemy has placed before them. They need to understand that what they are going through is only a test."

"Do you know what kind of specific problems these couples are having?"

"I've read their profiles, which state in black and white, the surface problems for which they've applied to come here. But it's the underlying problems that concern me most. But if you don't mind, I'd like to keep the specifics to myself—for now anyway. I want you to be able to look upon everything with fresh eyes. I'd like to see what you're able to pick up on as the retreat progresses. Then we'll talk about it."

"Sounds like a good approach to me. I can do that," Shelby said.

Phillip's stomach growled again.

"Let me fix you something light to eat. How about some cheese and crackers? Or some grapes?"

"Yeah, sounds good," Phillip said.

"Which one? The cheese and crackers or the grapes?"

"Fix a little of each. Can I have a glass of water too?"

Shelby kissed him again on the forehead and said, "You can have anything you want, my dear." Then she sat up to head for the kitchen.

Phillip pulled her back closer and kissed her again. "Ummm, keep kissing me like that, and I'll skip the food."

Reluctantly, Shelby pulled back. "Hold that thought. I am a little hungry myself. You know the saying 'we can have our cake and eat it too?' Well, we can eat a little and then explore on your idea." Shelby hopped up and took long strides to the kitchen. "We have this whole cabin to ourselves. I just wish it was cold enough for us to have the fireplace burning. And that faux fur rug over there is calling our names. Tonight, you, my dear, can have your cake and eat it too."

"With all the icing?" Phillip asked with anticipation.

Shelby sauntered back to her husband on the couch and kissed him long and hard on the lips. "With all the butter cream icing you want, baby."

Phillip shook his head as if he'd been in a daze. "Whew, I can't wait."

"Hold that thought." Shelby returned to complete her task of making snacks in the kitchen.

Phillip retrieved a thick down comforter and two fluffy pillows from their bedroom closet. He spread the comforter out on top of the rug, then placed pillows comfortably under his elbows and arms as he lay down on the floor.

When Shelby returned with a plate full of club crackers, cubed cheese, and red grapes, she nodded her head in approval. "You are anxious for your icing, aren't you?"

"You bet I am. And I'm not counting, but I do believe it's been at least two weeks since I've had any cake."

"That's not my fault," Shelby said. "You've been so focused on so many other things I guess I wasn't that high on the priority list."

Phillip nodded his head. "I know baby, and I apologize, but don't worry, I'll make up for it tonight."

Shelby sat next to him on the comforter and plucked a grape off the vine and tickled his lips with it. Then in one fluid movement she popped it into her mouth.

"Hey? Why are you teasing me?"

"I thought you said you weren't hungry."

"I'm not. I mean, I wasn't, but I am now. And I want to get all this eating over so I can have my cake," Phillip said.

Shelby plucked another grape, this time placing it between her teeth. She moved in closer, giving him a nose-to-nose kiss, just before thrusting the plump purple grape into his mouth.

Phillip savored the sweet juice as it burst. "Umm baby. Keep that up and we won't be finishing any of this food."

Without saying a word Shelby picked up a cube of cheese and traced his lips with it, then just as she'd done with the grape, she fed it to him.

"Quit playing, girl."

Shelby laughed. "Sorry, honey. I'll stop. Let's eat, I'm hungry."

In a famished manner, they both ate. Once they were finished, Shelby said, "Oh yeah, I almost forgot. I've got a surprise for you."

"What?"

"Wait a minute, you'll see."

Shelby left their pallet on the floor and headed for the kitchen. When she returned, she had two beverage glasses and a bottle of chilled sparkling grape juice in her hands.

After sitting back down next to him, she gave Phillip the honors of popping the cork and pouring the wine. Before taking a sip, they held their glasses up to toast.

"What would you like to toast to?" Phillip asked.

"Okay," Shelby cleared her throat. "To God blessing our marriage of twelve years. Even for the ups and downs. And blessing us so much that He placed us here to help three families with their marriages."

She lifted her glass toward Phillip's, and he did the same. "I can toast to that."

They sipped their fizzing juice.

"My turn." Phillip paused and looked dead into his wife's eyes. "To the most wonderful wife a man could ever be blessed with." He held his glass up to toast.

Shelby smiled, toasting with him. "Thank you. Keep this up and you're going to make me blush."

Phillip took another sip of his juice. "Give me a few more minutes, and I am going to make you do more than blush."

Shelby downed her remaining juice. "Well, what are you waiting for?"

At that, Phillip downed the remainder of his glass also, then took Shelby's glass to place them both on the coffee table.

He pulled her in to his arms, planting a passionate kiss on her lips. After what seemed like minutes had passed, Shelby pulled away with an abruptness that caused Phillip to jump.

"What's wrong?" Phillip asked.

"Did you hear that?"

"What?"

"I heard something outside."

"No, I didn't hear a thing. What you probably heard was my heart beating through my shirt."

Shelby rolled her eyes at him. "I could've sworn I heard something."

"You're just a little scared because we're out here all alone by this dark lake."

"You have to admit it is a little scary. It's pitch black out, and there probably isn't another person for miles."

"Maybe a quarter of a mile at best. This lake is full of cabins. Phillip flexed his muscles. "Don't worry baby, I'm here to protect you."

Shelby sighed with resignation.

Again Phillip pulled her into a kiss-filled embrace. "We'd better enjoy the quietness and time alone now, because tomorrow the people will start filing in."

"Are you ready to wade through the surface and figure out what everyone is really trying to say in order to get to the bottom of their problems?" Shelby asked.

"I'm definitely ready to help guide them on the road to recovery. It's the wading through part that'll be the hardest. You know there are three sides to every story: his side, her side, and the truth."

Just as Phillip stopped speaking, they heard footsteps on the porch, and then a knock at the front door. Both Phillip and Shelby stared at one another questioningly.

"Who the heck could that be?" Shelby whispered.

Part I

His Side

Chapter 3

Travis Highgate

Sunday: 9:30 P.M.

"It's pretty dark out here, Travis. It doesn't even look like anyone's here. Are you sure this is the right place?" Beryl Highgate asked. Travis could hear the fear and underlying anger in her voice.

"It's the right place; just trust me," Travis said, knowing that was the wrong thing to say; especially since his wife didn't trust anything that came out of his mouth. Hence the reason they were out in the middle of nowhere trying to get their marriage back on track.

Looking around the side of the wrap around porch, he saw a dark colored SUV. "See? Look over there." He pointed at the truck. "Someone must be here."

Beryl crossed her arms. "This is supposed to be a couples retreat and there's only one other car here? Something doesn't seem right." Disbelief seeped from his wife's voice.

Travis felt something wasn't right either, but he dared not say it. He *had* probably messed up. And the worst thing he could do was give Beryl the satisfaction of telling him what a failure he was.

Without saying another word to her, he returned to the cabin's front door and knocked. From inside he heard shuffling. *Good. Sounds of life.*

"It's freezing out here," Beryl said. "The temperature must have dropped at least ten degrees since we got on the road."

After a couple of minutes, Travis wondered what was going on inside the cabin. With a firmer knock, he tried again to get someone to come to the door.

"Who is it?" A male voice asked from the other side of the door.

Awkwardly, Travis said, "Uh, this is Travis Highgate. My wife and I are here for the couples retreat."

There was a pause. "Hold on a just a second," Travis heard the voice say from the other side of the door.

A minute later he heard the lock on the double doors click, and once opened, he looked up to see a man of African-American decent staring down at him. Travis was only five feet six inches tall, and this guy was well over six feet.

With a raised eyebrow and a forced smile, the guy said, "Hi, uh, come on in."

The man moved aside to let them into the cabin's foyer.

"Man, it's dark out there," Travis said. "We didn't think that dirt path we took down here was ever going to end." He looked over at his wife. Trying to lighten her spirit, he laughed, and then said, "She thought we were going to end up driving into the lake.

"And I was right. We did almost drive into the lake." She rolled her eyes at Travis, then extended her hand to the man. "Hi, my name is Beryl Highgate."

The man nodded his head. "I apologize for my rudeness. I'm Phillip Tomlinson." He shook both of their hands.

A woman sitting on a couch in the living room waved.

Phillip gestured toward her. "And that's my wife, Shelby."

"Hi," Shelby replied. The greeting was friendly, but the look on her face, as well as her attire, suggested they weren't expecting anyone anytime soon.

Travis wondered if it were because of the late hour. "Sorry we're so late. I know we were supposed to check in by five o'clock, but we ran into a few snags trying to get here."

Out of the corner of his eye, Travis saw Beryl roll her eyes again.

"Actually," Phillip said, "you are early—a day early."

Beryl pivoted her body and folded her arms in a fluid movement. "We're a day early?"

Even though Beryl was asking Phillip the question, Travis saw that she was staring directly at him.

"Yeah. Did you get the letter I sent with your itinerary? Check in is tomorrow from nine o'clock until ten o'clock."

Travis felt the familiar pressure of Beryl's finger nudging into his arm. She cocked her head to the side. "Did you hear that? We're a day early."

Refusing to face his wife, Travis said, "Yeah I heard him. I made a little mistake."

Out of the corner of his eye, Travis saw Beryl roll her eyes as she turned her attention back in Phillip's direction. "We got the letter all right, or shall I say my husband did. Then he lost it and swore we were supposed to be here today. So—what are we suppose to do now?" She tapped her foot as she spoke. "Do we have to drive four hours back home?"

"I made a little mistake, baby," Travis said.

She huffed. "Save it for someone who believes you. Honestly, Travis, just admit it. Once again you've gotten it all wrong. Your lack of attention to detail and irresponsibility has gotten us into yet another mess." Beryl shook her head. "We've only been here five minutes and already you're batting a thousand—a thousand in the red that is."

"Honestly, I—"

Beryl cut Travis off clinching her dreadlocks with both hands and saying, "Travis, I really don't want to hear you speak another word right now. That lake isn't too far from here, and so help me God, if you keep it up, I *will* throw you in."

"Whoa, whoa," Phillip said. "I'm sure it was a simple mistake. And you don't have to drive back home. Why don't you go ahead and get your bags, and my wife and I will show you to your room."

Travis smiled inwardly. This brother was all right. He was glad Phillip had his back.

Beryl waved her hand and rotated her neck. "Oh believe me, it wasn't a simple mistake. That's why we're here. It's always a simple mistake or a simple misunderstanding with Travis."

Travis looked toward Phillip again for help.

"And that's okay. Like you said, that's why you're here, and we're here to help you," Phillip said with reassurance.

This was gonna be all right. The brother had his back. *We brothers got to stick together,* Travis thought.

Shelby joined them in the foyer. "Yeah, Beryl, I can show you your room while your husband gets the luggage."

Travis realized the sister had jumped in to help Beryl. Under his breath, he mumbled, "I guess all is fair in love and war. If the sisters want to unite then let them go ahead and try."

Beryl clutched her purse and walked toward Shelby.

"Hey, man, let me put my shoes and coat on, and I'll help you get your luggage," Phillip offered.

"Thanks, man. I appreciate it," Travis said. He was relieved to be out of his wife's presence for a few minutes. She'd been nagging him on the whole trip up about how he needed to find a job as soon as they got back. That was . . . if things worked out at the retreat.

Travis stepped out onto the porch as he waited for Phillip to get his coat and shoes. He popped a piece of Big Red gum into his mouth. The temperature seemed to have dropped a few more degrees, but he'd rather be outside in the cold than to continue standing next to Beryl, with her poking and prodding accusing tone, reminding him of his incompetence.

Again, from Beryl's point of view, he was just proving what a failure he was. And for the life of him he couldn't understand why she even applied for the retreat in the first place. She was always complaining about money and how he needed to get a steady job. He couldn't count the times she'd nagged him about needing help with the mounting bills. But Travis knew Beryl kept a stash of money for rainy days because every time she claimed they needed money for a bill or something for the kids at school, those things hadn't gone lacking, and he hadn't given her a dime.

If he could just land the right job with the right boss, then everything would be fine. That would shut her up. But she'd have to be patient, just like he was.

Her latest thing was to nag him about getting some marriage counseling. When she told him that their pastor at church had mentioned a marriage retreat in the mountains, he'd almost laughed in her face. They didn't need marriage counseling; she just needed to give a brotha a break from all the nagging.

And when she told him they'd have to pay a little over a thousand dollars to attend, he'd told her he didn't have any money. But magically, Beryl had come up with the funds, and before he knew it, they were signed up to go.

On numerous occasions she'd threatened to kick him out if he didn't start pulling his weight around the house. But she'd never followed through on those threats, so he really wasn't too worried. Travis knew this was just another ploy to try to push him into doing something he didn't feel like doing. So to appease her, he decided to go along with her wishes for the retreat.

The more he thought about it, he actually started liking the idea, thinking of it as a week long vacation. He'd put forth just enough effort to keep her from nagging him—for at least seven days.

Phillip joined him on the porch. "Wow, it has gotten colder out here since we arrived."

Travis rubbed his hands together for warmth. "It has. And I didn't bring a heavier jacket. Hopefully we won't get snowed in or anything."

"I doubt it. Don't quote me on this, but I really don't think it snows this early in the fall. But then again, you know how unpredictable North Carolina can be with its weather; especially in late September."

Phillip gave him a pat on the back. "Try not to beat yourself up about everything that just happened in there. It's all working out. My wife and I just happened to come up a day early, and you didn't find an empty cabin."

Travis sighed. "It was a simple mistake. And she's just blowing it all out of proportion. Thanks again, my brother, for rescuing me."

"Just try to relax. I'm sure she'll calm down in a few minutes. Maybe she's just a little tired from the long trip you took." Phillip gave Travis another hearty pat on the back.

This Phillip guy was nothing like what Travis expected. When Beryl first told him about the Christian Couples' retreat, he immediately thought of some cult-like retreat in the mountains. He'd seen enough of the movies where the couples go get advice and counseling from a preacher and end up following the supposable man of God to the ends of the earth only to end up killing themselves in some sort of sacrifice.

Phillip wasn't a deranged looking old man. He actually looked like he was a couple of years younger than Travis. And the cabin, from what he'd seen of it so far, didn't look like any of the cult camps he'd seen in the movies. And he'd seen just about every horror movie there was. One of his favorites was the *Friday the 13th* series.

"Man, I wish that were true. I know she's going to leave me. She says this retreat is my last chance. After this, if I can't get it together, she's going to leave." Travis hung his head. After a minute or so, he raised it back up. "Well, there's nothing I can really do. Guess I'll let her do what she wants."

"Look, Travis. I'm sure you and your wife have probably tried to fix the problems you've been having yourselves, without someone neutral to intervene. You need someone with fresh eyes to help you see what's going on. And that's why you're here."

Travis nodded his head saying, "Right, right." What Phillip was saying did make a great deal of sense to him.

"Don't give up so easily. The next seven days may be the most crucial in your marriage. So you'll need to be at your best, just like the rest of us will need to be. And if you and your wife really want to make this marriage work, then you can. You may just need some professional and spiritual intervention. And my wife and I are here to help you with that."

"I hope so," Travis said, shaking his head in doubt.

"Come on, let's get those bags out of the car," Phillip said.

Phillip followed Travis to the early model Toyota Corolla. As Travis opened the back door, it creaked in need of oil. He pulled out a large duffle bag and a smaller travel bag, which he handed to Phillip. Then he retrieved two suitcases from the trunk.

"That's it. Thanks, man," Travis said.

"No problem."

Travis stalled, hesitant to return to the cabin. "About what just happened in there . . . I'm really sorry about that display."

Phillip placed a firm hand on Travis's back. "Look, what's going on with you and your wife is real. This is not the place where you have to, or need to put up false pretences. So face it. It is what it is. Stop worrying about how you look this weekend or what anyone else is going to think. It isn't about us or them, it's about you and your wife."

Travis felt as if a weight had been lifted off his shoulders.

"Be real, be yourself. That's the only way you'll be able to help your family," Phillip added.

Travis sighed. "I'll do anything it takes. I love my wife so much, and I don't want to lose her." It was true; he did love his wife, but just wished she would stop nagging him all the time, treating him like he was a kid or something.

With a firm pat on Travis's shoulder, Phillip said, "Why don't you go inside and try to relax? It'll probably get pretty intense around here soon enough. You don't need to be worrying yourself tonight. Go get some rest. You'll need it."

"I'll try," Travis said.

Phillip led him back into the cabin and to his and his wife's assigned room. Upon entering, Travis paused, looking at the separated twin beds on opposite walls of the room. "It doesn't seem like this retreat really wants couples back together if they've got us sleeping in separate beds."

"Actually, this cabin is used for various retreats. Not just for married couples. The beds can be pushed together."

"Oh," Travis said, knowing Beryl would probably welcome the idea of them having space away from each other.

Phillip chuckled. "I was bemused by the separated beds the first time I came to this retreat too. The reverend that ran the retreat told me I'd be surprised by how many couples first come here welcoming the idea of not having to sleep in the same bed with their spouse."

"I'll just bet my wife was glad to see the beds were apart," Travis said under his breath. In the other room, Travis heard the women laughing and talking. He couldn't think of anything funny at the moment.

"Why don't I let you get settled," Phillip suggested.

Travis nodded his head. "Thanks again, man."

"No problem," Phillip said.

After Phillip left, Travis commenced to unpack his duffle bag. He let out a huge moan when he realized he'd forgotten to pack socks and underwear. Actually, as he thought about it, it was Beryl's fault he didn't have any underwear. She normally packed his bag for him, but during one of her you-make-me-sick moments, she'd told him to pack his own stuff. So he had. And because of her, he didn't have any extra underwear or socks.

He shook his head in frustration. As soon as Beryl came into the room, he'd tell her what happened and she'd think of a solution—she always did. She'd probably packed some extra things for him anyway knowing he might forget something.

Now that was funny. She was always trying to teach him something. Travis laughed. This was another one of her teaching moments.

Chapter 4

Travis Highgate

Monday: 6:21 A.M.

Travis was jolted awake by the slamming down of what sounded like his wife's toiletry bag on the dresser. Then light spilled onto his face after he heard the curtains being slung open. He slid the pillow over his head.

When he heard the bathroom door close, he slipped the pillow off of his head and pulled his cell phone off the nightstand. He groaned realizing it was only a little after six o'clock in the morning. Beryl knew he didn't like loud noises in the morning and hated it when the lights were turned on in his face while he was still sleeping— much less the curtains and blinds being opened.

Travis figured Beryl was just trying to get back at him and get under his skin. He wasn't going to let it work. He felt if she wanted out of the marriage, it would be because she gave up on him.

He turned his back to the window in order to get more rest. Her plan to get him agitated was only going to back-fire. He'd stay in bed just to spite her. That would get under *her* skin. He hoped she'd be dressed and out of the room by the time he did get up.

It seemed as though only a few minutes had gone by when Travis heard Beryl rustling around the bedroom. After she left and closed the bedroom door, he again pulled the pillow from over his head to peek at his cell phone.

He shot up in the bed. It was already 8:50 A.M. "What in the world? Why didn't my alarm go off?" he asked himself aloud, knowing the answer before he finished the thought. He hadn't set the alarm on his phone. "Shoot!"

Travis threw the covers off. "I've got to get myself into gear." Hearing his voice out loud helped clarify things for him. He picked up the duffle bag and rummaged through it for some underwear, a pair of jeans, and a T-shirt. Then he remembered not packing any extra underwear, and he also remembered how things had gone the night before when he and Beryl finally decided to call it a night.

When Beryl came back into their room to turn in for the night, he'd told her about his packing mishap. She'd looked at him with a smirk on her face that asked *what do you want me to do about it?* He'd asked if she'd packed any underwear or socks for him and she said she hadn't.

Then she'd had the nerve to tell him for what seemed like the millionth time that she was not his mama, and he needed to stop waiting for her to do everything. Travis had heard it so many times he was desensitized to the words coming from her mouth. She whined on and on about how she wasn't appreciated and how she wished he'd take some initiative when it came to their marriage. After a while she sounded like the teacher on the Charlie Brown cartoon. The words bounced off his ears without comprehension.

After she finally paused from her insistent babbling,

Travis asked her what he was supposed to do about not having a change of underwear. She'd told him he'd have to drive an hour to a real store to buy some, or the ones he was wearing would have to be washed each night.

He'd thanked her for the idea and asked where he should put the underwear for her to wash. Beryl had laughed so hard that she'd had to hold her stomach. When her laughing finally calmed down, he'd asked what was so funny.

She'd rolled her eyes and told him to wash his own funky underwear. After that she continued to laugh as she pulled out her sketchpad to draw. As she sketched God knows what, Beryl's laughing continued in intermittent spurts until she'd finally gone to bed and fallen asleep.

Travis had been so upset with her that he'd jumped in the bed and went to sleep also. Now he stood with his jeans, T-shirt, toothbrush and toothpaste, but no clean underwear. He was wearing the only pair he had.

The bathroom was small but functional. Luckily someone had not only added some feminine touches, but had also supplied them with washcloths and towels. He hadn't even thought about packing any. Again that was something Beryl normally did. He was a grown man, and knew how to pack. And anyway, it seemed to be turning out okay. There was fresh linen folded neatly on a shelf over the toilet, and next to the medicine cabinet, Travis saw a mini blow dryer hanging from a hook.

Travis nodded his head. "This might actually be all right." All he'd have to do was wash the underwear and dry it with the blow dryer. In no time at all he'd have a pair of clean underwear. Beryl's attempts at trying to make him look bad weren't going to work.

He began humming a tune to the song "Lovely Day" by Bill Withers. He hummed the song throughout his shower and shave. And after washing and drying his only pair of underwear, he emerged from their room looking and feeling refreshed. That was until he rounded the corner to the dining room, and his eyes fell on the scowling face of his wife.

Travis dropped his head and looked the other way. All of a sudden, his stomach dropped as if it were speeding a downward slope of a roller coaster at Disney World, going fifty miles per hour. His stomach was the only thing that felt like it was at Disney World, because the rest of his body felt like he was in a low budget horror movie, starring as the villain.

"Good morning, Travis," he heard the voice of Shelby call from the direction of the kitchen. Travis hoped the woman had witnessed the angry looks Beryl had shot toward him.

"Would you like something to eat?" Shelby asked. Her voice was soft and sweet. Travis remembered a time when Beryl's voice had been just as soft and sweet. Not now though. Now her voice was hard and gruff. He wondered when it had changed, but couldn't put his finger on a specific time or date.

"I'm not hungry right now," Travis said. "My stomach is doing a few cartwheels."

Beryl rolled her eyes at him again and left the kitchen to sit in the living room.

"Do you have anything to take?" Shelby asked with obvious concern. "We've got a first aid kit."

Beryl's leaving the room had allowed the flipping of his stomach to subside. "Naw. It will probably pass with a little time."

"We also have some ginger ale in the pantry if you need some," Shelby offered.

"Thanks. If I need any, I'll get some," Travis said.

He took a deep breath, trying to think of a way to pass the time and stay out of his wife's way in the process.

Phillip entered the kitchen with a coffee cup in his hand. "Good morning, Travis. How'd you sleep, man?"

"Okay, I'd say. I guess I overslept." Travis laughed.

"I slept like a baby," Phillip said. "You want some coffee?" he added while heading back to the coffee pot to pour another cup.

"Nah. My stomach's been doing a few cartwheels."

With concern on his face Phillip asked, "Sorry to hear that, man. You need to take something?" He looked to his wife. "Shelby, do we have anything for an upset stomach?"

Shelby answered, "Yeah, I already asked him if he needed anything."

"Sorry, babe. I should have known." He turned his attention back to Travis. "You know my wife's a nurse, right?"

Travis shook his head. "No. I didn't know that."

"If you get sick, definitely let her know; only use me as a last resort." Phillip chuckled.

Travis nodded his head, and when Phillip headed back toward his bedroom, Travis was left to awkwardly stand in the area between the dining and living room. With the "Lovely Day" song still running through his head, he stepped closer to the living room. Hoping for the best, he attempted a conversation with Beryl. With a pleasant lovely day voice, he said, "Good morning."

She was obviously upset with him for some reason, and he didn't want to upset her any further.

Again, she'd pulled out her sketchpad and was drawing. Without looking up she said, "Morning. I see you finally decided to get up."

"Yeah, guess I overslept," Travis said, grinning.

"Guess you did, as always."

Travis closed the distance between he and his wife and sat on an opposite chair. With his voice lowered so that Shelby and Phillip wouldn't hear, he said, "Come on, Beryl. We haven't even been here twenty-four hours, and you're already honing in on me. Can't a man have a break? Relax and let's just enjoy this trip."

Beryl stopped drawing, huffed, and looked over at him. "When are you going to get a clue? This isn't a relaxation trip. We are here for a purpose; hopefully to save our marriage. And as for your break, I've given you more than enough breaks." The volume of her voice elevated with each sentence. "That's your problem. All you want to do is relax, and I'm sick of it."

Embarrassed, Travis motioned his hands in a 'calm down' gesture saying, "Come on, honey." He looked around to see if anyone was listening. He didn't see anyone. "Calm down. All I was saying was—"

Beryl cut him off, and with her ever rolling head and waving hand, she said, "I know what you were trying to say. But I really don't think you understand how important this trip is. This is it, Travis. If this doesn't work out, it's over."

"You don't really mean—"

Beryl cut him off again. Her eyebrows furrowed. "I do. Try me. If some things aren't resolved, you'll see just how serious I am."

Travis opened his mouth to speak again, but closed it when he heard a heavy knock at the cabin's front door.

Chapter 5

Travis Highgate

Monday: 9:13 A.M.

Travis watched as a woman and man, looking to be in their mid-thirties, entered the cabin. The man held the door for his wife and stood back so she could enter. The husband's smile was warm and radiant as he looked around the cabin. His face looked very familiar. And in an instant, Travis recognized who he was. With unbelieving eyes, his mouth dropped.

Walking into the cabin was the infamous Pastor G.I. Jones, a true soldier for the Lord. Pastor Jones was known for his often riveting sermons and the crowds who attended his services. He was also the author of at least five books that Travis knew of, and had appeared in a couple of Christian based movies as the pastor of a church.

Travis had only seen him once in person, but he might as well have been watching him on television, because he'd been sitting in the nosebleed seats of a coliseum with hundreds of other people. He hadn't been fortunate enough to sit in the floor seats with the thousands below them who'd arrived early.

Now he was in the same room with the man he'd admired so much. Whenever he could, Travis used to watch the pastor's broadcast. That was when they still had cable; before Beryl had put her foot down, saying that they couldn't afford a cable bill with all the other things they had to pay for.

And even though Beryl hadn't come right out and said it, Travis knew she was implying he was the reason they didn't have enough money. She was just trying to make him feel bad, but he wasn't going to let it bother him.

Lucky for him, she'd warned him about the deal on the cable. So before she had it turned off, he'd purchased VHS tapes and recorded his favorite shows. He'd ended up with eleven tapes, each filled with eight hours worth of programming. So whenever he wanted to watch cable, he just popped in a tape and it felt like they still had it.

He'd even had a few of Pastor G.I. Jones's programs. He'd watched the sermons so much he could almost recite them verbatim. Travis couldn't believe he was actually almost face to face with Pastor Jones. He wondered if the pastor was going to be one of the facilitators for the retreat. He knew it couldn't get any better.

Travis guessed they probably had to keep secret the fact that G.I. Jones would be here; otherwise there would probably be hundreds of people trying to register. He was going to meet a celebrity. Man, he was glad Beryl had made him come. This was truly going to be a trip of a lifetime.

Standing next to G.I. was his wife, Nina Jones. The first lady—as she liked to be called—looked just as she had on television. People often said she was the African American version of Tammy Faye Baker—only on the heavier side. She could have easily been a nice plus sized model. Nina's hair was always done in some sculptured style, and her makeup literally looked as if it had been painted on by the same makeup artist as Bozo the clown. But unlike the woman he saw smiling and grinning on television whenever the camera was squarely on her, she entered the room with a sneer sprawled across her face as she looked around the cabin without saying a word. She wore a black and silver jogging suit that definitely didn't look like it had been purchased at Wal-Mart, his favorite shopping place. She also had silver matching accessories and what looked like a brand new pair of black tennis shoes.

Travis looked down at his old, worn sneakers. He wished Beryl had bought him a new pair before they came on the trip. He'd tried to get her to loan him some money to buy some new shoes and a pair of jeans he'd been eyeing at Wal-Mart, but she mumbled something about there not being any money for him to buy new jeans and sneakers—again looking at him like it was his fault.

"Good morning," G.I. Jones said.

"Oh, good morning," Shelby replied. "I'm Shelby Tomlinson. Are you here for the couples retreat?"

Travis watched as Shelby's mouth dropped wide open with recognition, realizing who was standing before her.

"Ah, yes." G.I. strode toward Shelby to shake her hand. "I am George Jones." He gestured toward his wife. "And this is my wife, Nina."

Nina's smile was weak as she nodded her head and said, "Hi." Unlike her husband, she didn't move closer to greet Shelby and didn't acknowledge that anyone else was even in the room.

Dismissing the anger Beryl had previously been emitting, Travis took the opportunity to introduce himself. Turning toward G.I., he extended his hand and made his own introductions. "Hi. G.I.; I'm Travis, and this is my wife, Beryl."

Beryl, who'd had her face buried in her sketchpad, finally looked up to see what the spectacle was all about.

Then her eyes widened. She dropped her pen and did a slight wave to the Joneses.

G.I.'s handshake was strong and firm. "Nice to meet you. And please call me George." George sighed. "I wish it were under better circumstances, but such is life."

Nina Jones rolled her eyes at her husband's comment.

Travis was glad he wasn't the only one who had a wife with a rolling of the eyes problem, but Nina looked so weird doing it. It seemed out of character for the woman he'd seen so many times on the television.

Then after making a point of rolling her eyes at Travis again, Beryl finally spoke with a simple, "Hello."

Travis didn't understand his wife sometimes. Here she was sitting in front of a high man of God, and all she could say was hello? She hadn't even stood or offered to shake the man's hand. Travis was embarrassed by his wife's nonchalant attitude.

George nodded his head toward Beryl. The preacher wore a baseball cap with the letters JC embroidered on it. Travis had seen the emblem standing for Jesus Christ on baseball caps and jerseys. He himself owned a baseball cap with the same emblem, but just like his worn sneakers, the cap had seen better days. Unlike his underwear, Travis had packed his beloved baseball cap. But now after seeing the crisp new looking one George was wearing, Travis decided he'd leave it packed in the duffle bag.

Phillip emerged from the side of the cabin with the bedrooms. "I thought I heard someone come in." With a brisk pace, Phillip greeted George and shook his hand. "Hi, I'm Phillip Tomlinson, and this is my wife, Shelby."

"Yes, we've met your wife. I'm pretty sure you already know us," George said.

"And I must say, it's good to meet you, Pastor Jones."

"Please, please . . . you can all call me George and my wife, Nina. We aren't G.I. and the first lady here."

Nina had finally made her way next to her husband. She extended her hand to Phillip to offer a limp handshake. "Hello."

"Yes, Pastor Jones . . . I mean, George. We know of your ministry. We watch your broadcast on Saturday nights whenever we can get a chance," Phillip said. "How was your drive up?"

"Not too bad. Even though the church is in Greenville, we actually live about forty-five minutes from the church, closer to this side. So we didn't have to come through the Greenville traffic."

"Well, it's truly an honor to meet you both," Phillip said.

"I was just telling Travis and Beryl here I wish our meeting here was under better circumstances. So this week, I'm not G.I. or Pastor. I am just George. My wife and I are here to learn as your student, Phillip."

Now Travis understood George's statement. When he'd first said he'd wished they were there under better circumstances, Travis thought the man meant he wished he didn't have to be there helping couples in trouble. But now it was clear that G.I Jones and the first lady were having troubles of their own. Now he knew why Nina was acting so ill. She was probably embarrassed about having to be there.

Travis also noticed that after the pastor repeated his statement about their circumstances, his warm demeanor took on a distant coolness, making it seem like a cloud had just blocked the sun.

Nina spoke again. "Sorry to interrupt, but is there a bathroom around here anywhere?" She continued to sneer as she looked around the cabin.

"Oh yes. Right this way," Shelby said. Acting as if she hadn't noticed the snobbish attitude Nina Jones had, Shelby continued speaking. "You can use the one in the room you'll be calling home for the next few days."

With that said, Nina followed Shelby to the bedroom.

"George, let me help you get your luggage, and then I'll get your registration packet," Phillip said.

"Sounds good," George said.

Figuring two men were enough to gather the bags, Travis didn't volunteer to help. Instead, his stomach began to growl. The diversion of George and Nina's arrival had allowed his stomach to settle. Turning toward the kitchen, he grabbed a plate and some food.

As he sat and ate, he watched as Phillip and George made three trips to the SUV George and Nina owned. The luggage had the initials GJ and NJ on them—most with the initial's NJ. It reminded Travis of the scene from *Coming To America* when Eddie Murphy's luggage was unloaded on the streets of Queens, New York. He shook his head wondering how much luggage two people needed. They were only going to be there for a week, and as far as he knew, except for a few trails near the cabin and the lake, they weren't going anywhere else.

As Beryl had described it, this was to be an intense couples' retreat, trying to help people's marriages get back on track. He wondered what kind of problems Pastor G.I. Jones and the illustrious First Lady Nina were having. And why of all the places they could probably afford to go, they were there on Lake Turner with the common people. Especially since one of his hottest and best selling books, *I Do, I Don't*, was about helping married couples keep things on track.

But after looking at all the luggage that had been tracked into the cabin, Travis figured maybe George was just tired of all the baggage, especially all the baggage he'd just brought in belonging to his wife. Travis snickered at the pun he'd made.

So far, he hadn't seen anything intense except for the intense way Nina looked around like something or someone might touch her pretty new clothes or mess up her spritzed up hairdo. It was actually comical to him; so comical, in fact, that a laugh escaped his lips.

A glare from Beryl made him stop. But if things kept up the way they were, he was going to have a lot of fun people-watching the whole week.

Just as Travis finished eating his breakfast, there was another knock at the door. When the couple didn't enter, Travis took it upon himself to be the greeter, curious to find out who was behind door number two, like the whole thing was a game show.

Upon opening the door, Travis's mouth dropped for the second time that morning. He was face to face with the man who was known across Central North Carolina as "Pretty Boy." This guy reminded him of the guys on campus known as the Kappas he'd seen when he used to visit his sister in college.

They called the Kappas pretty boys also. These guys, a part of an African-American fraternity, were always clean cut and had an air of what some would call arrogant sophistication. But Travis just called it being stuck up.

Residents of Central North Carolina called the man standing in the front door Pretty Boy X. Pretty Boy was a well-known car salesman, often appearing as an actor in a series of ongoing soap opera like commercials. The commercials were always cleverly written and enthralling to watch with their action scenes and intriguing cliffhangers. Travis also enjoyed the commercials with the pretty girls who sometimes literally hung off the salesman.

Even though Travis was a married man and would never think about cheating on his wife, he still appreciated a beautiful woman. He'd never touch another woman, but he sure enjoyed looking—there was no harm in that.

After seeing the annoyed look on Pretty Boy's face, Travis finally said, "Hey, come on in." He extended his hand, receiving a firm handshake in return.

Standing just behind the man was a woman. Travis guessed it was Pretty Boy's wife. Travis greeted her also, then moved aside so they could enter. Introducing himself he said, "I'm Travis, and this is my wife Beryl."

Pretty Boy introduced himself. "I'm Xavier, and this is my wife, Charlotte."

Charlotte nodded her head and offered a weak smile. She was pretty enough with her petite frame, pecan brown skin, and short haircut which resembled Halle Berry's when she wore hers short. She reminded him of some of the women conducting business at the bank whenever he cashed his unemployment checks. Her demeanor wasn't exactly snobby like the women at the bank, but she did seem just a little withdrawn.

In a line up, he would not have picked out the woman as being Pretty Boy's wife. She didn't look anything like the women he often had salivating over him in his many commercials.

Continuing his host duties, Travis said, "Phillip or Shelby should be back out in a few moments. They're the ones running the retreat."

Xavier looked around the cabin, and his wife did likewise. He then pulled out his Blackberry, holding it up in the air for a signal. "Man, I can't believe I can't get reception out here."

Xavier's wife huffed out a breath of air and headed toward the living room area, finding a seat opposite Beryl. Charlotte shook her head in a how-am-I-going-to-get-through-this-week motion. Beryl replied with a silent I-know-what-you-mean-girl gesture with her arms and shoulders.

Travis shook his head. Pretty Boy X was here with his

wife. He'd wondered if Charlotte was a former pretty girl from any of the commercials. Then he wondered how long the two had been married. Many of the commercials showed women in skimpy clothing clawing at Pretty Boy, in hopes to get a good deal on a car.

Travis knew the women were only actors, but they weren't good actors. Travis knew good actors from all the many movies he had seen in his lifetime. It had to be hard for Xavier's wife to see so many women groping at her husband for the whole world to see—or at least the thousands of people in Central North Carolina.

Phillip reentered the room with George following. "Oh, I thought I heard more voices," Phillip said.

Travis changed hats and took it upon himself to be the liaison. "Phillip, this is Xavier and Charlotte."

Phillip crossed the room and greeted Xavier with a firm handshake. He then did the same walking over to greet Charlotte.

Shelby and Nina returned to the room. "Oh, hello," Shelby said to the new couple.

Phillip did his own introductions for everyone, then assisted Xavier in gathering the luggage from his car. Afterward, the new couples officially checked in, receiving their registration packets and room keys.

Travis knew God was smiling on him. The upcoming week was going to be better than any sitcom or movie he could've ever imagined. He was on a first name basis with two celebrities—who just might have some juicy secrets to reveal.

Chapter 6

Travis Highgate

Monday 11:00 A.M.

Once all the couples were settled, Phillip asked them to join him at "The Round Table" located in a meeting room, situated next to the dining area. The Round Table would comfortably seat up to ten people. With only eight of them, no one would be cramped.

This meeting room reminded Travis of boardrooms he'd seen in the movies. The Round Table had a glass top over it and meeting chairs like the kind executives sat in when conducting management type business. This meeting space, set out in the middle of nowhere, had all the amenities any New York City's high-rise office might have. The only difference in this room was that the window faced a lake instead of the Empire State Building.

As the couples took their seats, it was obvious to Travis that Beryl didn't really want to sit next to him. He also noticed that the Charlotte woman didn't really want to sit next to Pretty Boy X either, as if fearing they would possibly touch. But since all the other people were strangers, they ended up opting to at least have one familiar person sitting next to them. In the end, they sat in a boy/girl pattern.

Once they were all settled, Phillip began to speak. "First of all, I'd like to officially welcome each of you to this couple's retreat. As you know, my name is Phillip, and this is my wife, Shelby. While I'll be the main one facilitating this retreat, my wife and helpmate will be assisting with some of the lessons.

"Let me also say right now that I am not an expert on the subject of marriage. Meaning I don't have a PhD in the subject. I actually have an MBA. And let me also say that my wife and I aren't perfect. But we, like you, did go through some of our own problems in the past." Phillip paused to let the words sink in.

Travis wondered why they were sitting at this retreat with people who weren't experts, and how in the world this couple was going to be able to help.

"Shelby and I had some very rocky times, which took us to the brink of divorce. So the minister who normally conducts this retreat, with the blessing of my own pastor at home, felt Shelby and I would be viable candidates to assist in helping you three couples in your quest to get things back on track.

"Your journey this week should be a jolt in starting the process of getting things back on track. After this week is over, you can continue to seek professional counseling closer to your homes." Phillip smiled. "Professionals who may or may not be married, may or may not have had any marital problems, and lastly, someone who may or may not even be a Christian."

Again Phillip paused for his words to sink in. "So prayerfully, this week long retreat will give you some basic Christian marriage fundamentals which will help sustain you through the next weeks, months, and years to come; hopefully 'til death do you part."

Travis wondered what kind of problems Phillip and his wife could have had. They looked so happy together.

Even happier than he'd seen other couples who had marital problems and decided to stay together.

Phillip smiled again. "Okay, with that said, I'd like to take care of some rules and a few of the housekeeping notes that are detailed in your registration packets."

Each person flipped the registration packet open to the first page.

Phillip continued. "Please make sure you are each mindful of everyone else when it comes to cleanliness. Some of you may be used to others cleaning up after you, and if your spouse chooses to do so here, then so be it. But if your spouse does not, everyone is responsible for helping keep this cabin clean throughout the week."

Travis knew Beryl would get a kick out of that statement, especially since she was always fussing about him leaving things all over their house. A glance at Beryl confirmed his thoughts as she turned her body toward him, blatantly folding her arms and rolling her eyes.

Phillip continued as if he hadn't noticed the display. "We are all adults, and some very adult issues will be brought up. Make sure you respect the others here. Some of you may have different opinions about certain things, but you need to respect the other person's feelings and beliefs.

"Also remember that my wife and I are here to help you. We can only do this if you're open-minded and willing to participate in the discussions and exercises we'll be doing."

Trying to focus on something besides his wife's deliberate staring, Travis saw that he wasn't the only one who might have a problem with some of the things Phillip was saying. Xavier sat staring at the back of his own wife's head during Phillip's statements. His wife, Charlotte, had suddenly seemed to find fascination in a cobweb nestled in the corner ceiling of the room.

"Things may get a little hot at times, and this cozy little cabin could get even cozier as the days go by; maybe in some cases, too cozy for comfort. So as much as possible, please respect each other's personal space," Phillip said.

Travis saw that Phillip must have hit the nail on the head for Mrs. Nina Jones. Nina sat stolid in her seat as if gauging the distance between her husband on the one side and Phillip sitting next to her on the other side. She clearly didn't want her personal space to be invaded.

"The next topic is regarding confidentiality," Phillip told the couples. "In your registration packet, you'll also find a confidentiality statement. I'll ask you to all to sign it. Upon reading it, you will basically see that it states what goes on in this cabin, stays in the cabin. Many personal issues will come up during this retreat, and we don't want anyone to feel as if they have to guard their words or hold back things, for fear someone may talk about it outside later.

"This next part isn't in your packets," he continued, "but let's go ahead and talk about the obvious elephants in the room. George is a very well known pastor. And Xavier is also pretty well known across this state. There are many people who'd love to exploit information gained from this retreat about these men to use for their own personal gain." Phillip paused. "I'm sure this isn't the case for anyone in this room. But just as a precaution, I'll need you to carefully read the statement, and then pass them back to me."

Phillip stopped again, allowing everyone to read the entire confidentiality statement. After each person signed, they passed it over to him.

Phillip was serious about everyone being confidential. The statement said that anyone in violation could be sued. Travis wasn't the type to gossip. Well, actually, he was, but he could be confidential if need be. A couple of his friends would have jumped at the chance at having some tabloid news to report, especially if the price was right. Heck, if the price was right for him, he had to admit that he might throw the tabloids a few bones. But then he shook his head inwardly. Being sued, even if he didn't have any money, just didn't seem like a good idea.

"Does anyone have any questions?" Phillip asked. "If not, we'll move on. If you haven't already done so, please make sure you read over everything else in your packets. They are pretty detailed and should answer many of the questions you may have.

"Now, to get the ball rolling, let's have a little ice-breaker." Phillip opened a folder and pulled out a stack of sheets. "Please take one and pass the rest around the table."

After each person had a copy of the sheet, Phillip continued with his instructions. "On this sheet you'll find twenty questions. Please answer each completely and honestly." Then Phillip handed out pencils. He looked at his watch and said, "You have fifteen minutes to complete this, starting now."

Travis looked down at the questions on the page thinking they were pretty simple. The first question was easy. His favorite color was green, the color of money. The second question asked what his favorite pastime was. Travis loved watching television, and he loved movies; especially comedies. If he could, he'd watch movies all day long. That is if Beryl didn't nag him so much. His movie collection consisted of over three hundred fifty videos and DVDs, many of which he'd seen several times.

The third question threw him for a loop. It asked what he liked most about his job. Well, Travis didn't have a job and hadn't had one for over three months. And contrary to his wife's beliefs, he had been trying to find employment. He'd applied for several jobs, but they hadn't embraced his possibility of being a valuable employee. And the two years of college he had completed while trying to obtain his degree in general studies hadn't seemed to help on any of his applications.

So he decided to think back to the last job he held that he actually liked. Blockbuster. His employment at the popular video store was a dream job. He was surrounded by so many movies on a daily basis that it felt like he was in Disneyland. Not only did he get paid for working there, he got paid to talk about the thing he loved the most: movies. Travis's knowledge was pretty extensive before he started working at Blockbuster, but after his four month stint there, his knowledge increased exponentially.

Employees were able to get movies at a discount and checkout several movies for free each week. Travis had never actually been to Disneyland, but figured the way he felt each day he went to work was probably equivalent to the way a child would feel the first time he met Mickey Mouse or Cinderella.

Travis answered the next few questions with ease. They asked for his favorite meal and his favorite dessert. Then there was the question of his favorite movie. Without hesitation, he wrote *The Good, the Bad and the Ugly*, with Clint Eastwood, who was by far, one of his favorite actors.

There were other simple questions like did he have any sisters or brothers and if he were on a deserted island, what three things would he like to have with him. Other questions were a little more personal, seeking information about their wedding dates, full names, and height.

Travis smiled because he finished before anyone else.

He also relaxed a little more, figuring that if the rest of the week turned out to be as easy as the questionnaire, things would be a breeze.

Within a few moments, Charlotte finished her sheet also. And then she seemed to become fascinated with the eraser on her pencil. Beryl had completed some of the blanks, and was now going back to some of the ones she'd skipped.

Xavier placed his pencil down and seemed to be pleased with whatever he had written. Phillip and Shelby were filling out the sheet also. Travis thought this was pretty odd seeing as they were the ones conducting the retreat. But he hunched his shoulders and didn't dwell on it much.

George Jones was the next person to finish, and his face was completely peaceful as he looked back over his answers. And within the next few minutes, everyone except Nina, George's wife, was finished. From what Travis could see, the woman hadn't even written half the answers.

Seeing that Nina was not finished with her sheet, Phillip gave her a few more minutes, then finally asked, "Nina, do you need a little more time?"

Nina looked up as if perplexed by the question. "Oh, is everyone else finished already?" Her face flushed red. "Uh, just give me another minute or so."

She looked back down at her paper, and within a minute, filled out eight or so of the other questions she'd still had blank.

Travis, as well as a couple of the others at the table, sat dumbfounded. Why had it taken her almost twenty minutes to finish the first half of the questions and only sixty seconds to complete the rest? Even her husband, George, seemed a little baffled.

Phillip was the only person at the table who appeared not to have noticed the twilight zone moment. "Okay, everyone," he said. "Here is the second part of this ice-breaker." From the same envelope he pulled out another sheet. "Has anyone ever heard of the game Mad Lib?"

Beryl nodded her head. "I have. I used to love playing it as a child." She smiled. "We used to take Mad Lib with us on family trips. My brothers and sisters used to get a kick out of the funny answers." Beryl looked down at the paper she'd just been handed. "So this is sort of like Mad Lib, huh?"

Phillip nodded his head. "Yep, sort of. It has the same concept."

"Cool," Beryl said.

George and Shelby nodded their heads in agreement with Beryl.

"My sentiments exactly. I thought this would be a cool way to break the ice with everyone," Phillip said. "Even Shelby didn't know what the exact icebreaker was going to be."

"I love Mad Lib. I used to do them with my brother when we were little too," Shelby said, directing this statement to Beryl.

"Now for those of you who may be rusty in playing this game and the others of you who don't know how to play, this is what you'll do next." Phillip held out his blank copy of the second sheet to show it to the others. "On the second sheet I just gave, you'll find a narrative; a narrative that has twenty blanks that need filling in. Under each blank you'll find a number. For example, the first blank has the number ten under it. Transfer the answer you wrote on number ten on your first sheet to the narrative on your second sheet. Do this for each of the blanks so that you can complete the narrative. Your answers will help us get to know you all a little better, and depending on what you've written, some might even be a little funny."

Travis eagerly started filling in the blanks. The others did the same although some not as eager. This portion took only a fraction of the time it took to fill out the first page.

While reading over her completed paper, Beryl chuckled a little. She'd even looked over at Travis a couple of times and smiled instead of scowling at him. Travis didn't know what to think, but was glad something had finally made his wife happy. Only one day in, and this retreat had already started to work wonders.

George and Shelby looked over their papers and chuckled a little also. Travis read over his own narrative and thought it was pretty cut and dry. He couldn't see anything funny about what he had written. Nina sat stone-faced. Her sheet must have lacked life also.

"Okay." Phillip looked around. "Who would like to be the first to read theirs?"

Beryl continued to chuckle without being able to stop long enough to answer. Everyone else just looked around.

"Now don't everyone volunteer at once," Phillip said.

"I'll go ahead and read mine first," Shelby said, then proceeded to read.

After she finished reading her narrative, George volunteered to read his; followed by Xavier. The entire time Xavier read his short story, Travis noticed that Charlotte continued to direct her attention away from her husband.

Travis wondered what must have made Xavier's wife mad enough to not only ignore her husband, but make her stop speaking to him all together. Even though Beryl was mad at him, she still voiced her ever-mounting complaints and gripes to him. That's how he knew she still loved him. In Travis's mind, she wouldn't continue to take so much time out of her so called busy schedule to talk to him if she didn't care. Even if it were mostly complaining that she was doing.

As the others read their narratives, Travis wondered why Beryl kept chuckling. What he had written was sort of cute in a Mad Lib way, but nothing to snicker at. Before he knew it, the only two people left to read their sheets were he and Beryl. She had calmed down long enough to speak and decided to read hers. As she read it, she again started to laugh, but it was controlled enough for her to be able to finish reading it.

Travis looked around at the others at the table. Their expressions mirrored what he was thinking. What in the world was so funny? Nothing she had read seemed to warrant the laughing spell she was having.

Travis picked up his paper. "Okay, I guess it's down to me. Here it is; the life and times of Mr. Travis Wayne Highgate."

Beryl made an effort to calm down and direct all of her attention to Travis. He was glad she had. Her laughing was getting old and a little annoying.

Once he finished telling the group about his life, Beryl busted out laughing again. Travis was baffled. What was so funny about what he'd just read? It was pretty straight forward; not boring, but there was definitely no reason for his wife to be acting like Chris Tucker had just finished a set. Beryl excused herself to go to the bathroom, and Travis was relieved. By now he figured everyone at the table must have thought he'd married a lunatic straight from the nut house. He had no idea what had gotten into his wife.

He hadn't seen his Beryl laugh in a while. He'd actually forgotten how much she used to laugh when they first met. Her laughing was so intense that he'd actually heard her before he saw her. He was at the video store looking to see if they had put any new movies to sell in the previously viewed bin. He wanted to purchase a few to add to his growing collection.

Travis was deciding between a western and a comedy when he heard a woman laughing so loud that a few of the other patrons glanced her way. From where he was standing, he couldn't see the source of the laughter, but after it didn't let up, curiosity got the best of him. He maneuvered to the other side of the bin so that he could look in the direction the laughter was coming from.

When he did, his eyes fell upon one of the most beautiful women God had created. He couldn't believe that loud laugh was coming from such a petite woman. Her skin was smooth and the color of the chocolate mocha hot cocoa he liked to drink whenever it was cold outside. Her hair was pulled back in a ponytail of dreads, which fell midway to her back. Her eyes were the color of coal, and her laughing smile lit up the room. So much so that even the people who kept glancing at her didn't seem to mind and even smiled themselves.

She was on her cell phone, and the person on the other end of the line must have been saying something amusing.

Travis wasn't sure how long he stared at the woman, but he couldn't stop until he watched her leave through the front door. After a few moments, he awoke from his dazed staring and ended up deciding to buy three movies at the three for twenty-dollar discount.

As he left the store and headed for his car, he heard a woman's voice mumbling something in frustration under her breath. Looking toward the source, he saw the hood of a car raised, and the same woman who had mesmerized him moments earlier was shaking her head. She was off the phone, and the laugh lines were gone.

Travis looked up toward heaven and said a quick thank you to God. He was sorry the woman was having some sort of car trouble, but he was glad he'd have the opportunity to speak with her.

He quickly opened his car door and flung his bag in the passenger's seat. Then he slammed it and made a B-line for her raised hood.

Walking up behind her, he said, "Excuse me, Miss. Is there anything I can help you with?"

Startled, the woman turned around to face him. "Oh, you scared me." She placed her hand on her chest and started to breathe heavily.

"Sorry. I didn't mean to. It looked like you might need some help," Travis said. As he gazed upon the woman's face close up, she looked even more beautiful to him. Even in her frustrated state.

After a second, her breathing slowed, and she spoke. "Sorry, I'm just a little jumpy. This darn car has been giving me a run for my money." She kicked the tire and wiped sweat beads, which were starting to form on her forehead."

"What seems to be the problem?" Travis asked.

"Name something," the woman said. "Some oil valve thing has been leaking for a while. The breaks have been making this awful grinding sound, and now," she paused to look down at the ground, "there's green stuff leaking underneath."

Travis looked down and saw the green ooze she was referring to. "That green stuff is antifreeze."

"Great," the woman said, again wiping her forehead. "What does that mean?" She peered down under the hood of the car.

"I don't know. I need to look at it a little more closely. Your radiator might have busted, or it might be a leak in the hose or something," Travis told her.

"That's going to be a lot of money, isn't it? Then I'll have to get it towed somewhere." She shook her head. "Great . . . just great."

"Hold on," Travis quickly said. "Let me take a look before you work yourself up too much more." Travis touched the cap of the radiator to see how hot it was. It was warm to the touch. Then he touched the engine to make sure the engine wasn't too hot. Finally, he knelt down on the ground to try and determine where the leak might be coming from. Not seeing anything, he carefully opened the cap to the radiator, hoping it wasn't hot enough to burn him.

Once the cap was off, he peered into the hole and didn't see any fluid. He took a careful look at each of the hoses connected to the radiator. Seeing what he thought might be the problem he asked, "You wouldn't happen to have any antifreeze in your trunk, would you?"

Dumbfounded, the woman shook her head.

Travis looked around and spotted an AutoZone a ways down the street. "I tell you what, I'll run down the street to that AutoZone and get some antifreeze. Hopefully that will help me find out where this leak is coming from. Why don't you just wait inside the store and get out of this hot sun."

The woman huffed in frustration as she kicked the car again.

"Calm down. I'll be right back. Go inside and cool off a little bit. I'll be right back," Travis said.

The woman opened her purse. "How much does antifreeze cost?" She pulled out her wallet.

"I got it. Don't worry about it. Buy yourself some water or lemonade or something," Travis said.

She looked at him with skepticism. "Are you sure?"

Travis closed the hood and said, "Yep. Now go ahead inside, and I'll be back in a few minutes."

"Okay, thanks." Her demeanor softened a little. She closed her car door and locked it, then headed back inside the video store.

Travis returned to his late model Acura. Upon cranking it, he saw the bright red gas light indicating that his tank was close to empty. Instead of driving down the street to the AutoZone, he really needed to head toward the nearest gas station. He turned the ignition back off. He'd have to run down to the auto parts store instead.

Wearily he looked down the street to where the AutoZone was located, it was only about a half a mile away, but he was going to have to cross six lanes of traffic to get to it.

Looking up at the sun, he wiped his brow and took a deep breath before venturing off toward the store. After a great deal of heavy panting from the speedy walk/jog down the road, Travis finally reached the store. He welcomed the cool air blowing down on him from the air conditioner.

Scanning the aisles, he spotted the antifreeze. He picked up a bottle and saw it was seven dollars and twenty-nine cents and pulled his wallet out. In it he found the twenty dollars he knew was in there. He also looked behind old credit cards and his license to see if he had tucked away any other money that he might have forgotten about.

No such luck. This was the last twenty dollars. It was supposed to last him another two days until his next unemployment check arrived. After paying for the antifreeze he'd only have a little over ten dollars, not to mention the fact that his car was on empty.

"Maybe I should have let the woman give me some money for the fluid," he mumbled to himself.

He picked up two bottles of cold water and made his purchase, all the while shaking his head. Then he sprinted back to the video store. Once he returned to the woman's car, she quickly joined him outside. Travis's face and clothing were drenched.

"You ran all the way down to the store?" the woman asked with obvious concern.

"Yeah," he said, panting even though he was trying hard not to.

"It must be a hundred degrees out here," the woman said.

Travis wiped his forehead for what seemed like the hundredth time. "No problem. I figured I'd run down there real quick instead of fighting traffic." He pulled the bottles of water from the bag he was carrying and handed her one. "Here you go."

"Thanks." She took the bottle, opening it to take a couple sips.

Travis opened his too, but didn't stop drinking until the bottle was empty. The cold water felt good trickling down his throat.

"Pop the hood for me," he said.

After she unlatched the hood, Travis opened it and took the radiator cap back off. Then he poured antifreeze in. "Okay, crank the car up for me."

The woman did as instructed, and Travis looked around the radiator and hoses to see if he could detect a leak. Relief set in when he saw that one of the hoses had a crack in it, and her radiator hadn't busted. It was going to be a quick, cheap, relatively easy fix.

"You can shut the car off and come look at this," Travis said.

She came around the front of the car, and Travis showed her the source of her problem.

"Aw, man. What am I supposed to do now?" the woman asked.

"Well, the good news is that it isn't your radiator. That

alone will save you time and money. It's just a hose, which won't cost you much."

The woman nodded her head. "Okay I guess that is good news. But now I've got to get this car moved somewhere for it to be fixed."

Travis smiled. "Not necessarily. I'll be right back." He pulled his keys back out and headed for his trunk. After opening it, he rummaged through it for the pocketknife he kept in his fishing kit. After locating it, he returned to the car and commenced to pulling the hose away from the clamp it was attached to.

"Your hose is dry rotted and it's leaking where this clamp is connected," Travis said as he worked.

After he pulled the hose and clamp off, he cut away the part of the hose where the hole was located, and then reattached the slightly shorter hose and clamp. He then poured antifreeze back into the well of the radiator.

"Go ahead and crank your car again," Travis told the woman.

She did as he requested, and Travis surveyed the hose to again assess for any leaks. A couple of minutes passed before he fully determined that the problem had been fixed.

"There you go, Miss. You're all set," Travis said.

"What?" the woman asked, perplexed. "All set?"

"You can drive now. It is only a temporary solution, so try to get it to a mechanic soon. But for now you're good."

"Are you serious?" the woman asked.

"As a heart attack," Travis replied.

The woman smiled for the first time since he'd heard her laughing on the phone. Travis didn't know if he'd ever see that beautiful smile again.

"Thank you so very much." She touched her purse.

"Are you sure I can't give you something for all your help?"

Travis thought about the few dollars he had in his pocket and the empty gas tank that was awaiting him. But he wanted to impress the woman. He'd just ask his sister for a few dollars when he got home. She'd give him some money—like always.

"Nah, helping out a beautiful woman is enough gratification for me," Travis said.

The woman smiled at the compliment. "Well, thanks."

Travis wasn't sure if she were thanking him for fixing the car or for the flattering remark.

"I can't thank you enough." She paused for a moment. "Hold on a second." She rummaged through her purse until she found what she was looking for. "Here you go."

She handed Travis two pieces of paper. They were coupons for a free cup of coffee and breakfast sandwich at Hardee's. "I know it isn't much, but I'm a manager at Hardee's, and those are a couple of coupons, you know, for maybe you and your girlfriend."

The way the woman said it, he wondered if she were just fishing and flirting with him. "No girlfriend and no wife. No kids either, if you're wondering," Travis said, taking the bait.

"Oh . . . okay. So maybe one day when you need a caffeine fix or a sandwich for breakfast, they'll come in handy."

"Thanks." Both coupons would definitely come in handy in his current situation. As the woman turned toward her car, Travis thought quickly. He still didn't know who this beautiful young woman was. "Hey, I didn't get your name."

Turning, the woman smiled again, teeth wide and gleaming. "I'm sorry; how rude of me." She extended her hand. "My name is Beryl."

Travis shook her hand and held it a little longer than needed. "Beryl. That's different." Travis released her hand, though she hadn't seemed bothered by his extended handshake.

"Yeah, sort of like Cheryl, but with a B. My dad's name is Berry, and my mom's name is Cheryl," she said.

"It's a pretty name. My name is Travis. My mama's was Norma, and I don't know what my daddy's name was. So I really don't know where she got the name Travis from." He wanted to make as much small talk as possible. He wanted to keep Miss Beryl in his presence for as long as he could.

She wiped beads of sweat from her forehead and frowned. "Whew! It's so hot out here."

Reluctantly Travis said, "Don't let me keep you. Go ahead and get in your car and blast that air conditioning."

"You bet I will." She turned back toward her car and opened the door.

"Hey, uh . . . if I wanted to get some free coffee and a sandwich while being able to look at your beautiful face, where would I need to be and when?" Travis asked.

"The Hardee's on Main Street. I normally work the breakfast shift from six o' clock 'til two o'clock," she'd said.

As he reminisced about the first time he'd met Beryl, Travis nodded his head. He hadn't realized everyone at the table was starting at him until Beryl tapped him on the shoulder to ask him for his feedback.

Not having the slightest clue as to what the most recent topic had been, he said, "I think that icebreaker was nice, everyone has such interesting stories." He didn't really know what else to say.

"Okay everyone. Let's go ahead and break for lunch.

We'll meet back here at The Round Table at one o'clock," Phillip said.

Travis was glad his answer sufficed. He'd have to try and pay more attention during the sessions; after all, his marriage depended on it.

Chapter 7

Travis Highgate

Monday: 1:03 P.M.

Travis patted his stomach, full from the lunch Shelby had prepared. When he returned to The Round Table, everyone else was already there.

Once he was seated, Phillip said, "Okay, let's go ahead and get started."

Beryl rolled her eyes at Travis. He looked over at the clock on the wall and saw that is was just a little past one o'clock. He'd just lost track of time for a few minutes as he walked by the lake, but he wasn't that late. And what did it matter anyway? They had all week to sit around The Round Table and talk about all the gripes the women had about the men not doing something right.

"Again, I want to welcome you all to this marriage retreat. This week will probably be one of the most pivotal weeks in each of your marriages. I know for my wife and I, this retreat was vital during the reclamation stage of our marriage when we were literally sitting in the same places as you all are now," Phillip said.

Travis's ears perked up. Again he wondered what kinds of problems they could have had; especially with

Phillip being a minister and all. But then again, Travis knew that sometimes those ministers could be the most devilish of all.

"This week we'll be doing some exercises to help you communicate your thoughts and feelings to your spouses. We'll talk about the many facets of love. Not just the love you have for your spouse, but the love you have for yourself. We'll also talk about the way love can be used in the right and wrong ways," Phillip said.

"I'll be giving you some steps to improve your marital home and some marriage commandments you can use in your daily lives. Also we will delve into how important communication is in marriage and how to figure out what communication barriers you may have. There are five areas in marriage that you need to discuss and come to an agreement about, even if the agreement is that you disagree. You need to know where you both stand and how your spouse feels." Phillip looked around pointedly at everyone.

"Again, let me reiterate that you can voice any concerns you have. Ask any questions you need to ask pertaining to your situation. Please be assured that your information will not be shared with anyone outside of this room. Everything is to be kept confidential," Phillip said. "Are there any questions before we get started?"

No one had any.

"Okay then. The first thing we'll be talking about is the love we have for ourselves. The internal love we feel. In order to show others love—real love—you need to love yourselves first. And that love comes from within," Phillip said.

"You've also got to know that God loves you. He loved you enough to put you on this earth to live and breathe the same air as the other wonderful creatures He made. When God made you, He had a special plan in mind as to what you would look like, what complexion your skin would be, how tall you would become, and even the length of your big toe in relation to the other toes on your feet. He made your fingerprints just as He makes the snowflakes, unique and unduplicated. God loved you first. Now you also have to love yourselves."

Travis listened to Phillip as he went on about them having to love themselves. Travis thought about how much he loved himself. He loved himself very much. So that wasn't a problem. He also knew that God loved him, and he didn't have any doubts about that either. His mother had raised him in the church, and that was where he'd first learned about God's love. And he had even gotten saved at a young age. Each Sunday he was at church serving as an usher to show his love for the Lord.

Travis made sure he was always front and center when it came time to hand out programs and to help take up the offering. There shouldn't have been any doubt in anybody's mind about how much he loved the Lord. People could tell by the works he was doing in the church each Sunday.

Travis heard Phillip saying something about letting God complete you and not depending on another person to make you feel whole. Travis knew he didn't have a problem in that department either. He was a whole person and didn't need anyone else to validate that.

"Now I want each of you to take a mirror." Phillip pulled hand mirrors out of a box that was sitting on the floor. Once each person had one, Phillip continued. "I want each of you to take a look at yourselves in the side of the mirror that has the little heart sticker."

They did as instructed, examining themselves in the mirror, some holding the mirror closer to their faces than others. "Do you like what you see?" he challenged.

Travis nodded his head. "Yep, I like what I see just fine."

"I look good," Nina said.

George said, "I like what I see."

The others just nodded their heads, some more vigorously than others.

"Now," Phillip said, "turn your mirrors over."

There was a gasp from the 'I know I look good' Nina. "Oh my! My head looks enormous."

Looking in his own mirror, Travis saw how his nose looked three times its actual size, and he had something sticking slightly out of one of his nostrils that no one had bothered to tell him about.

"What do you think now?" Phillip asked. "How does it feel to look at yourselves up close and personal?"

"I must say, I do still look good," Nina said.

While everyone was focused on Nina's comments about herself, Travis decided to slip out to clean his nose. When he returned, Phillip was saying that they were to quickly jot down a couple of things they liked and disliked about themselves.

Travis pulled out his notepad and headed a piece of paper with two columns to list his likes and dislikes. First focusing on the positives, he wrote that he liked his physique. He worked out at least three times a week and had been doing so for years. The fruits of his labor had yielded him a body that often captured the attention of many women, especially when he wore fitted, sleeveless T-shirts. Travis wrote that he liked his skin. He had been blessed with what some people would call flawless skin. His mother and sisters didn't have skin like his, so he figured must have gotten it from the father he had never known.

In the dislike column, he noted the two things he didn't

like about his body. At only five feet six inches tall, he
hated his height. The second thing he hated about his
body was his teeth. Even though he had been blessed
with beautiful skin, his teeth were what some people
would call tore up. For many years, as a child, he was
teased about his teeth. He had a gap in the top center of
his mouth. But he also had gaps between many of his
other teeth.

Then to add to this eyesore, some of his teeth jutted
out and others were just plain crooked. His mother could
never afford to get him braces, and when he got older,
he'd never been able to afford them either. And now that
he was grown-up, he didn't know if having braces
would bring further scrutiny from adults. Adults weren't
as blatant as cruel children because they said things with
their eyes or behind a person's back.

"Okay, has everyone finished?" Phillip asked.

Nina shook her head. "I'm not. I could only think of
one thing I don't like about myself. Otherwise, I'm beautiful." Nina spoke as if she invented the word beautiful.
She sat with a straight back and stiff neck, poised like she
was being tested in the proper etiquette of sitting.

Travis's eyes widened. Beauty was truly in the eyes of
the beholder, because from what he could see, Nina didn't
look all that great. And he'd bet a million dollars that if
she took out some of her weave, popped off her fake
nails, and if her face came anywhere close to a wet wash-
cloth that would wipe off all the makeup she had caked
on it, she'd be not only plain and ordinary—she might
actually be knocking on ugly's front door.

"That's fine if you only have one thing. Not many people can say that," Phillip said.

Travis glanced over at some of the other people's
sheets of paper. His wife's paper had a long list of things

she didn't like about herself. He tried to read a few of them, but she slapped her hand over the paper before he could.

"Look at your lists and ask yourselves a few questions, and make some considerations. You don't have to answer these questions out loud," Phillip said. "For each thing you've written, ask yourself what can and cannot be changed. If there is something that is bothering you and it is in your power to change, then make efforts to change it. If there is something that cannot be changed no matter how much you dislike it, then you must allow yourself to accept what cannot be changed."

Travis looked again at the two things he didn't like about himself. He knew he could not change his height even though it bothered him to no end. But his teeth could be changed. He could get braces, but didn't really know if he wanted to go through all the ridicule, the hassle, or the pain. Plus he knew he needed dental insurance to get the braces in the first place. Beryl's insurance didn't cover him since she opted for the employee only coverage.

"Would anybody like to share what they've written?" Phillip asked.

Mr. Pretty Boy X spoke up. "I'll share. There are so many things I like about myself. First of all, my physique. I don't have to work very hard at making it look pristine because I've got it like that . . . naturally."

No longer fascinated with the cobweb in the corner, Charlotte rolled her eyes in disgust with husband's statement.

Ignoring his wife, Pretty Boy continued. "And I love the fact that my baritone voice can kick out a cappella songs like nobody's business."

Travis knew this to be true. Along with his good looks, the Pretty Boy often sang in his commercials, using this tactic to get people in to buy cars. But Travis couldn't carry a tune in a bucket, even if it were weighted down. He felt a twinge of envy toward this man. Xavier looked good, with his straight, white, pretty teeth, and his over six feet tall frame. The man seemed to have everything. Many of the things Travis wanted.

Xavier tapped his temple with his forefinger. "It's hard to think of anything I don't like about myself. But maybe the fact that if I wasn't so darn pretty, I wouldn't have to fight the women off so much." He hunched his shoulders and glanced over at his wife. She sat with her arms crossed, taking deep controlled breaths.

Nina piped up next and said, "I'll share." She held her paper up, and with an enthusiasm that seemed to come out of nowhere, began to read. "Okay, some of the things I like the most about myself are my big, beautiful, hazel eyes, my plus size, and especially my well endowed . . ." Her voice trailed off as she looked down toward the backside of her seat, and then up at her husband.

George smiled, saying, "Thanks."

"My husband thinks I'm a little too vocal, but you all know what I mean." Nina scooted from side to side in her seat. "And I had a hard time trying to figure out what I don't like about my body. I guess I'd have to say my toes. My big toe is shorter than the toe next to it. It doesn't look proportioned to me."

Travis had to stop himself from looking under the table. As soon as they took a break, he'd look to see what she was talking about, hoping she might have on some open toe shoes.

Next, Beryl spoke. "I'd like to share." She picked up her paper and read. "I don't like my weight right now. I've gained at least forty pounds since I got married. Specifically the weight in my abdominal area, my cheeks, my big flabby arms." She pulled at her dreads. "And lately I haven't been liking my dreads or the way my face has been breaking out."

Beryl stopped reading, putting her paper back down on the table. Travis wondered what Beryl was talking about. Sure she had put on a few pounds, but most women he knew put on a few pounds as they got older. He had noticed that her skin was a little dry and bumpy, but that hadn't bothered him either.

Travis and everyone else at the table waited for Beryl to continue with the things she liked about herself. But her paper remained on the table as if she were finished.

Phillip said, "Beryl, tell us what you like about yourself."

"Honestly, I can't think of anything," she said.

"Okay, maybe after you think about it a little more, something will come to you," Phillip said, not pressing Beryl to continue.

"Thank you all for sharing. Now look at all your dislikes and ask yourself if they are things you can change. If you can and want to change them, then make efforts to do so. But if there's something you can't change, then accept it and move on. And remember, before you can love anyone else, you've *got* to love yourself first."

"Why don't we take a short break before our next topic on the many languages of love."

Travis was glad they were finally taking a breather. He was starting to get bored. When Nina stood and walked out of the room, Travis made sure to look down at her feet. To his dismay, she had on a pair of slip on shoes that covered her toes. He made a mental note to try to check them out later on.

Chapter 8

Phillip Tomlinson

Monday: 1:35 P.M.

While the others had taken their breaks to grab snacks and visit the restroom, Phillip retreated in to his bedroom to reflect on the morning's events. Even though a couple of people were talking, he felt a heaviness floating around The Round Table during their first official session. Before letting the weight dishearten him, Phillip decided to go to his Father in heaven for strength and guidance.

Phillip knelt down beside his bed to say a quick prayer. "Dear Father in heaven, I come to you this afternoon to first thank you for this opportunity to impart into the lives of these couples in hopes to assist in saving their marriages. I know you don't put more on us than we can bear, so I trust in you, knowing this is a task you feel I am worthy of accomplishing.

"Lord, I come to you in prayer, knowing when to seek guidance and not work within my own strength and minimal knowledge, which pales in comparison to your infinite wisdom. With that being said, Lord, I need your guidance right now on how I can break through the ice for some of these people. I know they're hurting, and I know they're seeking wisdom and advice from me. I pray you'll give me the right words to help soothe their brokenness.

"I trust in you, Lord. You've never led me astray, and I expect positive results for this retreat and for each of these couples. I thank you in advance for the miracles I am sure you will perform here on this lake. Just as you performed the miracle for me just a short time ago, giving me the gift of eternal life.

"I thank and praise you, Lord, right here and now. In Jesus' name, amen."

Phillip stood with a renewed strength he hadn't felt just moments before the prayer. It still amazed him how the presence of God, and having an undying trust in the Lord, gave him an unexplainable kind of spiritual euphoria. He took a deep breath and stretched the full length of his body, almost touching the ceiling of his quaint cabin bedroom.

Shelby entered after a brief tap on the door. "Hey."

Phillip turned to face her, and with a mere step toward her, he pulled Shelby into his arms. Holding her tight, he gave her a kiss. Even after all their years of being married, the flame of love was still burning bright between them. Even through all the trials and tribulations he'd put her through, they were still as much in love as they had been when they met in college.

Shelby gave in to the kiss more than willingly, afterward saying, "What in the world was that for?"

"Do I really need a reason to kiss my wife?" Phillip asked.

"No, you don't. I just wasn't expecting it, that's all." Then she eyed him. "What's up? Were you having your own little personal revival in here?" She cupped his cheeks with the palm of her hands.

"You could say that. I had to come in here and talk to my Father above for a few minutes. I felt heaviness in the room and in my heart during that first session. I just wish they'd all loosen up some. I wanted to nip it before I let it get to me any more."

"I think the prayer worked. I did notice a slight furrow of your eyebrows earlier, and it's gone now," Shelby said. "I felt that heaviness also. I stepped outside for a little fresh air and said a little prayer of my own, for all of us. Hopefully our combined prayers will affect the group in a positive way."

"Whew, girl, how did I luck up and find you?" Phillip asked. "You are truly a Godsend."

"It was all in God's time and planning, P.T.," Shelby said.

P.T. had been Phillip's nickname from college and back in the days when he was the star of the football team. It was an ongoing joke between them whenever she called Phillip by the nickname, because Shelby hadn't met Phillip as 'P.T.' and knew nothing about his football star status. By the time she'd met him, he wasn't playing anymore due to a football injury.

It wasn't just the football fans that called Phillip by his nickname. Many of Phillip's many women, or conquests as he usually referred to them, had also called him P.T. By the time Phillip had met Shelby, his days of running women had decreased to a slow crawl. One, because he was a senior about to graduate, and two, because most of the upper-class females knew about his reputation of being a ladies man. His two-timing of women had gotten him into more trouble than he cared to remember.

Luckily, Phillip had met Shelby in the beginning of her freshman year—his senior year. He had been captivated. She was beautiful, but her beauty wasn't the thing that captivated him the most. It was the fact that Shelby hadn't swooned over him like almost every girl he'd come in contact with.

And after getting to talk to her and know her, Phillip found she had inner beauty and was also intelligent. These qualities brought even more of an appeal to him. And after only a few short weeks of getting to know Shelby, Phillip found that for the first time in his life, P.T. was truly in love. This love made him leave his two timing ways and want to actually settle down.

"Are you trying to be funny by calling me P.T.? It doesn't even sound right coming from you," Phillip said.

"It doesn't feel right saying it either," Shelby agreed.

Phillip looked at his watch. It was already one forty-six. The ten-minute break was up.

"Come on. Let's head back to The Round Table. I don't want to keep the couples waiting."

Phillip and Shelby returned to the table, and Phillip was pleased to see everyone assembled and ready to continue the next session.

"We all find ourselves at this table for different reasons. Yet there are many things we have in common, like the fact that we all fell in love and decided to get married. When you first got married you probably thought you'd found your soul mate, and we could only imagine a life filled with new beginnings and positive prospects. No one gets married thinking they'll one day want to separate and/or get divorced. Sure we've heard of couples who've had problems in their marriages and didn't stick it out until death parted them.

"I'm sure most of you have friends, cousins, an aunt or an uncle, or maybe even parents whose marriages ended in divorce. Sadly, just as marriages happen, so do divorces. My hope is that throughout this retreat, you'll be able to remember more of those fond moments in the beginning of your marriages and be able to weigh the costs."

Phillip looked around the table, making eye contact with each person. "I have a question for you. How many of you had some counseling before you got married?"

Nina and George raised their hands. The other two couples, Travis and Beryl Highgate and Xavier and Charlotte Knight did not.

"I ask this question mainly out of curiosity. I believe premarital counseling is an important and vital thing for marriage. My wife and I didn't have counseling before we got married either, and I wish we had. As you can see, marriage counseling does not guarantee that there will not be any problems. But I'm sure George and Nina can attest to the value of the premarital counseling they received," Phillip said.

George nodded his head. "Except for death and taxes, nothing else is certain. I will say the weeks of premarital counseling my wife and I received were very valuable. But without a crystal ball, no one knows what can and will happen in the future.

"Many of those basic teachings have helped my wife and me. But sometimes you need more. Sometimes life can throw you curve balls you never expected," George said.

Nina tapped her fingernails on the table, lightly at first, then gradually louder, as if perturbed by her husband's statements.

George took a deep breath. "Okay, let me stop before I start preaching in here."

Nina's tapping abruptly stopped.

Phillip held so much hope for the couples, and knew some of them were hanging on his every word, looking for sparks of hope that might help their marriage. But he also knew that in the end the decision to try to make their marriages work would be up to them. And he was going to try his best to give them all the reasons and as many angles as possible to try to make sure they thought about it multiple times before they decided to forever call it quits.

Phillip smiled at each of them with hope. "There are so many reasons marriages deteriorate. In general, most marriages are hit in one of three places: the pocket, the bedroom, or our spiritual walk. And sadly, some marriages are hit in two or all three of those areas.

"If you look at your own marriage, you should be able to pinpoint which area it has been hit. When the pocket is hit—in other words your finances—it can be very stressful; causing undue stress and tension between you and your spouse," Phillip said.

Phillip made sincere eye contact with the couples and noticed the uncomfortable squirming Beryl was making in her seat. He also saw the downward cast of Travis's eyes.

Phillip wanted to make a personal connection with each person, making sure they knew without a shadow of doubt he was there to help them and hopefully to get further insight on the specific problems each couple was having.

Phillip continued. "And likewise, when you're hit in the bedroom, this will definitely cause emotional and physical stress."

For the first time since she'd been at the cabin, Phillip watched as Charlotte nodded her head and made full eye contact with her husband. This time Xavier was the one to look away with guilt.

"The next way your marriage can be hit is via Satan. Being the serpent he is, he'll try to shake a marriage by preventing spiritual growth or making one question their spiritual soundness," Phillip said.

George clasped his hand together tightly while closing his eyes and taking a deep cleansing breath. Nina sat ridged in her seat.

Phillip felt he was a pretty good judge of character, and this upcoming week would prove whether his feelings were warranted or not. He stood picking up a dry erase marker. "Love misunderstandings," he said, then wrote the two words on the board. "What do you think this means?" He pointed to the words he'd written.

Travis spoke up. "I think it means, not understanding how much a person loves you."

Phillip nodded his head and wrote Travis's answer on the board in smaller letters with a green marker.

"I'd say in the sense of communication," George said.

"That's what I was gonna say. If there's a problem with communication, it can cause a big misunderstanding," Beryl said as she eyed her husband.

Phillip noticed the exchange but didn't comment on it. Instead, he wrote down the statement about communication causing misunderstandings.

"What about real love misunderstandings?" Xavier said. "I mean the misunderstandings in the bedroom. Because I always thought that once a man and woman were married, they belonged to each other. I mean, it shouldn't be like you are dating and hoping your wife will . . . well, you know," Xavier stammered. "Like you'll have to hope your wife will perform her wifely duties."

Again Phillip nodded his head with a straight face, glad to have more interaction than he'd had in the earlier session. "Misunderstandings in the bedroom, huh?" Phillip nodded to Xavier for confirmation. "Would anyone else like to add anything?"

This time Charlotte, Xavier's wife, replied. "What about misunderstandings about the vows you take when you get married, honoring your wife and forsaking all others?"

Charlotte reverted to ignoring her husband and kept her eyes square on Phillip. Everyone in the room knew the comment had been meant specifically for Xavier.

Phillip saw Xavier's upper body stiffen and his jaws clinch. Phillip could tell by the quick response made by Charlotte that this hadn't been the first time the couple had gone back and forth with each other, and it probably wouldn't be the last.

Nina said, "If you ask me, almost any and everything can be a misunderstanding depending on what it is. Sometimes a person can take the simplest of things and blow them all out of proportion."

This time it was George who exhaled a deep breath and shook his head. He shifted his body, fully facing his wife. "Nina, there aren't that many misunderstandings in the world. Tell the truth, and shame the devil."

Phillip spoke up. "Okay, okay. Let me make sure I've got everything jotted down." He wanted to stop any further escalation of George's comments to his wife before they got out of hand.

He wrote what each person said on the board.

"I'd like to add something," Shelby said. "Sometimes misunderstandings arise when a wife or a husband hides something from their spouse thinking this will protect the other person, only to find out their secrets could actually harm the person." She squeezed Phillip's arm and smiled.

Phillip knew his wife hadn't made the comment to hurt him or to remind him of the mistakes he made in the past—mistakes which caused them to come to Lake Turner during the time of their own marital turmoil.

No, Shelby wasn't the type to put salt in an old wound. She was just trying to impart her own words of wisdom. He also thought she brought up the comment just in case someone in the room was hiding something from their spouse; especially if they were thinking what their spouse didn't know wouldn't hurt them.

Phillip had learned the hard way that secrets shouldn't be kept from the ones loved most. He'd kept a secret about a son he'd fathered in college from Shelby, and the past literally ended up knocking on the front door of their home one evening.

Phillip shook his head, not wanting to remember that dismal time in their lives—a time when he almost lost his family forever due to his deceptiveness. He tried not to dwell on the negativity he experienced during that time. By the grace of God, his marriage had been saved. And because of that storm in his life, he was now standing in front of three couples that needed not just counseling, but someone who had once walked in their shoes.

"You all have brought up some very good reasons as to why people may have love misunderstandings. There is no right or wrong answer. It just depends on the couple and situation," Phillip said.

Phillip erased the board and wrote the word *communication*. "Communication is key when it comes to understanding others. Not just verbal communication, but non-verbal communication as well."

George and Beryl nodded their heads adamantly in agreement.

"Let me share some knowledge about love language skills. Maybe you'll be able to use some of these skills to bandage any love misunderstandings you may have," Phillip said. "As we go along, please feel free to take notes and ask questions. You don't have to wait until the session is over."

With his coaxing them to take notes, each person located the notepad in their packets and readied their pens.

"First let's talk about verbal communication. When you think about verbal communication, what comes to mind?" Phillip asked.

"Very simple," Beryl said. "Talking to someone and making your thoughts known."

"Right," Phillip said. "And what else?"

Beryl didn't have anything else to add to her comment. Charlotte spoke instead. "Verbal communication can be affected not only by the words a person chooses to use, but also by the tone a person speaks in."

"You are correct also," Phillip said, glad to have so much increased participation from the group. "In addition to tone, there are non-verbal actions which often negate what's being said. "For example . . . " Phillip stopped speaking, and in a swift movement, he stood behind Shelby and hooked his arm around her neck in a headlock, acting as if he were going to choke her.

The women jumped in their seats in surprise. The men's eyes widened at the display.

Phillip smiled, and in a calm loving tone said, "If I told you right now that I love my wife unconditionally and would never harm a hair on her head, would you believe me?"

"Nope," Travis said.

Phillip released Shelby's head and gave her shoulders a tight squeeze. "You okay, baby?"

"Yeah. Thanks for forewarning me about your experiment, or else I might have elbowed you or something," Shelby said.

"So as you can see, actions speak louder than words. Even though I was syrupy sweet with my words, the choking didn't make me too believable."

"Um-huh." Beryl heartily nodded in agreement.

"So the words we use and how we use them can make the difference between our loved one fully understanding our true feelings or intentions. But they can also contribute to a love misunderstanding if there is a conflicting tone and/or body language associated with what we are saying."

Beryl looked at her husband, Travis. Her non-verbal stare said that she'd been through similar displays many times before.

Chapter 9

Travis Highgate

Monday: 3:29 P.M.

In their bedroom during their free time, Travis attempted to hug Beryl, but she pushed him away. "Beryl, honey, will you please sit down for a moment so we can talk? Can I show you my love language abilities?" Travis was referring to the seven love language skills Phillip had taught them in their most recent session.

"Travis, weren't you listening at all during the last session?" Beryl huffed in exasperation.

"Yeah, I was listening. I heard everything Phillip said."

Beryl was always accusing him of not paying attention. So he decided to prove to her that he had been listening in the previous session. He rattled off the list of things he'd memorized. "There are seven different ways people show their love to others: words, touch, serving, quality time, gifts, providing physical wellbeing, and making a special opportunity." Travis grinned wide, showing his crooked teeth. He was proud of himself for memorizing the list in such a short time.

"Umph," Beryl said. "I guess you were listening."

He took Beryl's hand and pulled her over to his twin

bed. "See, baby. So please just sit down for a second so we can talk."

Even though there was reluctance in her eyes, Beryl did as Travis requested and sat down next to him. He then turned toward her, taking her hands into his.

"Baby, don't you see how committed I am? You asked me to come up here with you for this retreat, and I did. And let me tell you, I can already see that we don't need this counseling." Travis looked deep into Beryl's eyes. "I know things haven't been the best lately, but we don't need someone else telling us how we can get our relationship back on track," Travis said.

Beryl pulled away. "Travis—"

"Baby, let me talk." Travis pulled her back, squeezing her hands as he pleaded.

She pursed her lips together and allowed him to speak.

"I know what your concerns are, and I promise to try even harder to find a job when I get back home. And I am going to try to do better with helping out around the house and with the kids. Baby, I promise I'll do better about keeping the grass cut." As Travis spoke, he felt his words must have been getting through to his wife. Tears welled up in her eyes. He took this as a good sign.

"So baby, I know you spent a lot of money for us to come here," Travis told her. "And since you're already off for the rest of the week, I guess we can stay and just consider this a long overdue, well deserved vacation." He smiled. He and Beryl were going to be able to get things back on track. He would do better at home, and Beryl would once again be proud of him.

He looked over toward the other twin bed that sat against the opposite wall. "And why don't we go ahead and push these beds together? I've missed you, baby."

Travis missed his wife so very much. He'd missed the

way they used to talk about simple things like their favorite TV shows. He missed the way they used to hold
hands whenever they were out in public walking around—
be it at the park, in the mall, or even in the grocery store.
But most of all he missed the oneness a husband and
wife should have behind closed doors in the bedroom.

It started off with her coming up with excuses as to
why she didn't feel like making love to him. Then one
day she told him straight out, that if he didn't do better
around the house and start bringing in some money, he
wouldn't ever feel her warmth next to him in the bed.
After that, it was as if there was an imaginary line drawn
down the middle of their queen size bed, and he knew
not to cross it.

Beryl started to laugh again, this time pulling away
completely. She stood and started pacing the room. "You
just don't get it do you?"

"Huh?" Travis asked.

"When in the heck are you going to get a clue? Is this
all just a game to you?" Beryl hit her forehead with the
palms of her hands. "You're serious, aren't you?" She
laughed again, looking up toward the ceiling.

Travis sat looking at Beryl with bewilderment. What in
the world was she talking about?

"Darn it! Once again I've wasted my hard earned
money on you." She shook her head, continuing to look
up at the ceiling. "Now tell me again what we talked
about in the session today?" Beryl asked.

Travis thought about the list he'd memorized earlier,
and he rattled off only six of the seven things. And after a
couple of uncomfortable moments, he finally remembered the one he'd forgotten. Again he smiled at himself.

"No, Travis, not the list of skills. Tell me about the
skills."

Travis hadn't really paid attention to the specifics of

any of the skills. He was so determined to remember the list.

Beryl folded her arms impatiently as she waited for an answer. "You don't know the answer, so forget that question. How about if you tell me what love language skill I prefer?"

Again Travis was a loss for words. He didn't really have an idea. But he was tired of Beryl looking at him like he was a dunce. So he picked out the first one that came to his head and said, "Quality Time."

"No, Travis. And I won't waste my time asking you to guess again, because that's all you are doing is guessing. You'd know if you were really listening this afternoon, instead of trying to memorize some list to impress me. It doesn't impress me. The sad thing is you really only had to remember two things on that list." Beryl held her index finger up and said, "First, the skill of providing physical wellbeing." She stared at him like *that* was supposed to jar his memory. Then she held up her middle finger along with her index finger. "And second, the skill of words. Does either one of those two things mean anything to you?"

He still didn't know what Beryl was talking about. Now he wished he had paid a little more attention. Inwardly he chastised himself.

Without waiting for a response, Beryl continued. "Well, once again, let me school you a little bit, since for some reason, you missed what everybody else heard. Everyone else in that room knows what my preferred love language skill is. I wouldn't want you to feel left out."

Travis wasn't sure, but he felt a twinge of sarcasm in his wife's last statement.

"You prefer to use the speaking of words as your love language skill when it comes to our relationship," Beryl said. "And here's the newsflash. I am sick and tired of hearing your words. I can't believe a thing you say. You'll say anything to try to appease me and anyone else who'll listen, and I am tired of it."

Then Beryl deepened her voice as if to mimic Travis's voice. "I'm gonna get a job, baby; I promise. I'm gonna keep this job; I promise. Baby, it wasn't my fault they fired me." Then she returned her voice to normal. "It's baby this and baby that. If it isn't lies about you trying to find or keep a job, you're lying about why something doesn't get done around the house."

Travis spoke up. "If you're talking about the grass not being cut last week, you know the lawnmower was out of gas. And you also know that since you had the car at work that day, I couldn't get to the station to get more gas."

"That was Tuesday. What about the rest of the week? What's your excuse for that?" Beryl asked.

"Well, ah, let's see. On Wednesday, I uh—"

Beryl spoke again. "And that's not the worst of it. When I do catch you in a lie, you want to play word games. Forget it. Whether it's more lies or excuses, I don't want to hear them. Bottom line is the grass still hasn't been cut, and by the time we get back, the house will probably look like it needs to be condemned. I just pray our landlord hasn't put another note on our door threatening us."

"Come on, baby, I'm not trying to come up with excuses. I was just giving you the reason why the grass hadn't been cut yet. And don't worry about the landlord. I called him before we left and assured him that as soon as we get back, I'll be cutting the grass. It's all under control," Travis said, stretching the truth a little.

"Oh really? Is that the truth or are you just lying to make yourself look good?" Beryl said.

"I'm not lying." Travis rubbed the back of his neck with his hand as he spoke. She was always catching him in lies and exaggerations. He wondered how she was always able to do so.

Travis had no idea why he lied so much. For some reason, the lies and embellishments just flowed from his mouth as freely as the air that came through his nostrils.

"Well, I hope you are telling the truth, because if I do find out you're lying—" She stopped mid-sentence and shook her head. "Maybe it won't even matter. We're a long way from Sunday, and you're failing to show me you really want things to work between us."

"Come on, baby, give me a chance," Travis said.

"I've given you chance and chance again. Most other women would have probably left you already. But no. Stupid, trusting me just keep on thinking things are going to get better and that one day, you'll do the right thing."

"I am going to do better. You might not believe it right now, but I'm going to show you; just believe me," Travis said, pleading.

"Words again? Wah, wah, wah, you sound like the teacher off of the Charlie Brown cartoon," Beryl said.

Travis was tired of hearing all the complaining. "That's all I've got right now, baby, so you'll just have to trust me."

"See, that's the problem, all you've got are your words; words I haven't been able to trust in years. And while you're using your empty words to try and convenience me, what I really need is for you to provide a physical wellbeing for me and the kids." Beryl's eyes began to well with tears. "You know I've only given birth to two children, but for the past few years I've felt like I actually have three."

"Huh? What's that supposed to mean?" Travis asked.

Beryl started pacing. "It means it feels like I have to treat you like a child. I have to think for you, remind you to do things, pay for your food and shelter, and even wake you up when you've overslept. Some days I can't even distinguish you from the kids." Beryl's face was now streaming with tears. "I need you to take care of me and the kids. I need you to be the man of our household. I need to feel secure knowing I can lean and depend on you. But at this point, I don't feel that way."

"How are you going to say that Beryl? I'm not a child." Travis couldn't believe she had just compared him to a child. "I carry my weight when I can. But it's hard out here for a black man. I can't help it when a company downsizes and decides to fire people."

Beryl stared at him. She threw her hands up and headed for the bathroom. Travis saw her pull tissue off the roll and wipe her face. Then she turned and left the bedroom, slamming the door behind her.

Travis called out saying, "Beryl, you can't just run away. We need to finish our conversation."

Chapter 10

Travis Highgate

Monday: 6:05 P.M.

"Let us bow our heads," Phillip said. "Dear Lord, we thank you for bringing us together at this moment in time. Only you, Lord, know the outcome of what will happen within the next few days, and we thank you for the divine intervention you'll impart into all of our lives.

"We also thank you for this food we are about to receive. Please bless the hands that prepared it, and let it be nourishment to our bodies. In Jesus' name. Amen."

Travis looked down at his plate filled with two turkey cutlets, mashed potatoes, and salad. He didn't have an appetite. Ever since his conversation with Beryl, he hadn't felt like doing much of anything.

"Shelby, these turkey cutlets are good," George said.

"Thanks," Shelby said.

As the couples sat around the dinner table making small talk, Travis merely nodded his head on occasion. He didn't feel like making small talk with any of these people. He needed to talk to his wife and get her to understand his point of view. He had to get her to understand his side of everything.

She just wasn't giving him a chance to do so. He couldn't understand why she was in such an uproar about the way things were going. It wasn't like he hadn't tried to look for work. And it wasn't like he hadn't worked most of the time they'd been married. He'd been a limousine driver until he got the speeding ticket doing sixty-five miles per hour in a thirty-five mile per hour zone. Then he'd been an apartment grounds keeper until complaints had been made to his boss about him not being on the grounds too often during work hours. He figured one of his jealous co-workers had made the complaints against him.

Next he'd been a newspaper carrier until he got fired for delivering the papers to the wrong houses and because of the number of times he'd gotten up too late to deliver the papers in a timely manner. It seemed that some people actually wanted their papers to read while they were eating breakfast. Travis had never really been a morning person and couldn't understand why anyone would want to get up so early to read a paper when the words on the page would be the same at noon as they were at eight.

He had also worked as a taxi driver, meter reader, and as a security guard at a few businesses. And for one lame reason or another, he was let go.

"Hey, Beryl, are you feeling okay?" Shelby asked.

"Uh, yeah. I'm good. Why do you ask?" Beryl offered a disbelieving smile.

"The way your eyebrows are furrowed, it just looks like something might be wrong," Shelby said.

"No, I was just thinking about something," Beryl said.

Travis felt eyes glancing over at him. He knew everyone had probably heard Beryl ranting earlier. He was embarrassed and wanted to crawl under the table. He still couldn't understand why Beryl was the way she was. When they'd been dating, he hadn't been working and she'd seemed to understand how hard it was for a black man to find a job. She'd even understood when he lost the first couple of jobs in the early part of their marriage.

He had to admit that Beryl was different from the women in his family. Travis's sisters had always understood how hard it was for him. They'd always been helpful to him whenever he found himself between jobs.

Actually, he couldn't remember a time when his sisters weren't there for him. They'd stepped right in after their mother died, taking care of his every need. He never had to worry about where his meals were coming from, never had to worry about having clean clothes, or a place to live. His sisters made sure their brother hadn't wanted for a thing.

In the beginning, Beryl had been like his mother and sisters. She'd catered to his every need. Cooked for him and cleaned after him. But after their first child was born, the meals degraded from full courses to get it yourself. And she stopped picking up his clothing, telling him it was time to start pulling his own weight.

Travis had tried to cook, but burned everything, even down to pots of boiling water. He'd tried to wash clothes, but washed the whites and colored clothes together and in the wrong temperature. Not only had the white clothes turned out pink, but the colored clothes had shrunk to an un-wearable size. Beryl fussed for weeks about the money she'd had to spend buying new clothes to replace the ruined ones.

She'd finally taken over washing the clothes again, but Travis was lucky if she folded his clothes or put them away. She had totally flipped the script, and he hadn't felt it was fair.

Travis had tried speaking to a few of his friends about

his ordeal, but they'd just said he had been spoiled since he was a child, and it was time for him to grow up. They sided with Beryl, saying he needed to help out more, especially with the kids. His friends said all this even though he kept stressing the fact that his wife had flipped the script. Their reply to them was that everybody flips some sort of script during marriage, and Travis just needed to go with the flow.

Travis knew most of his friends were just jealous of the fact that his mother and sisters had been so loving and caring to him. And because he'd found a woman who was also attentive to his needs and they hadn't.

"Travis, what's up?" Phillip asked.

Coming out of his thoughts, Travis looked up from his plate. Everyone else had finished their food and had left the table. His plate had barely been touched.

"Oh. I'm not really that hungry," Travis said.

"You can always wrap it up and eat it later. I'm sure there is some foil or plastic wrap in there somewhere."

Travis pushed his plate away slightly. "Thanks."

Phillip took a seat next to Travis. "Is there anything you want to talk about?"

"Nah. I'm good, man. There are just a few things I need to work out for myself."

"Well, I just want you to know I'm here if you need to talk. No matter what time." Phillip firmly patted Travis's back.

Travis nodded his head.

"Hey man, we're about to gather in the living room for a couple of rounds of the newlywed game. We've changed it a little to better resemble the oldiewed game, since you've all been married for more than two years." Phillip smiled.

Travis looked to see if Beryl was anywhere around, but

didn't see her. He stood. "I might join you guys in a few minutes."

"It would be good if you and Beryl could join us. Rome wasn't built in a day, but just think if they'd taken breaks building that city? It might not have ever been completed," Phillip encouraged.

"Let me see what Beryl wants to do," Travis said.

"Okay, we're going to start in about ten minutes. As soon as Shelby and I can finish getting the kitchen cleaned."

Again Travis nodded his head, wondering where his wife was. He picked up his plate from the table and headed for the kitchen. After wrapping up his food and placing it in the refrigerator, he headed toward their bedroom to see if Beryl was in there.

Not seeing her, he left, casually looking around the cabin. But he still didn't see her. Instead of asking anyone if they knew where she was, Travis decided to look outside. As soon as he stepped onto the porch of the cabin, he spotted her silhouette leaning against a tree only a few feet away.

Gently he closed the door. At first he stood just outside of the door, staring at his wife's back, not wanting to disturb her. Then gingerly he shuffled off the porch and made his way to the tree where she stood.

"You okay?" he asked not wanting to startle her.

She didn't answer him at first. He didn't know whether she'd heard him or not. But after a moment, she finally spoke.

"As okay as I'm going to be, I guess." Beryl spoke without looking in his direction.

Travis listened as insects made their various screeches and as an owl hooted from somewhere nearby. "I'm surprised you came out here all by yourself. It's pretty creepy out here."

Again Beryl paused before speaking. "I just needed some fresh air, that's all. And besides, I'm not crazy enough to walk that far off. Plus I've got the keys to the car." Beryl jingled the keys, showing him how she already had her thumb poised on the panic alarm button.

He should have known. Beryl wasn't the type to do just anything on a whim. She always thought things through—often over and over again—especially when it came to safety issues. She was one of the most safety conscious people he knew.

Travis looked down at his glow in the dark watch. They'd be starting the newlywed game in about five minutes, and he didn't want to go back into the cabin with a sour feeling on his stomach. Or have his wife sitting around with a sour look on her face.

"Baby, about earlier," he started, but Beryl cut him off.

"Don't, Travis. Don't do this. I don't want to talk about it anymore."

"Please, baby, just hear me out. I know you are tired of hearing me talk without anything to show for what I've been saying. But I pledge to you right here and now that I will do better and I will be a better person. You'll see. I will be a changed man."

Beryl shook her head with hopelessness, not saying a word.

"I know you think I'm just talking, but you'll see. I'll stop the talking and just start showing you. I want to show you that I can be the man you want me to be. I will prove that to you. I promise." In his heart of hearts, Travis meant every word.

When he got back home he was really going to look for a job. Not just circle a few ads in the paper and leave it on the table, making it look like he'd actually been job hunting. He'd do everything in his power to make sure he was following all the rules to prevent getting fired—

starting with getting to work on time. He'd set two alarm clocks if need be, to make sure he got up on time so that Beryl wouldn't have to wake him up. He'd even take it upon himself to help with the kids in the morning.

Additionally, he was only going to watch his taped television shows after he'd helped with doing some of the household chores. And even though he didn't want to, he'd refrain from renting any movies from the video store for a few weeks; until he could get into the swing of things with his new work schedule.

Travis was excited about his new ideas and even more excited about the fact that very soon, Beryl would see that he wasn't just talk.

"You'll see, Beryl. I am a changed man. All I ask is that you give me one more chance." Beryl turned her head toward him and stared. "You know Rome wasn't built in a day," Travis said, borrowing the words Phillip had spoken to him. "But I promise I'll keep on working at this until I prove it to you."

"Two words, Travis," Beryl said.

"What's that?"

She placed her forefinger on his lips indicating that she wanted him to stop talking.

"Show me," Beryl said.

Without speaking, Travis nodded his head with enthusiasm. Beryl was giving him another chance, and this time, he wouldn't do something stupid to mess it up.

He looked down at his watch. "They're about to start playing the newlywed game in a few minutes. You want to play?"

While Travis loved television and movies, Beryl's thing was board games. She loved them and was very competitive. So Travis figured the game would bring out Beryl's competitive side and hopefully help her forget the events of the last few hours.

"It might be fun," Travis added.

"You know I don't play for fun. I play to win."

"Now that's the Beryl I know," Travis said as he led Beryl back into the cabin.

Upon entering, they saw the women gathered in the living room. The men were nowhere in sight.

"Oh, you guys are just in time," Shelby said. "Travis, the men are in my bedroom answering some questions. Why don't you join them while we women answer our questions out here."

Travis and Beryl did a Barack and Michelle Obama fist dap—touching fist-to-fist—wishing each other good luck.

Once Travis found the men, they filled him in on the rules of the game and gave him pieces of eight by ten-inch cardboard paper to answer his questions on. After they were finished, Phillip left the room to consult with his wife, ensuring the women were finished with their questions and answers so they could all continue the game.

Once they were all assembled back in the living room, Beryl, Nina, and Charlotte sat in a row in front of the fireplace, ready to begin the game.

"Okay, men, are you ready?" Shelby asked.

The men all answered yes.

Shelby continued. "Gentlemen, I asked your wives three questions, and they've written down the answers they thought you might say. Each question has a point value and the couple with the most points at the end of the game will win. Phillip and I will keep score.

"In the event of a tie, there will be a bonus question asked as the tie breaker. Any questions?" Shelby asked. Hearing none, she continued. "Travis you first. This first question is worth five points. What sport or sports did you play in high school?"

"I played football," Travis answered with ease.

Beryl flipped her card over which read: FOOTBALL.

Travis and Beryl both clapped their hands.

"All right, good going," Shelby said. "George?"

"I didn't play any sports in high school. I was all into the books," George said.

Nina flipped her card over and it read: NONE. And with an air of boredom she placed it back down.

"Good for you both also." Shelby jotted the points down. "Okay, Xavier. What about you?"

"Oh, let's see. I played football, basketball, and baseball." Xavier said this as though it were a matter of fact everyone should know. I helped my high school football team go to State all four years I was there."

Travis wanted to gag. He was surprised the Pretty Boy had played any kind of sports. Surely he had to have been scared someone might scratch his pretty face with a foul or a fly ball.

Shelby smiled, looking to Charlotte for her answer, "Charlotte?"

Charlotte flipped her card over and it read: BASKET-BALL, FOOTBALL AND BASEBALL.

"Yeah, boy," Xavier said, acting like his team was going to State again on his account.

"Looks like everyone's tied. Maybe these questions are a little to easy for you all." Shelby shook her head. "Next question. Men, we asked your wives how old you were when you got your first kiss."

In the same order in which they had gone before, the men gave their answers. By the end of question number two, only Beryl and Travis had scored. And by the end of question three, only Charlotte and Xavier had scored.

"We're now at the end of round two. Beryl and Travis, you have fifteen points. Charlotte and Xavier, you have twenty points, and Nina and George, you have five points," Shelby said.

Travis saw the fight in Beryl's eyes. She wasn't happy

about the fact that they were losing, and Travis knew they'd have to get all the answers right in the next round. He didn't even want to think about how tense things would be back in their room that night with an angry Beryl on his hands if they lost.

The women moved out of the way, trading seats with their husbands. Likewise, Phillip switched places with Shelby.

"Okay, ladies, we asked your husbands three questions," Phillip said. "First question. Where did the two of you meet?"

Travis and Xavier got their answers right, but George did not. George said that he and Nina met at a church conference in Greenville, but Nina was adamant about the fact that they'd first met at a church conference in Atlanta.

Question two asked what the womens' favorite movies were. Travis and George got the answer wrong, and Xavier got it right. For the final question Phillip asked where the couples went on their first dates. Travis was the only one who answered correctly, saying he'd taken Beryl to the Olive Garden for dinner.

"It looks like we have a tie between Travis and Xavier. So we'll have to go with the bonus question," Phillip said.

Shelby stood back up. "Gentlemen, we asked your wives who your favorite superhero was as a child."

Travis answered the Super Friends and Xavier said he didn't really have a favorite superhero, but if he had to choose one, it would be Superman since he was so much like him.

Beryl turned her card over with a smile and Charlotte frowned when she turned hers over. Beryl's card said: THE SUPER FRIENDS and Charlotte's said: UNDERDOG.

Travis jumped up shouting, "Yes, yes, yes," then stepped over to Beryl, giving her a victory hug.

"Underdog, Charlotte?" Xavier asked.

"Don't act like you don't know why I wrote it, Xavier," Charlotte said.

"I mean, come on. You could have written something a little better than that." Xavier looked around at the others in the room as he spoke. His ego had taken a major hit.

Travis smiled inwardly. He guessed like, Superman, Pretty Boy must have had his own type of Kryptonite.

Chapter 11

Xavier Knight

Tuesday: 6:17 A.M.

Xavier strained as he counted. "Four hundred ninety-eight, Four hundred ninety-nine, five hundred." Reaching five hundred, he finally allowed his body to relax from all the crunches he'd done. He'd been up since five o'clock that morning doing as much of the daily workout he normally did in his home gym.

As he lay catching his breath, Charlotte rolled out of her bed, and without saying a word, she stepped over him. After picking up her toiletry bag, she headed into the bathroom.

Xavier shook his head. He wondered how long it was going to take his wife to cool off enough to talk to him. He sat up and pulled his Blackberry off of the dresser. Turning it on he saw there still wasn't a signal. He desperately needed to check his emails and wanted to see how sales were going at the dealership.

In one way, he was actually glad there wasn't a signal. That way he wouldn't have to worry about what had happened. A few miles before they had reached the cabin, one of his former clients had called. A female client named

Yasmine. The same Yasmine who had been the main reason he and Charlotte were at the retreat. He hadn't spoken
to Yasmine in almost a month, and though he wondered
why she was calling, in his gut he knew. The woman only
wanted to cause him more trouble.

But he hadn't had a chance to find out what she
wanted because as soon as he'd said hello and spoke Yasmine's name, he'd lost the signal. Simultaneously, Charlotte turned her head with neck breaking speed, looking
at him with questioning eyes.

Seeing the signal had been lost, Xavier flipped the
phone shut only to have Charlotte cross her arms and roll
her head in a why-is-Yasmine-calling-you motion. He
tried to explain that he didn't know why the woman was
calling and told her the signal was dropped before he
could find out.

Charlotte rolled her eyes. She didn't believe him. Xavier
couldn't blame her for her distrust. But he *was* telling the
truth.

The problems first started when the dealership began
running a new series of commercials that starred him
and featured women often wearing little of nothing. The
commercials were already starting to draw people in
droves. Charlotte started developing insecurities one day
during one of the commercial shoots after seeing some
women groping on him like he was an R&B star.

The women—actresses—had been wearing bikinis
while he wore his swim trunks. He played the part of a
lifeguard and they were damsels in distress, drowning
from the high car prices of the competitors. At the end of
the commercial, the women gathered around Xavier,
thanking him with hugs for his rescue abilities. Xavier
hadn't touched any of them as he held a lifesaving device.

Charlotte was so livid about the display from the commercial shoot that it had taken him two weeks to finally get her to calm down about it. Two weeks of assuring her there was nothing going on with any of the women and that all they were doing was acting. Also during that time, she'd become paranoid about his every move. So to appease her, he'd started updating her on his where-abouts, and that seemed to diminish her paranoia.

Xavier knew Charlotte's suspicions weren't totally un-founded because of the history of extracurricular activi-ties he'd had during his first marriage. Activities he'd vowed to not bring into his current marriage.

When he and Charlotte had started dating and he saw that things were getting serious, he sat down with her and had a long talk about the reasons his previous mar-riage had come to an end. He'd been sorry for what he'd done and apologized to his first wife, but she'd sought divorce on grounds of adultery instead. He'd learned his lesson. He assured Charlotte that his old ways were be-hind him, and the slate was clean.

But ultimately, he hadn't kept that promise to Char-lotte. It ended up being harder than he thought it would be. He loved his wife. She was everything he could ever want in a woman. She was intelligent, caring, and beauti-ful. At home he hadn't lacked for anything from Char-lotte. She was attentive to his every need. But for some reason, Xavier had a strong proclivity for women.

When he wasn't around his wife, the women were lur-ing eye candy. He couldn't avoid them. There were so many of them around, especially at his job. Since the dealership had started the commercials, the influx of women had gotten even worse. They seemed to come in multitudes. He'd tried his best to ignore them.

And if that weren't enough, the Internet complicated things even more. One afternoon while he was sitting at home checking his emails, a window popped up on the screen, showing women in suggestive poses. He clicked on it and the screen opened with an array of beautiful eye candy from which he couldn't avert his eyes. These women weren't real. It wouldn't hurt to look at them. It wasn't like anyone could see him, and it wasn't like these women could make any advances toward him. It was totally innocent, and it gave him a rush of a lifetime.

In the weeks that followed, he'd returned to the website, whenever he needed a fix. When he got bored with that website, he'd found others with more pictures and varieties of things to behold. Xavier found that surfing the websites helped him keep a better focus at work, especially after he found a site in which he could chat with the women.

Charlotte emerged from the bathroom, covered in her terrycloth robe. She'd forgotten to take her clothes into the bathroom with her. Again doing her best to ignore her husband, she pulled a pair of pants and a top out of the bag, already ironed and ready, then she returned to the bathroom. Minutes later, Xavier heard the shower turn on.

He finally sat up and shook his head, wondering when Charlotte was finally going to stop her nonsense and talk to him. They didn't need to waste precious days during the retreat for her to come around. They needed to use the time wisely.

Looking back at his phone, his thoughts trailed back to Yasmine. He shook his head again, wondering why the heck the woman had picked that exact moment to call. This was the time in which he and Charlotte were finally on a course to getting their relationship back on track.

Yasmine had been his nightmare for months, and then the nightmare turned into reality. Xavier tried to use the alluring images from the websites to control his need for being with other women, but the Internet had only been a temporary solution.

Slowly some of his old ways returned as he made small talk with the female clients during test drives. It wasn't hard since so many women flirted with him on a daily basis. He didn't see a problem with taking their phone numbers to continue talking to them over the phone.

Remembering how his last marriage ended, he didn't want the same results. He was going to have to be more careful this time and let the new women friends he was talking to know that he was not looking for a long-term relationship, making sure there weren't any misunderstanding on the womens' parts. He also told them to only call his cell phone during working hours. He figured the women should be able to deduce that he was a married man by those instructions and the ring he wore on his left hand. It was all innocent enough. He hadn't done anything with the women, he just liked to talk and flirt.

For months his personal life was on top of the world. He had his beautiful trophy wife at home, newly found friends on the side, and handy websites at the touch of his fingers when he needed an extra fix. On the business side, he was the top-selling salesman in the dealership and across the state of North Carolina.

Things were going pretty smooth until Yasmine entered—stage left, as the thespians might say. From day one, meeting Yasmine had been like something out of a dramatic play debuting on Broadway.

There were signs of trouble from the first time Xavier had met her at the Starbucks down the street from the dealership. Starting with the low-cut red dress that looked like it had been painted on. Her cleavage hadn't been hard to miss, neither had been the devil's horns he saw extending from her head . . . or at least he thought he saw a pair. He'd done a double take until she changed positions in her seat. There had actually been a mural behind her on the wall which gave the illusion that she had horns.

She'd introduced herself as Yasmine and made herself comfortable at his table without asking if he were expecting anyone else. She'd recognized him as the guy from the commercials and talked and asked questions for the better part of his thirty-minute break. When it was time to leave, she gave him one of her business cards. She was an IT specialist for a local company.

A few days later, he'd come across the card and thought about calling Yasmine to see if she might be in the market for a new car. The thought had only been on his mind for a fleeting moment before he saw Miss Yasmine strolling around the dealership looking at the cars on showcase. She was wearing another painted on dress, but this one was hot pink and was even lower cut in the front than the dress she'd worn a few days prior. Surprised, he made his way over to her and asked if he could be of any assistance. She said she'd been thinking about getting a new car and had seen some she liked. She wanted to test drive a few, but only if Xavier went along to tell her about the cars' features.

Xavier ended up going with her on three test drives until he realized the woman was only a fan trying to get as much free time alone with him as she could. Time was money, and he'd wasted enough of both on her already.

Xavier shook his head again as he remembered. He so wished he'd taken the red dress, the horns, and her pushy aggressiveness as a sign to run and hide. Instead, trying to make a buck, he pressed her about whether she wanted to buy a car or not. She said she did, but was trying to make up her mind on which to choose.

After a week of her coming to the dealership on a daily basis, supposedly making up her mind, she finally purchased a vehicle. Xavier wondered if all the time he'd spent had really been worth the commission. But he was glad the woman—cleavage or not—was finally going to be out of his hair.

A mere week after the purchase, Yasmine again strolled into the dealership offering to buy Xavier lunch to thank him for all his help and time. Something told him to decline, but his growling stomach got the best of him. And when he really thought about it, he didn't see any real harm in grabbing a bite with the woman.

During their lunch, Yasmine made a number of suggestive overtures that could not be ignored. Xavier did his best—in the beginning—to disregard those advances, but had ultimately been unable to. From there everything was a blur. Before he knew it, he was seeing her more often and spending time with her at her apartment at night when he couldn't be seen. Whenever he was at Yasmine's place it felt like he was in his Cyber-world—in 3D. She was everything the websites promised and more.

He was in a virtual heaven; at least until the pain started each time he went to the bathroom. Then after a while, in addition to the pain, he also noticed a discharge. He went to the doctor and found out he had gonorrhea. This totally freaked him out. The only other person he had been with besides his wife in the previous couple of months had been Yasmine. He hadn't seen a need to pursue any kind of relationship with the other women he'd been corresponding with, especially after seeing how easily accessible Yasmine was.

He broke contact with Yasmine as soon as he found out about the STD. He didn't answer her calls and told coworkers the woman was stalking him. His coworkers had laughed at him, but obliged with his wishes to assist in breaking any contact she had with him.

At first, the messages Yasmine left sounded urgent. Then she just sounded hurt. After that, she started leaving messages threatening him to contact her. He took the threats as idle and figured she'd get the message sooner or later and leave him alone.

Meanwhile, he'd gotten the medicine he needed to treat the STD and prayed to God he hadn't spread the disease to his wife. After he'd found out about the diagnosis, he'd even avoided sleeping with her for a few weeks, making up excuses—excuses which sounded like the ones most women would use to get out of sleeping with their husbands. He had to buy time until he could figure out a way to tell his wife.

But he'd waited too long, and before he knew it, Charlotte had confronted him with her own test results, saying she had gonorrhea. He fessed up and told her about Yasmine. Not everything. Just enough to let her know he'd slept with another woman. But he didn't tell her about his other female friends. He wasn't trying to dig an even bigger hole for himself.

Things had been worse than tense at his house for months, and Xavier feared Charlotte would have probably left him already if he hadn't set up the marriage counseling at the retreat for them. Waiting for the date of the retreat had bought him some time, and ever since, he'd been doing his best to make amends. He felt lower than dirt for what he'd done to his wife.

So now here he was, sitting on the floor of a cabin in the middle of nowhere without contact with the outside world. But it would all be worth it if he could get his wife to forgive him and give him another chance.

If only Yasmine hadn't called. And why had she called,

anyway, he wondered? How stupid could he have been? He should have known Yasmine wouldn't give up so easily. Xavier thought he was finally free of the woman. One day she was calling almost every other hour, and then it was as if she had fallen off the face of the earth. He truly wished she had.

Chapter 12

Xavier Knight

Tuesday: 8:06 A.M.

"Something sure does smell good in here," Xavier said.

"Thanks." Shelby smiled. "I am cooking omelets to order. What would you like in yours?"

"What kind of ingredients do you have?" Xavier asked.

"She's got just about anything you can name," Travis said.

Xavier noticed Travis's lack of appetite from the previous night had heartily returned. His plate held what looked like two omelets.

"Yep, I've got a smorgasbord over here." Shelby turned an omelet in a pan.

Xavier cracked his knuckles and took a seat at the table. "I'll take one with bacon, ham, cheese, onions and green peppers."

"Coming right up. I've got one order in before yours. Go ahead and help yourself to some juice," Shelby said placing an omelet on a plate. "Here you go, George. One omelet with extra cheese and ham," Shelby said.

"Thanks, Shelby. This omelet sure does look good. I can't remember the last time I had one," George said.

"Nina, you just want veggies in yours, right?" Shelby asked.

Nina didn't answer. Her head was down and she seemed to be dozing at the table. George nudged her.

"Huh? What, George?" Nina asked.

"Shelby is talking to you," George said.

"I was asking you if you want just veggies in your omelet," Shelby said.

"Yeah, I don't eat pork," Nina said.

"I've got some turkey bacon I can put in there for you if you'd like," Shelby said.

Nina wrinkled her nose. "I tried that stuff once, and it tasted pretty nasty to me. Just vegetables will be fine."

"Okay, one vegetarian omelet coming right up," Shelby said.

"So, Xavier," Travis said between bites of his omelet, "do you have your own dressing room and a makeup artist?"

"Huh?" Xavier asked. He had no idea what this guy was talking about.

"You know, when you do your shoots for your commercials."

"Oh no, man. It's nothing like that. They might put a little powder on my skin to absorb any oil, but that's where it ends. I don't wear makeup." The furthest thing from Xavier's mind was shooting commercials.

"So how long does it take you to learn your lines?" Travis asked.

Xavier felt Travis was asking him questions like he was some type of movie star or something. "The commercials don't really have that many lines. Some days I get the script an hour or so before shooting, it just depends on my general manager. But the cue cards help.

And by the time we've shot it a few times, I pretty much have it memorized."

"Right, right." Travis nodded his head as he spoke, still chewing on his food. His eyes sparkled with awe.

Xavier was used to women looking at him with awe. They'd done so since he was in high school and college. After his acne cleared up, the braces were removed, and he'd had a growth spurt of five inches within a year, the sorely picked on Xay Xay, as the neighborhood kids called him, had metamorphosed like a caterpillar into a butterfly.

Xavier stared at the crooked teeth of the man sitting in front of him and shuttered to think what his teeth would have looked like if his parents hadn't seen fit to put braces on them. He was also thankful to God that he'd had his growth spurt in high school or else he might have been a squat in stature just like Travis. Sometimes he felt bad for the little guys of the world.

"I've seen all the commercials you've done. I really liked the mini series you did around Christmas last year," Travis said. He smiled, showing a few of his crooked teeth.

"Oh, that series was called Santa Claus is coming to town," Xavier said. He figured he might as well appease the man while he waited for his omelet.

Travis closed his eyes for a moment as if remembering something. "It was so nice how everyone got the gift they wanted in the end; especially the old lady with the foster kids."

"I actually came up with the ideas for that series. I told my general manager we should do a series of commercials sort of like a soap opera with a story that viewers could follow. Our sales increased by fifteen percent over our Christmas sales in previous years." This was an accomplishment Xavier was very proud of.

"But I still don't understand how that nurse ended up

getting her SUV. Especially with all the problems she was having with her credit," Travis said.

"You don't? We did a whole commercial on how she was able to get a co-signer and won money off of a scratch off ticket. Enough money for her to be able to place a down payment," Xavier said.

"Ah, man. I must have missed it," Travis said. His face was truly perplexed.

Xavier wondered if all the man did was watch TV all day, because even he hadn't seen all of the commercials on the airways.

"Here you are, Nina. One vegetable omelet." Shelby handed Nina her plate.

Without a word of thanks, Nina took the omelet and started inspecting it with her fork like she was in an anatomy class, dissecting it.

Xavier thought this woman was the epitome of rude, and wondered how the famous G.I. Jones could have ended up with a woman like her. Opposites must truly attract; especially when it came to George and Nina Jones.

"Xavier, you said cheese, ham, bacon, onions and green peppers, right?" Shelby asked.

"Yes, please," Xavier replied. "You remembered all that without writing it down? Were you a waitress or some-thing?"

"Nope, just a good memory that's all," Shelby said.

Upon looking back at Travis, Xavier saw the same look of perplexity still covering his face. The commercials ran for six weeks prior to the week of Christmas. Each epi-sode ran for seven days at various times during the day and night. So it didn't seem too farfetched that the man could have missed a commercial.

"Did you say you've seen all my commercials?" Xavier asked for clarification.

"Yep," Travis said, nodding his head as if he'd won a

blue ribbon prize or something. "Although from what you just said, I must have let one slip by."

Xavier was even more perplexed that the guy had said he'd seen all of his other commercials. Not just the six they shot for last Christmas holiday, but forty-something others. Xavier didn't really keep up with the count, but was pretty sure they were getting close to the fifty mark.

Curious as to what line of business Travis was in, Xavier asked, "So what type of work do you do?"

At this question, Travis, who was about to put another bite of omelet in his mouth stopped the fork in mid-air and glanced nervously at his wife. Beryl looked expectantly at her husband for an answer.

Travis put the fork down and picked up the glass of water to drink before he answered. "Well, I'm between jobs right now. I had a few problems at the last place I worked." He nodded his head as if trying to convince himself. "I have an associate's degree in General Studies, so I am a jack of all trades."

Xavier nodded his head at this.

"I've been looking, but it's hard out there trying to find a job. And I don't just want any job. I want a job where they'll appreciate my experience and educational background," Travis continued. "There are a couple of jobs I was looking at in the paper before I came here, and I am going to call them as soon as I get back home."

"Here you go, Xavier. One hot and cheesy omelet," Shelby said as she handed him his plate.

The omelet looked just like the ones Xavier had seen pictured on the menus of the IHOP restaurant. Steam rose from it, and the cheese glistened as it dripped through the sides. His mouth watered. He couldn't wait to take a bite.

After saying a quick, silent grace, he took the side of his fork and cut a piece. Upon tasting the meat and vegetable filled masterpiece, he hummed with delight. It tasted even better than the omelets at IHOP. "Are you a chef?" Xavier directed his question to Shelby.

"No, I'm a registered nurse," Shelby answered.

Xavier took another bite of his omelet. "I see what you mean now, George. Shelby, I really think your missed your calling. You cook as good as any of the chefs from many of the restaurants I've been to."

"Thanks, Xavier. There is a secret I assure you. I might share it with you before you all leave and go back home." Shelby smiled.

"My wife can cook too," Travis said. "That's what she does for a living."

"Are you a chef?" Xavier asked Beryl.

Beryl cut her eyes at her husband. "No, I'm not a chef. I manage a Hardee's back home. But you know how managers are in fast food restaurants. We can do just about anything. Sometimes we get a high rush of people, and my cooks may need help. Or you just never know when someone might call in sick or just up and quit."

Travis nodded, pride glowing from his face at his wife's comments. "She sells makeup on the side also; so if any of you ladies need something, call my wife, and she can hook you up."

With the volume of her voice rising, Beryl looked directly at her husband and said, "Sometimes you've got to get the job done whether you like it or not. Sometimes you gotta do what you gotta do."

Travis's look of pride fizzled into a look of embarrassment and shame. Xavier figured he'd try and help prevent any further escalating heat in the room by directing his question to Travis. "Have you ever thought about car sales?"

"No, can't say that I have. I don't know if I'd be good at trying to get people to buy cars."

Beryl put the cup of orange juice she was drinking down on the table with a thud. And with her neck shaking like a bobbing head doll, she said, "But you could at least try. People need cars. I'm sure there are people who come in already planning on buying a car; they just need a little help choosing the right one. Isn't that right, Xavier?" Beryl rotated her whole body toward Xavier and crossed her arms as she waited for the answer.

All Xavier wanted to do was enjoy the rest of his omelet while the cheese was still running warm. He had his own problems to deal with, and right now he was feeling like he was some sort of counselor.

"Uh, yeah, lots of people come in knowing they want to purchase a car. They might not know what they want, and sometimes they're dealership hopping, looking for just the right car. But that's when the skills of salesmanship kick in. If you're a people person, with the right training, you might do well as a salesman," Xavier said.

Beryl rotated her body back toward Travis. "But you'll never know if you don't try."

Travis picked up his napkin, wiped his hands, and balled it up. He dropped it into his plate.

"Hey, everybody," Phillip said as he entered the dining room. "What's going on? I thought I heard a couple of voices in here."

"That was me," Beryl said. "I didn't mean to be so loud. I was just trying to make a point." She waved her hand in a dismissive gesture. "But whatever. I honestly don't know why I try so hard."

Travis let out a deep breath, picked up his plate and headed for the kitchen. He mumbled something to Shelby while throwing an entire omelet into the trashcan. Then he rubbed his stomach and headed toward his bedroom.

Xavier wondered how he had gotten sucked in to the whole argument between Beryl and Travis. No one else had said a thing. George sat in his seat looking as if he were meditating the whole time. His wife, Nina, finished dissecting the omelet she was eating, barely taking two bites. Xavier wondered how the woman had gotten so big with the minimal caloric intake she'd been displaying so far at the retreat.

Charlotte, who was sitting in the living room, had barely even acknowledged there were other people in the cabin with her, much less having an escalating argument. It was as if she really didn't care, and this bothered Xavier.

He only had a few days to try to convince his wife that he was truly sorry for his infidelity and to assure her that he was a completely changed man. And so help him God, he was going to do it somehow.

Chapter 13

Xavier Knight

Tuesday: 9:02 A.M.

"I trust you all have eaten and enjoyed your breakfast. My wife can cook, can't she?" Phillip gently patted Shelby on her shoulder. They were seated back at The Round Table.

Shelby looked into her husband's eyes, and Xavier could see the mutual love the couple had for each other. He wondered if he and Charlotte would ever again have that same type of mutual love.

"Tell the truth, Phillip, she's really a chef, right?" Xavier said. He smiled, patting his stomach.

George piped in, "I agree, I haven't had cooking like that in a while."

"Not every woman can be domesticated. Some of us have other talents and skills," Nina said. She looked at George as if daring him to challenge what she was saying.

George shook his head in exasperation. Without saying a word, he picked up his agenda and read the day's information.

"Thanks, Xavier and George, I know you're just trying

to find out what my cooking secrets are, but like I said, at the end of this retreat, I just might share a few of those secrets with you," Shelby said. She smiled and turned her attention back to Phillip.

Phillip wordlessly looked around at everyone with the biggest smirk Xavier had ever seen on a person's face. He did this for so long, that after a while, a couple of people, including Xavier, looked at everyone else with question, wondering if they knew what was going on or if they'd missed something in their notes.

After what had probably only been a full minute, Phillip said, "I bet you're all wondering why I am sitting here with this bigger than normal smirk on my face."

"Yeah, I thought I might have missed something," Travis said. "Or at least thought we all must have done something wrong."

"When I smirk like this, Shelby knows something is up. And when she does the same to me, I know something in our marriage is a little off kilter."

Phillip stood and faced the dry erase board. "You may have done something wrong, but only you'll be able to determine what it is."

Phillip wrote the acronym S.M.I.R.K. on the board in uppercase letters.

"Today we'll be talking about agreement as it relates to marriage. Please know that there is power in agreement. Matthew 18:19 says, *Again I say unto you, That if two of you shall agree on earth as touching any thing that they shall ask, it shall be done for them of my Father which is in heaven.*

"Just like communication, agreement is vital to a relationship. Marriages and families require not only structure, but the responsibility of some type of agreed upon agreement; whether it is to agree or to agree to disagree. This will require much discipline. There are five vital areas of agreement which will be pivotal to the restructuring of your marriages."

Phillip turned to the board again, writing what each of the letters in the acronym meant.

"Sex, Money, Intangibles, Religion, and Kids. These are key areas in which you and your spouse will want to make sure there is some type of verbal agreement. You'll need to sit down without disruption and know what your feelings are on these subjects. You may even need to discuss each of these areas in more than just one sitting," Phillip said.

The whole while Phillip spoke, Shelby nodded her head, agreeing with what her husband was saying. Xavier wasn't sure if she was actually conscious of her movements. It looked like the agreement between them came so naturally.

Xavier figured whatever problems they had in their marriage must not have been any where near the magnitude he'd been having with Charlotte. But he longed to one day have his wife sitting next to him supporting him one hundred percent, patting him on his back.

"There may be some areas which you and your spouse have discussed and other areas which you've only allowed the grey matter in your brains to play with, letting things take their own course. So like a toddler walking around in a China shop, you can't let some things go unsaid, waiting for whatever results arise. You've got to be proactive when it comes to your marriages and the topics which can cause your buttons to be pushed," Phillip said, smirking again. "That brings me to the first area of agreement: sex."

Dread enveloped Xavier. Why did the first topic of the day have to be about sex? Why did they even have to talk about sex at all? Sex was the thing that got him in trouble in the first place. Why couldn't they just continue talking about communication? That's all he really needed. He just needed for Charlotte to get over the phone call he'd received and talk to him so he could try again to reassure her that he was a changed man and would do whatever she wanted to make amends. He'd go to more counseling if need be. He'd stay off of the Internet. And he would definitely be changing his cell phone number. The last thing he needed was for Yasmine to start calling him again or to start stalking him.

"I guess I could have said love instead of sex, but I couldn't think of an acronym that would suffice with the letter *L*. Nonetheless, sex is actually a more appropriate word," Phillip said. "Sex should be seen as something beautiful between a husband and a wife. When you talk to your spouse on this subject, you want to understand what specifically attracts you to the other person. You also want to know what the other person deems as romantic. Is it a candlelight dinner, or is it the candlelight without dinner?" Phillip smiled.

At this comment, Nina grinned and George smiled also.

Phillip continued. "We are all adults here. I'm not here to try to give you any ideas about what you should or shouldn't do in your bedroom, bathroom, dining room or kitchen. What is done within the auspices of marriage is not defiled by God.

"You just have to know what the other person likes or dislikes. With dialogue, come to some sort of agreement."

Phillip cleared his throat. "There are times when people think of the word sex with a negative connotation—mainly when it involves people who are unmarried. There are instances when one person is married but the person they are sleeping with isn't.

"Let me make this real clear to you all. There are two categories: married and un-married. Everyone falls into one of these categories. When an unmarried person is brought into the equation of a married couple, the only thing it can lead to is disaster."

Xavier cracked his knuckles. It felt like Phillip was talking directly to him. Charlotte started moving uncomfortably in her chair.

"And if there is a third wheel in a relationship, that's a red light warning that you need to stop and talk," Phillip said.

Xavier hoped Phillip was going to impart some great words of wisdom or give him some other angle on how he should talk to Charlotte about the third wheel he'd been responsible for bringing into their marriage. Everything he'd tried so far hadn't worked, and the more he talked, the more he felt like he was digging an even bigger hole for himself.

He was just thankful Charlotte hadn't found out about the other women he'd contacted and chatted with on the Internet. He was truly glad she didn't know about the two other women he'd gotten extremely close to sleeping with: a girl named Angel that he'd actually met from the Internet, and Carly, their neighbor.

"On the subject of sex, agree on what you will and will not do, what you can and cannot accept, and what your full expectations are with your spouse," Phillip said.

Charlotte ran her fingers through her hair while continuing to fidget nervously in her chair.

"Any questions or comments so far?" Phillip asked.

Xavier had lots of questions and even more comments, but remained closed mouthed. He hoped Charlotte wouldn't pick this time to have a kumbaya moment with the group, sharing all of the intimate details and problems about the sex in their marriage. Luckily she hadn't.

Phillip moved on to the next topic: money. Stating couples should look at all the aspects that dealt not only with the handling of the money in a marriage, but spending plans and even career decisions.

Xavier was glad that he and Charlotte hadn't had any financial problems. In that area, they were sound. He just wished the same could be said when it came to his history of stepping out in his marriage.

During the time Phillip spent talking about the importance of finances in a marriage, Nina had taken on a nervousness Xavier was surprised to see. George, on the other hand, looked like he could be popped with a safety pin if poked. The grin and smile they'd held when reminiscing about their behind closed doors undefiled activities were now wiped clean—without a trace.

Xavier thought this odd. He knew G.I. Jones who'd been featured in *Essence* magazine and who had one of the fastest growing churches in the Eastern United States, had probably been enjoying millionaire status for at least a few years. The exposé the magazine had written and shown pictures of a ground breaking ceremony for his new church edifice, his and her luxury cars they had, and the sprawling two story mini-mansion he owned.

Travis stared out toward the lake, his mind somewhere else. Eerily, Xavier wondered if the guy was daydreaming about the car commercials. His wife, Beryl, stared at Phillip, absently nodding her head every now and then. She looked tired and drained, as if she hadn't rested well in a while.

Phillip went on to discuss the intangibles, the little things in a marriage that can bother a person like a splinter imbedded just under the skin. Saying a splinter under the skin couldn't sometimes be ignored, but eventually, if not taken care of, it could grow into an unwanted infection. Next he spoke about the importance of religion in a marriage and how couples need to discuss beliefs about denominations, salvation, and even levels of church involvement.

Last he spoke about kids. At this, Xavier raised an eyebrow, as did Charlotte. Xavier had children from his previous marriage that his ex-wife hardly ever let him see. Even though the courts had awarded him designated holidays and three weeks in the summer with his children, his ex-wife was always coming up with last minute excuses as to why the kids couldn't visit him.

In addition to Charlotte being upset with him about his infidelity, she had also been frustrated because they hadn't been able to have any children yet. They'd been trying ever since they'd gotten married. Charlotte was an only child and wanted at least two children, if not three. She'd often told Xavier how lonely she was as an only child and envied her friends who had siblings to play with or even exchange clothing with. She didn't want to have just one child who'd have to endure the same loneliness she had.

To date, after four and a half years of being married, Charlotte had not gotten pregnant. Xavier had encouraged her on more than one occasion to talk to her doctor about it. He'd even done some research on the Internet, finding there were medical procedures that might be able to help them; especially if there were any problems.

But Charlotte hadn't wanted a doctor probing and prodding her. She just wanted to trust that if they were meant to have children, God would make it happen. Some days she let the fact that they didn't have any children roll off her back. Other days, Xavier saw the sadness in her eyes; especially when they went to church and saw many couples with their newborn babies, or whenever her church friends would tell her they were pregnant.

Xavier could tell by the look in Charlotte's eyes that

today, the subject of children wasn't going to roll off her back with ease.

"Oh yes, the loving and sometimes touchy subject of kids," Phillip said. "Children are wonderful gifts from God. We must always remember this. But when children are added to the marriage equation, your need to communicate and agree increases. With children involved, you are at a whole new level.

"They come into this world needing everything. They can't even hold their little heads up, so you as a parent have to help them even with that small thing. Someone has to take on the task of feeding and cleaning them. And in the beginning, it is all so new and exciting.

"Then after a while things get a little more intense, ever so gradually. Those cute little diapers with the little bit of poop turn into bigger diapers with a load you'd never imagined could come from such a little person."

"Uh-huh." Beryl nodded her head in agreement.

"Early on, you might find yourself having to discuss and agree on the smallest things like how many children you want to have and how you'll raise them," Phillip said.

Phillip looked at Shelby. "Sometimes life throws us a curve ball, adding a little baby mama or baby daddy drama."

Shelby looked into her husband's eyes and moved her hand to squeeze his forearm.

"But with communication, mutual respect, and a little give and take, you can master raising the children God has blessed you with," Phillip said.

Shelby nodded her head and raised her hand in a church type waving motion.

"And any curve balls life throws your way," Phillip added, placing his hand on his chest. "I'm a witness."

At this statement, Xavier, as well as everyone else, did

a double take. Now he was really curious as to what type of problems Phillip and Shelby experienced during their marriage. He didn't have the nerve to ask, but he figured sooner or later, Travis would open his big mouth and bring up the subject.

Chapter 14

Xavier Knight

Tuesday: 12:00 P.M.

Xavier stepped out on to the wrap around porch of the cabin, pleased to find Charlotte alone sitting on one of the four oversized rocking chairs. The air had chilled, but it wasn't cold enough for them to need a sweater or coat.

He took a seat in the chair closest to his wife, but didn't say a word. He was just glad to see she wasn't fleeing off the porch to get away from him. Just being close to her was enough. He appreciated not being in a tense room full of people talking about subjects like sex and children—subjects that seemed to be pushing him and his wife farther apart instead of bring them closer.

There was so much he wanted to say to Charlotte; he just didn't know where to start. So instead of talking, he sat silent listening to the rippling of the water from the lake and a boat's engine somewhere in the distance.

From the corner of his eye, he saw Charlotte staring at him. He remained facing forward, looking out on to the rippling waters of the lake, not wanting to push his luck with his wife.

After a few moments, Charlotte also turned her attention back to the lake and finally spoke. "You know, sometimes I just wish none of this ever happened. I wish we could just go back to the days when we didn't have all the curve balls, as Phillip would say."

Xavier nodded his head. He felt terrible for being the one to have caused the stress their marriage was now undergoing. Charlotte didn't deserve all he was putting her through.

"Sometimes in the morning, I wake up, and for the briefest of instances, I've forgotten, and all is well with the world. But then everything floods back to me, and I feel a dreadful sickness in my stomach," Charlotte said.

Her tone wasn't angry or spiteful, but the hurt in her voice was unmistakable. Xavier could see the tears starting to trickle down her face, and he wanted to jump up and grab her, to hug her and let her know that everything would turn out okay. It had to. He couldn't imagine his life without her. But he knew better. He hadn't held his wife or even gotten so much as a handshake from her in months. But he was committed to working as hard as he could to put the smile back on her face.

As Charlotte's trickling tears turned into sniffles, and then sobs, Xavier couldn't hold back any longer. And before he knew it, he was in front of her, on his knees, embracing her as if she held the key to life itself. At first she protested, trying to wriggle free of him. But his strong arms and her need to release a built up anguish won in the end.

Xavier held her until the sobs turned into moans and continued to embrace her as the moaning subsided into intermittent sniffles. He didn't know how long they'd been out on the porch, but was glad no one had been looking for them. Their being able to hold one another at that moment in time was the best therapy any doctor could have ordered. With reluctance, he let Charlotte go once he felt her tense body relax.

Continuing to kneel in front of her, Xavier moved back slightly, giving her some space. She looked down, staring directly into his eyes.

"I hate what's happened to us, Xavier." She wiped lingering tears from her face.

"I hate it too," Xavier said. "But we can get through this; I know we can."

Charlotte shook her head.

He took her hands into his. "We can, Charlotte. We just have to take everything a step at a time. One day at a time."

"It won't be that easy."

"I know it won't be easy. I have no illusions about that. But if we work together we can get back to where we were." Xavier caressed her cheek with the palm of his hand. "Baby, I want you to smile again, laugh again. I want you to be able to wake up in the morning and only think of this horrible time in our lives as a distant memory."

Charlotte took in a deep breath, and then slowly released it. "I can't trust you. Ever since that horrible day, I can't trust you. And I don't know when I'll be able to trust you again. This isn't something that can simply be forgotten."

"But hopefully, with time, things will get better. I don't expect you to forget this. Just know that I am sorry, and I am going to do absolutely everything in my power to earn the trust you've lost in me," Xavier said. He took both her hands and kissed them.

Charlotte stared with intensity as she looked into his eyes.

Xavier knew her trust in him had been severely severed the day she'd receive her test results about the gonorrhea. The memory was still fresh in his mind as he thought back to the most sobering day in his life, when his world came crashing down. It was on a Friday evening. He'd called Charlotte earlier in the day to let her know he'd be home for a short break around four o'clock. It was the first of the month, which meant it was payday— payday for the military at nearby Fort Bragg Army base and Pope Air Force base and also for county and city employees.

As soon as he walked in the door, he sensed something was wrong. At first he wasn't sure what it was, but then it hit him. The ticking of the grandfather clock in their living room seemed louder than usual. The house had been quiet—as quiet as it usually was in the wee hours of the morning when he got up to go to the bathroom.

Charlotte was a praise dancer at her church, and that upcoming Sunday, the dance ministry was set to minister. For days she had been playing a song over and over again, getting into the spirit. She always did this before she was about to minister.

When he rounded the corner of the dining room, calling her name, he was startled to see her sitting at the table with an envelope in her hand.

"Have a seat," Charlotte said.

Xavier wondered what was going on. "What's up?" he asked, but did as Charlotte told him.

She thrust the envelope into his hand and crossed her arms.

"What's this?" Xavier asked.

"You tell me." Charlotte's voice was calm and controlled.

Xavier opened the envelope hoping and praying it didn't have anything to do with the disease he'd gotten from Yasmine. But his heart dropped when he saw the medical report listing various tests performed for sexually transmitted diseases. The paper with Charlotte's name showed she had tested positive for gonorrhea.

He stared at the paper thinking if he looked at it long enough, the results would change or he'd realize he was really dreaming, and at any second, he'd wake up. But there was no such luck.

"So you tell me. What is this?" Charlotte said.

Charlotte's voice had been unbelievably calm. Xavier wondered what was going on.

"I . . . uh, it's a test result that says you're positive for gonorrhea," Xavier said, stating the obvious. He didn't want to say anything that would take him directly into a hole he might not be able to get out of.

"I can read. I can see that. I am asking you what this is all about. I need for you to tell me," Charlotte said. She shifted in her seat, moving slightly closer to him.

"Baby—"

Charlotte interrupted. "Cut it, Xavier. Tell me who it is? Where did you get it or do you even know?"

Xavier felt like he was having déjà vu. Only it wasn't really déjà vu because he'd had a similar conversation with his ex-wife before she filed for divorce. With his ex, he'd denied everything.

But this time he figured he'd go ahead and tell Charlotte about Yasmine. He'd have to come semi-clean about the relationship. He couldn't lie his way out of a positive test result.

"There was this woman. I met her at a Starbucks." He paused. "Baby, I don't really want to go into the details. But I did sleep with this woman a couple of times."

Charlotte's eyes widened, and Xavier saw the first crack in her calm demeanor.

"It was a mistake. I broke it off with her," Xavier said. He'd said it with enough of a mixture of the truth for it to be believable.

Charlotte continued to stare at him expectantly. "What's her name? And why? Why did you feel like you had to sleep with someone else?"

"Her name doesn't matter. What matters is that it's over," Xavier said.

"You could have fooled me. I'm the one with a sexually transmitted disease. Doesn't feel like it's over to me." Charlotte sat back. "You could at least tell me that much. Who is she?"

"Her name was Yasmine. And again, it's over. I don't have any contact with her anymore."

"Yasmine. It sounds exotic or something," Charlotte said. Sarcasm dripped from her voice.

"Baby, don't even think about it or her," Xavier said.

"Did you know you had this disease?" Charlotte asked.

Without fully thinking it out, Xavier said, "No, I've been having a little pain lately, and I went to my doctor the other day. I hadn't received my results yet. I didn't want to tell you if there wasn't anything to worry about."

Xavier was lying through his teeth, but he couldn't really justify telling her that he'd known for weeks that he was positive. And he knew there was no way she would understand.

Charlotte took a deep breath. "Yasmine; well, isn't that cute?"

"No, it isn't cute. Like I told you, it's over."

"Is she the only one?" Charlotte asked. She drummed her fingers noiselessly on the table.

He couldn't believe she was asking him about other women, and he wasn't about to tell her about the women he'd gotten intimate with or the various women he'd chatted with on the Internet. "No, there isn't anyone else. I am so sorry. I made a terrible mistake."

He reached across the dining room table to touch her

hand, but as soon as he did, she slapped him across the face. The open handed slap stung, but the fact that his wife knew about his infidelity stung even more.

"Get away from me. Don't touch me," Charlotte said. The calm exterior had instantly evaporated. She stood, backing away from him.

He rubbed the stinging spot on his face, knowing the slap was well deserved. And he knew he probably deserved more than that.

"I need some space. I want you to leave," Charlotte said.

"Leave? Where am I going to go?" Xavier asked.

"I don't know. Why don't you just go to your little friend or something? At this point, I really don't care."

The calm exterior Charlotte had held only a few short minutes ago was now being replaced with a stream of tears. Her body had become visibly shaky.

Xavier stood now also. "Charlotte, I'm not going anywhere. We need to talk about this."

Charlotte turned and headed toward their bedroom. Xavier figured she needed the space, so he gave it to her. He walked over to their living room window and gazed out. His worst fear had been realized. His wife knew that he'd been unfaithful and worse, she'd contracted a venereal disease.

He hadn't heard Charlotte walk through the house or the garage open. But he did hear Charlotte's car as it was being cranked. And before he had a chance to go to the garage to see where she was going, Xavier saw his wife pull out into the street in record speed. She had backed out and stopped so hard that he heard the tires squeal on the car.

With the way she was shaking during the end of their conversation and the way she was driving, he was scared she might get into an accident. He fumbled while pulling his cell phone out of his pocket.

When he dialed her cell number, he'd heard it ringing from somewhere in the house. Following the sound, Xavier found the cell phone on the bedroom dresser. He also saw that Charlotte had hurriedly pulled out drawers and hangers with clothes from her side of the closet. Remnants of strewn clothing dotted the bed and the floor.

Xavier snapped his phone shut. Upon further inspection of the room, he saw that his wife had taken one of her suitcases as well as some of her toiletry items from the bathroom. She was gone, and from the looks of it, she wasn't planning on coming back any time soon.

Charlotte stayed away for three days, and he had no idea where his wife was. He hoped she was okay, but was hesitant to call friends or family to ask if they'd seen her; partly because he knew Charlotte was a private person and wouldn't want everyone in her business, but mainly because he was ashamed of the reason she'd left in the first place.

The sound of a speedboat zooming by on the lake brought Xavier back to his current reality. He was thankful that for the first time in months, on a porch in the middle of the mountains, he was finally able to hold his wife's hand again.

Charlotte rocked forward in the rocking chair. "Trust is so important, Xavier. You've damaged my trust in you so much."

"I know, and I promise I'll do everything in my power to earn your trust back again. Okay?"

"I hear you." Charlotte didn't look like she believed what he was saying.

"I promise, Charlotte. No secrets, no messing around, no more drama."

"I hear you, Xavier," Charlotte repeated, still seeming unconvinced.

She looked down at her watch, then wiped her eyes again. "I guess we'd better get back inside. They've probably already started the next session."

Xavier looked at his own watch. They were late for the beginning of the afternoon session. Even though his legs felt stiff and heavy as he stood, his heart was light.

Chapter 15

Xavier Knight

Tuesday: 1:14 P.M.

Charlotte and Xavier reentered the cabin and tried not to disturb the other couples who were already in the midst of conversation. They took their respective seats at The Round Table.

Noticing a few of the eyes glancing at him and Charlotte, Xavier said, "Sorry, we had to discuss a few things."

"It's all right," Phillip said. "We were just going back over the S.M.I.R.K. acronym. Feel free to join in."

Xavier appreciated the fact that Phillip had smoothly welcomed them back to the group without a be-on-time-next-time undertone. Even though Phillip hadn't been out on the porch with them, it was as if somehow he knew they were trying to focus on getting their marriage back together.

"George was giving us his take on how the differences in religion that a husband and wife might have, can impact marriages," Phillip said.

"You wouldn't believe how many people I have coming to me with arguments about their religious beliefs," George said. "Many of them got married with the understanding that each would continue to participate in their respective religions or dominations." George shook his head. "It's often such a mess. One person goes to church and the other doesn't, or the husband worships at one church and the wife is at another church with no spiritual unity at all. Then they wonder why many of the other areas of their lives were so askew. They didn't understand that God wanted them to be unified, coming together with an agreement that would entail oneness."

"How'd you get the couples to come in for counseling, especially if one of them wasn't a member of your church?" Phillip asked.

"Only about a quarter of who I counsel are actually my members, believe it or not. Many people enjoy watching my broadcasts. And the couples know I am real and tell it like it is. They may not like what I have to say, though, by the time they leave my office. But they do respect the advice I've given them," George said.

Travis nodded his head. "So George, how do you find the time to counsel people with all the services you have and the traveling I see you doing?"

"I make the time. People say I am a soldier for the Lord. I am also a soldier for married couples. My book, *I Do, I Don't*, has a workbook that accompanies it. Whenever I counsel couples, I encourage them to read the book and work on the exercises in the workbook. If a couple does this and is serious about making their marriage stronger or repairing damage, I continue to counsel them as needed. But if I see people are playing games with their time and mine, I'll quickly let them know to take it elsewhere."

Xavier felt George came off as not only a spiritual man of God, but also a knowledgeable one. The man had sold millions of books and often appeared on talk shows talking about his ministry. And he definitely acted as if he were a no-nonsense kind of guy. So Xavier wondered why a man who was sought out by so many for his spiritual guidance was sitting at the same table with him, getting advice from a man no one really knew—as far as the religious world was concerned.

George shook his head. "Sadly disagreements about religious beliefs have contributed to the demise of many a marriage."

Charlotte stood, excusing herself. Xavier touched her arm, wondering if she were okay. She smiled, reassuring him she was fine; mouthing she needed to use the bathroom.

Xavier beamed inwardly, glad to finally see a smile on his wife's face for the first time since she found out about the STD. Things were looking up for him.

"What about the little things? You know . . . the intangible things as Phillip called them?" Beryl asked. She'd directed her question to George.

"Ah, the intangibles. The things we don't often know about until after we've said I do," George replied.

"Yeah. How often do you find couples who can't overcome the intangibles? Little things do mean a lot, and after they pile up, they're sort of hard to overlook," Beryl said.

"Compared to the problems of sex, money, religion, and kids, the intangibles are things that don't always seem as big. But if enough intangible things pile up, and especially if it is coupled with one or more of the other big four, the little things can cause unbelievable marital strife," George said.

Xavier was glad he and Charlotte didn't have any money problems. Early on, they'd decided who would take care of which bills. They also decided that Charlotte would handle the budget; not because Xavier was bad with money, but because she happened to be better than he was with it.

They'd also never had any problems with religion; not in his eyes anyway. Charlotte was a saved Christian woman when he met her. And although he wasn't saved, his mother and grandmother had been, and he'd been raised in a loving Christian home. He went to church on Sundays and paid his tithe along with his wife. He didn't see a real need to become saved like the people he'd seen going to the altar at the end of each service. Because except for his proclivity toward women, he knew deep down he was a good guy. And now that he had been given a second chance, obviously from God, to save his marriage, he swore to himself that he would never stray again. He'd do whatever it took. He'd already ruined his first wife's life and would make sure he didn't ruin Charlotte's with any more of his shenanigans. It was only by the grace of God he hadn't contracted AIDS, and from Charlotte's test results, she didn't have the disease either.

The subject of kids was a different story. He knew Charlotte wanted kids and hoped one day she'd at least consider being open to going to have some tests done to see if there might be any problems. Until then, he'd be patient and be ready to discuss the subject whenever she might be ready to talk.

Xavier could only think of two things that still irked him after all the time they'd been married. The first thing was that whenever Charlotte washed dishes, she always faced the dishes in the wrong direction in the dish drainer. His mother and grandmother always faced the front of the plates away. The other thing she did was to put the toilet paper on the roll backward, so that the tissue hung down in the back instead of the front when pulling it down. He always had to pull from the back, and it was awkward to him. So without saying anything, he'd change the roll whenever he saw it had been turned the wrong way.

These two things irked him, but weren't anything he'd have to go see a counselor about. The dishes always dried whichever way they were turned, and the toilet paper still did its job when needed.

As far as Xavier was concerned, he and Charlotte were in pretty good shape. Especially now that she was warming back up to him and giving him another chance. He was looking forward to their free time that evening. He couldn't wait for their one-on-one time, without the interruption of others. The marriage retreat was turning out to be the best thing they could have done for their marriage.

Charlotte returned from the bathroom with a thick, brown, expanding accordion file in her hand. He hadn't seen this folder before and hadn't noticed it packed among the things in her suitcase. Xavier looked at her questioningly, wondering what it could be.

She smiled as she sat next to him, but her smile wasn't that of love and hopeful reconciliation. It was a smile that more closely resembled the smirk Phillip had displayed earlier that morning. The smirk gave him an uneasiness in his stomach.

Charlotte placed the folder on the opposite side of her on the floor, well away from him. "What did I miss?" she said. Her voice—unlike her smirk—was delightful and pleasant. Her demeanor continually caused Xavier's stomach to feel uneasy.

Phillip filled her in. "George was just telling us how sometimes the intangible things in a marriage can compound any other problems that may be present. The little things can often mean a lot; especially when there are quite a few little things to factor in.

"We've reviewed the intangible problems and problems with religion. What would you all like to discuss next?" Phillip asked.

"How about the subject of sex and lies?" Charlotte asked.

Xavier didn't know exactly where Charlotte was going with what she was saying, but he had a sinking feeling that it couldn't be going anywhere good.

"Sex and lies?" Phillip asked.

"Yeah. I mean you've discussed the fact that couples need to let the other spouse know where they stand when it comes to sex. But what if you've done that, but a spouse doesn't adhere to what you've established verbally and doesn't adhere to what should be understood in a marriage?" Charlotte asked.

"That's a very good point," Phillip said. "When talking about the areas of S.M.I.R.K, I did so with the understanding that each spouse needs to be open and honest in each of these areas. When you add lies into the equation, they lead to dishonesty. If there is dishonesty, you will not be able to effectively work out problems you may be having."

Phillip looked around at each person in the room with utmost sincerity. "You've got to be open and honest with your spouses. If not, then you're wasting your time at this retreat and taking up space where another couple could have been sitting."

Xavier clearly heard what Phillip was saying, and he had kept the whole truth from his wife. But he wasn't about to start divulging extra information about the other escapades outside of his marriage, especially when Charlotte didn't know anything about them. He'd had friends who hadn't been loyal to their wives. Often times, the wives did find out about some of their extra curricular activities, but none of the guys had been dumb enough to let the women know everything. What the women didn't know wouldn't hurt them. And for the most part, the guys cut back on what they were doing or completely stopped, realizing the grass wasn't always greener on the other side.

Charlotte didn't have to know about his other activities. Knowing about Yasmine was enough. The Yasmine subject alone had almost brought their marriage to an end. Xavier shuttered to think what she would do if she found out about any one else, especially their neighbor, Carly, a supposable good friend of Charlotte's, who smiled in her face whenever she got the chance; especially when they had book club meetings.

"Okay, so on the subject of sex, what if you've talked to your spouse about being honest and they tell you wholeheartedly they're being open?" Charlotte asked.

"Then it's at that point you have to trust in the person you've married. You have to take them at their word," Phillip said.

"But what if you can't do that? What if you know they're not telling you the truth?" Charlotte asked.

"Well, that depends on what you mean by knowing the other person isn't telling the truth. Let's just say it's a wife for instance?" Phillip said.

Charlotte nodded her head in agreement.

"And let's just say she doesn't trust something her husband is saying because she has that strong women's intuition you ladies often have. Or maybe even a friend who might be voicing their own personal concerns to the wife," Phillip said and smiled.

Charlotte sat unsmiling at Phillip's statements about intuition and friends.

Xavier, as well as the others sitting around the table, watched the conversation between Phillip and Charlotte like it was a tennis match.

"Then again, you still need to trust what the other spouse is saying. Later on this week we'll be talking about communication barriers." Phillip chuckled. "Believe me when I say the brain often distorts stuff."

"What if it's not intuition?" Charlotte asked. "What if you just know without a shadow of doubt that this person is not being honest with you? You know they're downright lying, or shall I say withholding information?"

"Again, that just depends on what you might have. Or shall I say the hypothetical person might have. I would encourage that person to talk with their spouse again and call them on it. Maybe that person is scared and just needs some encouragement. Especially when it comes to us guys. Sometimes we get scared when we think there might be something you women will hold against us or just go completely off on us."

Without even knowing it, Xavier nodded his head in agreement, ever so slightly.

"So you think the hypothetical woman should talk to the hypothetical man again and show him that she knows he's lying?" Charlotte asked.

"Or withholding," Phillip said. He smiled encouragingly at Charlotte and Xavier.

Charlotte nodded her head in understanding.

Xavier knew everyone in the room knew who the hypothetical wife and husband were. But surely Charlotte hadn't found anything concrete for which she could hold him accountable. He'd seen the test results for the STD. That was concrete, but they'd already discussed it at length. She'd tried time after time to get him to tell her the exact details of the affair, but he held firm in keeping everything else to himself.

Xavier had also held fast, saying the affair was completely over. He didn't have, and had never had, any real feelings for the other woman. And he adamantly tried reassuring Charlotte that she didn't have to ever worry about him sleeping with another woman again.

The tennis match spectacle had all eyes landing on Charlotte. She seemed oblivious to the fact that everyone was focused on her. Taking a deep breath, she turned her body and attention to her husband. "Xavier, is there anything you want to tell me?"

Without even allowing his mind to complete a full thought, Xavier said, "Nah."

Charlotte leaned over and pulled the thick accordion file off the floor. She opened it and pulled out three sheets of stapled paper. Upon further inspection of the file, Xavier saw that it had tabs separating the compartments by months. And from what he could tell, each compartment had something in it.

"Xavier, I've tried and tried to get you to tell me the truth about what you've been doing behind my back, but you continually tell me there's nothing going on. I've asked you time and time again to just be honest with me. You continually tell me you're being honest. Even less than an hour ago, out on that porch, you held my hands, looked in my eyes, and tried your best to assure me that you have been and are being honest with me," Charlotte said.

Even though Charlotte had asked the question, Xavier sat stone still with tight lips.

"What? You don't have any reassurances for me right now?" Charlotte said.

Her tone and demeanor mirrored the way she had been acting just before she sprung the STD test results on him. Xavier knew he'd better say something. That day sitting at their dining room table, Charlotte had only had one thin little envelope with just enough damaging information to cause his wife to leave him for a few days. That one sheet had caused her to almost leave him for good. If not for the reassurances he'd given her, Xavier was sure she'd have left him long ago.

It was as if he had lockjaw. His mouth refused to move, which was a good thing because he had no idea what would end up tumbling out.

"Go ahead and admit it, Xavier. Admit you've been lying to me," Charlotte said.

His body seemed to have contracted the lockjaw also. He couldn't even nod his head to answer her question.

"Charlotte, do you and Xavier want to go into another room so you can discuss whatever is bothering you?" Phillip asked.

Without looking in Phillip's direction, Charlotte said, "No, we can discuss this right here and now. Nobody is perfect in this room, and everybody has skeletons. I'm just the only one in here who is about to let those skeletons breathe."

"Yes, but Charlotte—" Phillip attempted.

Charlotte held up her hand to stop him from speaking. "Honestly, I don't have a problem with talking in front of you all. And unless my husband says he has a problem, we can finish this right here."

The tennis match spectators turned all eyes to Xavier. This was the time to say something, the time to save face and go into another room with his wife so that they could talk about whatever was on her mind. But his body still refused to obey his brain.

"So, there you have it. He doesn't mind either," Charlotte said.

Charlotte picked up the piece of paper she was holding in her hand. "For the month of May there were fifteen phone calls made from your phone to the number 555-1837 and twenty-eight calls received from the same number. In the month of June there were fifty-one calls to the same number and forty-seven calls received by you from that number." Charlotte paused and looked at Xavier. "Do I need to continue with July and August?"

Xavier couldn't believe what he was hearing. How had she known about all those calls? The only way was if she had a detailed phone bill for his cellular phone. He had to think of something to say quickly.

"Those were all business calls. You know how my work cell phone goes out. I started using my personal cell phone to take care of needed business transactions for work. That's the phone number for the new sales guy who started a few months back. I was his mentor." Xavier chuckled with nervousness. "He was a slow learner at first, so I had to keep on top of things with him until he fully learned the ropes."

"Oh really, Xavier? Is this new sales guy named Angel? What is he? A transvestite with an unusually high soprano voice?" Charlotte taunted.

How did Charlotte know the phone number belonged to Angel? He wondered if Charlotte had called Angel and gotten her voicemail or something. Angel had never mentioned talking to his wife.

He stammered, "Baby, what are you talking about? Who's Angel?"

Charlotte pulled a sheet out of the July section of the accordion file. "And I quote, 'Hey, baby, it's Angel. Where you at? I've been waiting for over thirty minutes. You said you'd be here thirty minutes ago. You know I gotta go to work in a few hours. I wanted to spend a little time with you. Call me as soon as you get this to let me know when you'll be here.' That was a phone message Miss Angel left you on July 21st," Charlotte said. "Funny, I don't remember hearing anything about any sales tips in that message." Charlotte's voice was full of facetiousness.

He didn't remember getting that particular message

from Angel, but it sounded like one of her typical messages, vernacular and all. Had Charlotte been listening to his cell phone messages somehow?"

Charlotte directed her full attention to Xavier as if there was no one else sitting in the room. "Do you want to hear more?" She paused. "I've got more."

Xavier shook his head.

"Oh no, humor me, please." She pulled another sheet out of the accordion file; this time from the label titled July. She traced her finger down the sheet. "Okay, here's a real good one. 'Hey, Xavier, I got your message, and last night was absolutely wonderful. I just hate that things got cut short. Let me know when Charlotte is scheduled to be out of town again. I'll check and see if the date coincides with any of the times Quincy will be out of town. Call me back after six o'clock. Quincy has a meeting and won't be home.'"

Xavier's mouth dropped. He couldn't be hearing what he thought he was hearing. He remembered that particular message well. It was from their neighbor, Carly. And even though Carly hadn't left her name on the message, Xavier knew good and well Charlotte had known who the voice belonged to. Carly had left messages on their home answering machine many times, especially about their book club meetings.

"Charlotte, I—" Xavier began to say, but Charlotte cut him off.

"No no. There's one more thing I want you to listen to." She pulled out another sheet of paper. "Now this one is a little different, a dialogue of sorts which went as follows.

"PrettyB: What's up with you?

"Sunshine627: Nothing much. When are we going to hook up?

"PrettyB: That's up to you.

"Sunshine627: Told you I'm game. When you gonna post a picture? I want to see if you look like you described yourself.

"PrettyB: LOL, I told you I am still new at this whole chatting thing.

"Sunshine627: Yeah right. We been chatting for over a month. Even I can tell you how to post your picture.

"PrettyB: Okay. Truth is, I am a little shy, and I don't want to put a picture on this site. You know there are a lot of weirdos out on the Internet.

"Sunshine627: You could always email a picture to me.

"PrettyB: Nah, I want you to meet me up close and personal. Pictures don't do me justice.

"PrettyB: You still there, Sunshine?

"Sunshine627: Uh yeah, I gotta go. I just heard my boyfriend's car pull up."

Charlotte looked up at Xavier, and then at the others seated around the table. "That was one of the tamer messages. I'll spare you all the details of the many other Internet correspondences my husband has been having."

"Okay, Charlotte. We need to talk," Xavier said. He had no idea what else his wife might pull out of the file, and didn't want to find out in front of the others.

"Oh, so now you want to talk?" Charlotte said. She folded her arms. "Go ahead and talk."

"Not in front of everyone. We need to talk this out in private."

"What? Is all this too uncomfortable for you? Can't stand the heat?" Charlotte asked.

Phillip interjected, looking at his watch. "Hey, everyone, it's time for our scheduled break. And after the break, I'd like for you all to talk one on one with your spouse about each part in the S.M.I.R.K. acronym and how it relates to your marriage. Don't worry about meeting back here at The Round Table." His eyes darted toward Xavier and Charlotte. "I want you to find some place where you and your spouse can talk privately.

Phillip directed his attention to the others at the table. "And if there is anything either of you two other couples need to talk about, then I strongly encourage you to do so. As John 8:32 says, *And ye shall know the truth, and the truth shall make you free."*

Amen, Xavier thought, hoping finally telling his wife the truth would make him free.

Chapter 16

Xavier Knight

Tuesday: 3:33 P.M.

Charlotte sat on the twin bed opposite Xavier. With folded arms, she stared him down. He could feel her eyes on him.

In his lap he held the expanding file Charlotte had pulled all of her information from. She'd been silent for the past fifteen minutes as she watched his trembling hands go through the entire contents of the file. From the months of February through July, he'd found sheet after sheet of damaging information. He didn't set the file down until he'd scanned the last sheet.

He dropped his head, not knowing what to say.

"What are you dropping your head for? No need to be ashamed now; now that you've been caught," Charlotte said. "Do you want to explain?"

"Explain what? It looks like you've done quite a good deal of investigation yourself."

Charlotte stood, crossing the room to pick up a copy of one of the detailed cell phone bills. "Explain this. What was so important that you and these Angel and Yasmine women needed to talk over five hundred times in a six-month period? And you and Carly talked a hundred times or more. Since I can't get a detailed phone bill for land line calls, I am sure it's been way more than that."

"I don't know. It doesn't seem like I talked to them that many times," Xavier said. And it was true. He hadn't realized it had been that much.

"I'm surprised you found time to work, talking to them so much. And it's a wonder I talked to you at all. But let's see, I did at least get the chance to talk to you one hundred and eighty times. Maybe I am a little special."

"Charlotte, don't."

"Charlotte don't what?"

"Don't do this. You know you are special to me."

"No, not really; not for the past eight months or so it seems," Charlotte said. "And Carly . . . I can't believe you slept with her. She was supposed to be my friend. How could you do that to me, and with her of all people?"

"Charlotte, baby, first of all, I didn't sleep with her. And please believe me when I say it wasn't all that cut and dry. It wasn't all that simple, and I didn't have feelings—I mean any real feelings—toward any of these women."

"Oh, I am supposed to believe you now? Now that I've done everything but get your fingerprints matched, I'm supposed to believe whatever you decide to let fall out of your mouth?"

"It's true. I didn't and don't have any feelings for any of those women."

"So what were they? A hobby or something? Most people get regular hobbies, but not you; you have to get a hobby that could jeopardize our lives, not to mention eventually cause you to end up getting someone pregnant."

"I used protection," Xavier quickly said.

"So, I guess that gonorrhea must have slipped through the condom somehow?" Charlotte rolled her eyes.

"Charlotte, that was low," Xavier said.

"No, Xavier, you are low."

She was one hundred percent right. How could he have even formed his lips to say that to her? He was one of the lowest pieces of scum on the earth. Why couldn't he have just learned his lesson losing his first wife? And why couldn't he have just found something else to occupy his time? Now he was right back to where he was years earlier; trying to explain his actions to his second wife.

His mind was reeling; he couldn't believe the extent in which Charlotte had gone to gather information about his escapades. And he wondered why she'd kept it all a secret from him for so long.

"There's no excuse for what I've done," Xavier said.

Continuing to fold her arms, Charlotte stared at him.

"I'm sorry for lying to you. I'm sorry for withholding information. There's just no excuse."

"What about the women you chatted with online? How many of them did you sleep with?"

"None," Xavier said.

"Come on, Xavier. You're just saying no because you've seen everything in that file. Don't you know this could be another test for me to see if you'll tell me the truth?"

"You don't have any proof of me sleeping with any of the women online because there isn't any evidence to find. Yeah, I chatted with them and probably led them on in many cases, but it was all just fun to me. I didn't sleep with any of them. I'll have to admit that I did meet Angel once. But nothing happened." Xavier was stating the truth. He'd set up a meeting with Angel at a restaurant in a city over an hour away from his home. With anxious anticipation, he waited for Angel, who said she'd be wearing a camel colored top and mini skirt. When she'd rounded the corner of the front doors and introduced herself, Xavier had been completely turned off.

The picture she'd posted on the Internet had been old. It was a picture of her wearing a bikini on the beach. In the picture, she was every bit of a size three, if that—pretty and petite with a smooth hourglass figure. The woman he'd met that night at the restaurant sounded the same as the Angel he'd spoken to on the phone, but the long gone hourglass figure had now turned into a Coke bottle shaped like a two liter. And she was nowhere near a size three; more like a size twenty-three. Xavier couldn't make enough excuses fast enough as he tried to get away from her.

He'd made it back home in record time that night, hoping Angel hadn't gotten a glimpse of his license plate.

Charlotte paused, thinking about his response. Xavier knew she couldn't comeback with any proof that he'd slept with Angel either.

"Look, I know you've spent a lot of time finding information to back up all you've been saying. And you're right; much of the truth is here in black and white. But believe me when I say I'm a changed man. Getting that STD really scared me, and giving it to you scared me even more," Xavier said.

He took a deep breath. Keeping secrets and telling lies wasn't going to work anymore. He needed the truth to make him free. "I did know I had gonorrhea before you confronted me. I was afraid to tell you and was really hoping you wouldn't get it."

"I knew," Charlotte said.

"You knew what?"

"I knew you knew about the gonorrhea before me. When I went on the Internet to find out more information on the disease, I saw that you'd already done searches," Charlotte said.

Xavier wasn't sure, but for a flicker of a moment, he thought he might have seen relief on Charlotte's face because he was finally telling the truth. But it was only there for a moment, quickly replaced with a furious scowl.

"What the heck were you thinking? What if it had been some other disease; an incurable one? Or what if I hadn't shown any symptoms and it was too late for me to be treated?"

"I wasn't thinking straight, I know that. Everything happened so fast. I went to the doctor, got my results, and just got scared. I immediately broke it off with Yasmine. She wasn't too happy I'd broken it off, but at that point I really didn't care. She'd given me a disease, and because of her, I gave it to you."

"No, Xavier. Because of you, you gave me the disease. I married you, not that woman," Charlotte said.

Xavier nodded his head. Now was not the time to start blaming someone else. He had to take ownership for what he'd done and face it like a man. Whether it led him down the same road he'd been down before or not.

"I did break it off with her." Xavier picked up a handful of papers off the bed. "And somewhere in this tall stack of investigative paperwork, you should see that I haven't had contact with Angel or Carly in months. I'd broken it off with Angel before I met Yasmine. And Carly ended up getting a conscience herself, and stopped talking to me."

"So, what are you supposed to be, a saint or something? Am I just supposed to forget all this because you say you're turning over a new leaf?" Charlotte asked.

"Yes, something like that. We can start with a fresh slate. No more secrets, I promise. And again, I haven't had contact with any other woman in months. And there aren't any other women in the woodworks for you to find out about. From what I've seen in these papers, you've been extremely thorough." Xavier was sincere in all he said.

"Don't you understand that you've demolished any amount of trust I've had in you?"

"Can I ask you something?" Xavier said.

"What?" Charlotte snapped.

"If you knew about my stepping out for months, why didn't you call me on it before today? Why gather all this information for months?"

"Your ex-wife tried to tell me that you had numerous affairs during your marriage to her, but you'd only told me about the one affair. So who was I to believe? I believed you of course. You're my husband. But then I started seeing some things that just didn't add up. So I checked here and there.

"There is a saying that goes, be careful what you look for, you just might see it. That's when I started noticing the increased number of calls on your detailed cell phone bill. I was in denial and kept thinking there had to be an explanation for all the stuff I was finding. Then when I got the disease, and you wouldn't give me the details I wanted, I found myself doing even more investigative work. And after looking in the right places, I found more than I could handle."

Charlotte stared at him with contempt. "I wanted so badly to believe you. I truly hoped there was an explanation for everything. I gave you chance after chance to tell me the truth, but you never did."

"I'm telling you the truth now." He held the papers up again. "Look at your papers again. Look at the dates again. You'll see. A couple of weeks prior to your confronting me about Yasmine, my correspondence with her stopped. And the correspondence with everyone else in real life, and in cyberspace, ceased also. I am a changed man. I promise you."

He hopped off the bed and handed her the stack of papers he'd been holding. "Just look. You've got to believe me." Then he scooped up the rest, giving them to her as evidence.

Instead of looking at the papers, she stood and threw them back. Some landed on the bed, but most scattered to the floor.

"You're like the boy who cried wolf, Xavier. Prove it to me," Charlotte said. She stepped past him, leaving him in the pile of papers.

Chapter 17

Xavier Knight

Tuesday: 6:10 P.M.

At dinner, Xavier felt like he'd traded places with where Travis had been the night before. This time it was he who was unable to finish eating his supper, while Travis ate just fine. Even though the spaghetti tasted fantastic, he just didn't have an appetite.

Charlotte, on the other hand, didn't seem fazed by their earlier conversation. She was eating her second helping of spaghetti and garlic bread. And unlike the previous day, she was talking with everyone like she didn't have a care in the world. Talking to everyone except him, that is.

"Don't you want to go ahead and share your fabulous recipes with us now?" George asked Shelby. He also was on his second helping of spaghetti.

"Can't do that just yet," Shelby replied.

"I have to give it to you, Shelby," Nina said. "This spaghetti is almost as good as my mother's, God rest her soul. She used to make the best spaghetti in the world. I've never tasted anything that has ever come remotely close."

"Thanks. Do you have your mom's recipe?" Shelby asked.

"No, she died when I was seven. And at the time, I took my mom's cooking for granted and I thought everyone's cooking was as good as hers." Nina's eyes turned downcast and her tone saddened. "But I found out the hard way that everyone wasn't like my mom."

It was the first time Xavier had witnessed Nina's lack of arrogance. She actually seemed human as she spoke about her mother. He watched as George started rubbing his wife's back.

"Sorry to hear that," Shelby said. "I'll make sure to give you my secret for the spaghetti, and maybe you can make a few modifications to get it to taste even more like your mom's."

"Thanks, I'd really like that," Nina said. She actually looked grateful for Shelby's offer.

"My baby can make some of the best Italian food in the world. You name it: spaghetti, lasagna, baked ziti, chicken parmesan. Just name something, and Beryl can whip it up," Travis said. He patted his wife's back. "She can tell you some of her cooking secrets also."

Halfheartedly, Nina nodded her head.

Xavier didn't know why, but Travis was really getting on his nerves. It was like he was trying to impress somebody and like he didn't want to feel left out of their conversations. The guy was always thinking of any and everything he could to add to what was being said.

He was surprised the guy hadn't said anything about something on television or a movie yet.

"My wife can cook so good that one day I gave her a recipe from a movie I was watching, and she made it look just like it did on the TV. I don't know how it tasted to those actors, but it sure was good to me," Travis said.

Xavier's head was starting to hurt, and the ramblings of Travis were only making it hurt worse. He wanted the guy to be quiet and knew that if he didn't tune him out quickly, he might just tell him to shut up. He didn't have the luxury of time to listen to Travis's trivial comments, especially when he needed to focus on how he was going to get Charlotte to believe he was a changed man.

He recounted the events after Charlotte charged out of their bedroom. Instead of running after her, he'd quickly gotten to work, knowing there was no time for a pity party. If he had caught up with her, she'd probably have just told him to get out of her face anyway.

He needed to quickly figure out what he was going to say to Charlotte the next time they got a chance to talk. Since she was so enamored with dates and numbers, he figured he'd use the documentation she'd gathered—the only resource he had—to help his case.

He'd gathered the pages, reorganizing them by category instead of by month. After he had the categories sorted out, he then organized them by date. Once all this was done, he was able to pinpoint—on paper, at least—the last time he had either talked to or corresponded with any other woman.

As he had told Charlotte, all communication with the women had ceased the day he found out about the STD. There were a few sporadic places where some calls from Yasmine had gotten through to him. But the timestamps never logged more than a minute. He always either told Yasmine not to call him again, or hung up as soon as he realized it was her.

Looking over the numerous times and dates he'd talked to the women, had made his stomach churn. What had he been thinking? He hadn't been thinking anything really. He'd just gone on his impulses, never thinking of the consequences and never thinking he'd get caught.

He'd been so stupid. Most men weren't blessed to ever find a good woman. And God had blessed him with two. Surely he wouldn't get that chance again if Charlotte left him. And he didn't want to look for woman number three anyway. He'd done enough of that and was just plain tired.

He circled dates and times, which would hopefully help Charlotte see that he was serious about being faithful to her. Then on his own separate sheet of paper, he jotted down key points he wanted to show her.

After an hour of studying the papers, he had all the information he could scrounge. Then with heavy legs, he set out to look for Charlotte, hoping that within that time she'd had enough time to cool off.

But when he looked around throughout the cabin and out on the porch, there was no sign of her. With flashbacks of her leaving the day she'd confronted him with the test results, he looked to see if their SUV was still parked around the back of the cabin. He was relived to see the SUV, but she was still nowhere in sight. So he sat on the porch waiting for her to return from wherever she had gone.

The last time she disappeared, he didn't hear a word from her for three days. Three days filled with him pulling out his hair.

After she finally returned, Xavier had asked her where she'd been. Charlotte told him not to worry about where she'd been. And to this day, he still didn't know where Charlotte had been for those three days.

Just before dinner, Charlotte emerged through the trees and returned to the cabin. She was sweating and breathing hard. When Xavier stood to greet her, she'd placed her hand up saying she was tired and needed to clean up before dinner. She kept walking right past him and entered the cabin. She hadn't really talked *to* him, but at least she was talking *at* him.

Now, at dinner, she was talking around him. But at least she was talking. And Xavier didn't want to push. He decided to wait until they could talk in private again, after dinner.

"Did you hear what I said, man?" Xavier heard someone say.

"Huh?" Xavier replied.

The source of the question was Travis. He was still talking. "I said, did you ever see that movie with Glenn Close and Michael Douglass, *Fatal Attraction*? The part where they boil the rabbit?"

"Ah, yeah." Xavier wondered how they had gotten on the subject of boiled rabbits. And the interruption had caused him not to be able to make his thoughts detour any longer. "Travis?" Xavier said.

Travis looked at Xavier expectantly, as if glad to finally have the man's attention.

"Silly rabbit; tricks are for kids." It was the closest thing Xavier thought to say without straight out telling the guy to just shut up.

Chapter 18

Phillip Tomlinson

Tuesday: 9:07 P.M.

Doing a silent attendance check, Phillip mentally checked off where each of the couples were. Xavier and Charlotte were in their room, Beryl and Travis were playing one of the board games, and Nina and George were outside by the lake, roasting marshmallows.

He decided to take time out to spend with Shelby. They decided to go for a walk on the walking trail they'd become very familiar with during their first stay at the cabin. After grabbing two flashlights and donning a couple of light jackets, they set out for a stroll.

That afternoon, the warmness of late summer had turned into a coolness of early fall. The weather in North Carolina was notoriously known for being wishy-washy. One day the temperature might get up well into the eighties, and the next day it might only get up to forty-something. And likewise, one day it might be dry, and the next day it might pour cats and dogs.

This particular evening, the temperature had gotten down into the sixties, and luckily, it hadn't rained since they'd been there. The weather forecast hadn't predicted any rain the whole week.

The moon was full and bright. Near the cabin there was no need for a flashlight, but as they reached the thick foliage of the trees surrounding the trail, it became a little harder to see. As soon as Phillip and Shelby reached the opening of the trail, they cut on their respective flashlights.

Phillip took a deep breath. "Umm, smell those Carolina pines. Don't they smell good?"

"Fresh and strong," Shelby said.

They guided the flashlights up and down and back and forth in front of them on the ground, so they wouldn't trip and fall or run into any trees.

"Nice, fresh, smog-free air. That's one of the things I love about being up here in the mountains." Again Phillip filled his lungs with air, and then let out a deep breath.

They walked along gingerly, avoiding sticks and tree limbs.

"I wonder if that log is still out here," Shelby asked.

"I figured you'd want to forget about that log," Phillip said.

"Except for tripping over it and falling face first, no, I don't want to forget it. We had some good times talking on that log—our own little get away from all the other couples and their roller coaster arguments," Shelby said.

"You know, before coming here, I really didn't know people could have so many problems. Those couples we met our first time here really had some problems. And I don't mean to diminish the problems we had, but we were actually pretty well off compared to them," Phillip said.

"Yeah, you never really know what goes on behind closed doors with people."

Phillip figured she was alluding to the fact that even though they had only been there two days, two of the couples had already discussed their mounting frustrations out in the open. He was glad the couples were finally starting to warm up and share. A lot of their concerns were being manifested through not only their words, but with their body language as well.

"Speaking of arguments," Shelby said, "what about Xavier and Charlotte?"

Phillip nodded his head. "It's a start. At least they are talking."

"I know they're talking, but I meant about all that stuff Charlotte had on him. I didn't know what she was going to pull out of that file next. I was scared she might have a video or something," Shelby said.

This time Phillip shook his head. "Baby, I'm so glad my days of running around were over by the time I met you."

Shelby stopped dead in her tracks, causing Phillip to jerk back slightly. "Come again? Your running days were over when you met me?"

"You know what I mean. Once I realized how serious we were, I quickly let the other couple of girls I was talking to go. I hate to think what could have happened if I'd brought the same kind of mess I was doing from college into our marriage. I could have ended up like Xavier." Phillip shuddered at the thought.

"You know, that's right. But I don't think I could have sat around acting like nothing was wrong with me while I collected evidence for months on end." Shelby started walking again. "I would have freaked the first time I saw you making more than twenty calls to the same number in a month, much less over a hundred."

"I know what you mean. But you never know what you'd really do unless you're in a person's shoes. We all have different reasons for doing what we do," Phillip said.

"I hear you, but I'd be doggone if I'd keep collecting copies of your little chats on the Internet. For real. I'd be all over you like white on rice after I saw the first message."

"Violence, honey? That's not like you at all."

Shelby positioned the flash light under her face to illuminate a smile she was displaying. "Like you said, baby, you never know what a person might do, given the circumstances."

"You didn't go off on me when you heard about Jeana," Phillip said.

"That's because I was all banged up in a hospital. With all those wires and IVs hanging from me, I couldn't reach you. Besides, I was so confused about what she'd told me and what I'd seen, I thought you were up to no good for sure," Shelby said.

There was once a time when Phillip's ex-girlfriend Jeana's name couldn't be mentioned in their house. And soon after, Phillip had to tread lightly when mentioning anything about Jeana and her son Taren—who had also turned out to be Phillip's illegitimate son. But now, after a couple of years and numerous counseling sessions, they'd gotten past those problems and moved on.

"And for the most part, it was all a misunderstanding," Phillip said.

"No, not for the most part. But yes, some parts were very pivotal," Shelby said.

"Okay, when you take some truth and add a few lies, and then you add a sprinkling of misunderstanding, then what you have is an ungodly mess," Phillip said.

"Which is what we had," Shelby said.

"Which is what Xavier and Charlotte seem to have right now."

"We got through it," Shelby said.

"And with the help of God, I hope they can get through it also."

"Prayerfully," Shelby said. Then she shook her head. "But I don't know. Charlotte had some pretty damaging evidence."

"Baby, how many times have you watched *Matlock* and seen where the person being accused has a mound of evidence against them, but in the end, Matlock always finds out the truth, clearing the person of the supposable wrong doing?" Phillip said.

Shelby laughed. "Now you sound like Travis."

"Ah, you got jokes now? I'm serious. Sometimes things look worse than what they are. Even when all the evidence seems to point in a certain direction, there's always hope and sometimes, even a legitimate loophole."

"You must have the faith of a mustard seed to believe that. She's got cell phone details with date and time stamps, copies of online chats, and full voicemail messages," Shelby said.

"And with all that, she still doesn't have this man red handed on tape, nor does she have a personal witness to any of the alleged activities," Phillip said, trying to convince his wife that anything was possible.

Shelby stopped walking again, causing Phillip to jerk backward for the second time.

"Baby, I might need my arm for writing tomorrow. If you keep stopping, sooner or later you'll dislocate my shoulder."

Now Shelby was the one with the serious look on her face. "My dear husband. Let me let you in on a little something. I know I've only known Charlotte for a couple of days, but she looks like a very smart woman to me. And if she is the smart woman I think she is, then she wouldn't have pulled out everything she had on her husband.

"She might have a video somewhere or credit card receipts for hotels. She's not going to let him know everything she's got, for two reasons. Number one, she might need the other information if she has to go to court for divorce. And number two, she may really want her husband to fess up to anything else he might be hiding from her, to once again give him a chance to redeem himself."

What Shelby said made sense to Phillip, but he still asked, "Do you really think she has something else on the guy?"

"I'm willing to bet she does."

Phillip shook his head. "You women are something else."

"You men are something else. The difference is, we women pay close attention to detail, and we have memories like an elephant. Often, not because we are looking for anything, but when we think something is off kilter, we pay even closer attention until we find out where the problem truly lies."

"Are you serious? I think I pay pretty good attention to detail," Phillip said.

"And don't discount our women's intuition," Shelby added.

"So pretty much what you're saying is, when women pay attention to detail, remember things, use women's intuition, and all these modern resources available today, y'all can be lethal?" Phillip asked.

"Bingo," Shelby said.

"Whew. Remind me never to make you mad at me again," Phillip said.

"All I know is that when you finally called for a break in that session, Charlotte didn't look like she was losing any steam. And she probably did have a couple of other things she might have to pull out in their bedroom," Shelby said.

Phillip pulled at Shelby's arm again so they could continue walking. "I hope not. You know I'm being impartial because I have to be. I do have to admit that all that stuff Charlotte has on him does look pretty damaging."

Shelby nodded her head in agreement.

"There it is." Phillip pointed his flashlight in the direction a little ahead of them. "Our log."

They walked up to the log they had so many fond memories of.

"Somehow it doesn't seem as big as I remember it," Shelby said.

Phillip examined the bark closely with his flashlight, looking for dirt and bugs. They both took a seat after seeing that it was safe to do so. The so-called log was actually the trunk of a tree which had fallen along the path of the trail.

"Ah, it's just right," Shelby said. "I wish we could take a chunk of this tree home and have it carved into a bench or something. I'd sit it in the backyard and we could pretend like we're out here in the woods."

"Yeah, right. How are we going to tune out the sounds of traffic and the smell of smog?"

Shelby smacked Phillip playfully on his arm. "We could still listen to the crickets and swat mosquitoes."

They sat for a few moments, enjoying the silence and the smell of pine.

"Okay, enough about poor Charlotte and Xavier. What about Beryl and Travis? What are your thoughts there?" Phillip asked.

"I see the love in Beryl's eyes as well as the frustration. Travis seems to be a fast talker, when he isn't zoning out in one of his daydreams."

"You've noticed that too?"

"Yeah, but with his fast talking, he's actually trying to cover up the fact that half the time, he doesn't really know what is going on," Shelby said.

"I wonder if all the guy does all day is watch TV, because that's all he talks about."

"Deep down I really feel like Beryl wants to try to make things work out between them, and Travis only wants to do enough to get by, whether it be getting a job and keeping it just long enough to collect an unemployment check, or only helping around the house when Beryl asks him to."

"Wow. You gathered all that?" Phillip asked.

"That and more," Shelby said. "Beryl and I had a chance to talk this morning before anyone else came into the kitchen. She confided some things in me. I think she's been itching to talk to someone about her situation, but was too ashamed. Many of her friends and family don't know she's the one who's been carrying their family financially, and she hates the fact that she has to basically beg her husband to do stuff around the house. She feels like she is dealing with an adult sized child to go along with her two young children."

"That's got to be frustrating. Maybe Travis has a side to the story, and it isn't as bad as Beryl is making it out to be," Phillip said, still trying to remain neutral.

"I think his job turnover indicates that something isn't right, and playing the race card, saying the establishment is trying to keep a brotha down is just a copout." Shelby rolled her eyes.

"Bottom line is that a man knows when he isn't working, he isn't contributing to the financial health of his home. Just like he knows that every time a light switch is turned on, the phone rings, and the toilet flushes, that means that somebody pays for it, and that somebody isn't him."

Shelby held up her finger and started rotating her head. "Instead of making excuses, Travis should be making arrangements to find and *keep* a job. With all the time he spends making excuses and probably watching the television trying to catch the next segment in a commercial saga, he could be earning something to help his wife put food in his kids' mouths."

Phillip placed his hands on Shelby's shoulders and massaged them. "Whoa, baby; calm down."

"I will. I promise I'll be calm by the time we make it back to the cabin, but that stuff he allegedly is doing is a pure mess." Shelby rolled her eyes again. "And I tell you one thing, I would not put up with that kind of mess. You can say what you want about being in someone else's shoes, but taking care of a grown, able-bodied man is something this sister just wouldn't be doing."

Phillip shook his head, knowing what Shelby was saying was true.

"If he wants to watch TV so bad, then he can go to Best Buy. They've got a whole wall full of TV's, all shapes and sizes, that he can look at while he's working," Shelby said.

"Well, all right," Phillip said. He would be as neutral as he needed to be. But Phillip knew his wife had a point about taking care of a grown man.

"That was more feedback than I expected. What are your thoughts about Nina and George?" Phillip asked.

"Truthfully, I can't believe G.I. Jones is here and seeking advice from us. I read his book, *I Do, I Don't,* and it was wonderful. Much of the book went over some of the same things we're doing here at the retreat."

"You don't understand why George is here? Matthew

13:57 explains it pretty clearly. It says, . . . *But Jesus said unto them, A prophet is not without honour, save in his own country, and in his own house.*"

"So he can teach thousands, but can't teach his own wife?"

"Bingo," Phillip said with a smile.

"They really haven't said very much about their problems," Shelby said.

"They're probably used to being guarded about their private lives. Unlike some people who can run their mouths all day, I just think George is the opposite. He's probably feeling everyone out. James 1:19 says, *Wherefore, my beloved brethren, let every man be swift to hear, slow to speak, slow to wrath.* I think we both know that G.I. Jones, the soldier for the Lord, is a very wise man," Phillip said.

"I don't quite know how to read Nina. It sort of seems like she is bipolar, but the symptoms don't exactly match. Sometimes she seems like she's dragging and tired, and other times, she talks a mile a minute."

"My grandmother would just plain call it being wishy-washy," Phillip said.

"Maybe so, but it seems a little clinical to me," Shelby said just before she dropped her flashlight and slapped the backside of her hand. "Ouch."

"What was that?" Phillip asked. "A mosquito?"

"No, it's too cool out for a mosquito," Shelby said.

Phillip took his flashlight to shine it on the spot she'd just hit. On her skin was a dead ant.

"That really stung."

Phillip shined his flashlight back down on the bark of the tree where he saw a stream of ants coming from underneath. "There are more of them. Let's go ahead and get back to the cabin."

Shelby hopped up off the log, vigorously patting and wiping her jacket and jogging pants. "What time is it?"

Phillip looked at his watch. "It's almost eleven o'clock."

"It's that late already? Time really does fly when you're having fun." Shelby scratched at the spot on her hand. "It's still stinging."

"Must have been a fire ant. Those little jokers don't play. I'm glad a swarm of them didn't bite you," Phillip said. He put his arm around Shelby's shoulder as they returned to the trail.

"I just wish each couple at the cabin could just squash their problems like I just did that ant. Then we could all relax and enjoy the rest of the week like second honeymoons."

"The week is still young," Phillip said.

"It's not that young. In a little over an hour it will officially be hump day."

Shelby was right. Two full days had passed and it didn't look like the miracle he'd been waiting for was going to happen any time soon.

Chapter 19

George Jones

Wednesday: 5:30 A.M.

George Jones opened his eyes. He'd been trying for an hour to go back to sleep, but figured it wasn't going to happen. Looking over at the alarm clock, he saw it was already five thirty. He'd be getting up in thirty minutes anyway.

He'd slept fitfully with concern about his wife. She'd been changing and seemed to be deteriorating on a daily basis. She had been acting strange lately. It all started a couple of months prior, just after he'd uncovered some of Nina's secrets.

There was a time when Nina had secrets she didn't think George knew about. But instead of confronting his wife in a room full of strangers, he'd done so in the comforts of their bedroom at home, with the door closed so the maid and cook wouldn't hear them. George hadn't done the investigating himself. He'd hired a private investigator to do so.

When his wife first started acting strange, George started paying more attention to her, watching her as closely as possible. There were inconsistencies in things she was saying about her whereabouts and time lapses which she couldn't give him straight answers on. Often she got short tempered with him whenever he asked her simple questions about the household or how her day had gone.

Then there were times when she acted as if she didn't want to talk to him or be touched by him. George figured some of her actions were because he had been spending a great deal of time focusing on his ministry and a new book he'd been writing. Many days he and Nina didn't have any quality time. So he decided to take a break so they could take a vacation. But Nina had come up with excuses as to why it wasn't a good time for her.

George hadn't fought the subject, but wondered what could be keeping his wife so preoccupied. She had a part-time job working at the church as one of the administrative assistants, she didn't have many friends, and she didn't have any real hobbies to speak of. There were times when she volunteered in the church daycare, but he had no idea what his wife did in her spare time.

Then his mind started working overtime. He put all the pieces together. She was acting strange, didn't want to be touched by him, and was barely speaking to him. George came up with the only conclusion that made any sense. And though George didn't want to believe it, he figured his wife must have been stepping out on him.

He had to find out what was going on. He hired a private investigator to watch the house and follow his wife. After two months of monitoring, the investigator found out exactly what his wife had been up to. Nina hadn't been stepping out with another man, but she had been stepping out to play Bingo.

Upon first hearing the news, George laughed, relived to hear she wasn't with another man. But as the investigator completed his report, the number of Bingo halls she'd been to and the amount of money she'd been spending there weren't adding up. It wasn't a laughing matter after all.

Within the two-month investigation, Nina had played Bingo ten times. Once, she'd driven down to South Carolina, and another time, she'd even gone to Jacksonville, NC and played Bingo all night. Upon reviewing his calendar, George realized he'd been away speaking at church conferences during that time.

The investigator also reported that in the two months Nina had been gambling, she'd spent over $3,000 and had only won back $250. George wondered how many other trips his wife had taken and how much more money she had spent. The investigator also reported that Nina had visited several check cashing places, opening a new proverbial can of worms.

Their entire marriage, Nina had been the one to handle their accounts. The bank accounts and other credit accounts were managed by her. She'd told George he only needed to focus on the ministry, and she'd take care of everything else.

She had taken care of everything around their home too. George didn't even know how much they paid the maid and cook. When it came to their home, Nina was always on top of things. The house was immaculate, George never missed a doctor's appointment, and their vehicles were always serviced on their proper maintenance schedules.

With the can of worms opened, George called the bank to look at their accounts. He requested a year's worth of statements. What he found made his mouth drop. Their personal joint account had dwindled in the first couple of months of statements, and then began going into overdraft. Their emergency fund account, which was connected to their personal account, had been dwindling also to cover the overdraft fees. So the emergency account, which had been opened with over $20,000, was now down to only $6,666.23. It was then that George began having a sinking feeling, knowing the devil was truly at work.

After receiving the information from the investigator, George did further self-investigation. He found mail Nina had been hiding in the bottom of her desk draw at the church. He also uncovered some of the bank statements, along with credit card bills and rejection letters for personal loans which were not only in Nina's name, but his name also. The biggest surprise he found was letters from their mortgage company stating they were about to be foreclosed due to their house payments being in arrears for over $30,000.

Later that week, he'd asked his secretary to pull some of the church's bank statements—the ones in which Nina had access to. He'd found copies of checks Nina had cashed. Her distinct, and clearly legible, script was neatly written on the bottom right corner of each check. He'd stuffed all the papers in his briefcase and confronted her with all he found that evening at home.

Now, in her twin bed, Nina stirred under her covers and mumbled something in her sleep that George couldn't understand.

He sat up on the edge of his bed, then slipped down to the floor, turning to face the bed and pray. With his head bowed he said, "My dear Father in heaven. Lord, thank you for this, another day—the third day. On this day I'll remember the trinity—God the Father, God the Son, and God the Holy Spirit. I'll remember that three represents divine perfection, and I'll be relying on you to step in today during this retreat and show your divine intervention.

"Dear Lord, I pray for each couple here this weekend. I pray that you will continue to bless Phillip and Shelby Tomlinson's marriage. Continue to impart wisdom into their lives during their quest to help married couples. I pray also for Travis and Beryl, Lord. I pray that you'll open their marriage for effective communication, and Lord, I pray to bind the spirit of a reprobate mind when it comes to Travis.

"Lord, I pray that Xavier and Charlotte's marriage will be saved. Loose Xavier from any unnatural appetite for women he may have. I pray this couple will come out stronger after this storm in their lives. Bless them, Lord, and show them what you have purposed for them to do.

"And Lord, I pray for my dear wife. I pray that whatever demon is trying to keep hold of her, will be sent back to the pits of hell. I plead the blood of Jesus in my marriage, and I thank you in advance for the miraculous things you have in store for us. I know you will help us turn this around. I have faith in you, Lord, and only you. I say thank you. Hallelujah, hallelujah, hallelujah unto you. Amen."

Concluding his prayer, George rose and took a shower and dressed. Then he gently shook Nina to let her know what time it was.

She stirred awake.

"Good morning, honey," George said.

"Morning," Nina mumbled.

His wife's hair looked as if it were matted to the side of her head due to the sweating she'd done during the night. And the other half of her head was a tangled mess. She had slept even more fitfully than George had. He couldn't actually remember the last night she'd slept well. Nina had forgotten to wrap her head with the scarf she normally used to keep her hair in place. She seemed to be forgetting a lot lately.

George knew once she realized her mistake, she'd be upset about it for a while. He wondered how she was going to fix the mess since she usually let her hairdresser at home do her hair at least once a week.

"How'd you sleep?" George asked.

Nina groaned. "Awful. I feel like I've been hit by a train. My body is achy, and I still feel tired."

"I wish you would go to a doctor and get checked out. You've been entirely too tired, and your self remedies don't seem to be working."

"I told you, I'm fine. I just need to get up and start moving around, that's all. And once I take one of my vitamins, I'll feel a lot better."

George shook his head. For weeks he had been witnessing his wife's overwhelming tiredness that sometimes caused her to lose coordination. Then there were days when she had unexplained sporadic surges of energy. He'd encouraged her to go to the doctor to see why her body was acting so strangely, but she refused. Likewise, she had also started having mood swings, especially when George or someone else corrected her about something she'd said.

Nina had been trying some home remedies, ranging from doing yoga to drinking herbal teas. Now she was taking some kind of vitality vitamin she'd said a friend told her about. So far they had been the only thing that remotely seemed to work. But in the past week, even the vitamins didn't seem to have the positive effect they once had.

Nina pushed herself up into a sitting position and felt her head. "Oh my, where's my scarf?" She felt around the bed.

"You didn't put it on last night."

"I didn't?"

"No."

"Oh, man? I need to call Vera."

"For what?"

"I need to get my hair done!"

"We are in the mountains, and I am not driving all the way back to Greenville just so you can get your hair done. You'll have to figure out something," George said.

"But G.I.—" Nina started to say, but George cut her off. She always called him G.I. when she wanted something.

"No, Nina. There's some shampoo and conditioner in the bathroom, and I brought along some hair grease. Work it out, and use a few of those hairpins already in your head. We're at this retreat for a reason, and we will be staying to see it through to the end."

Nina pouted, poking her lips out. After taking a few deep breaths she said, "I could use some tea. Do you mind making me some?"

"What kind?" He knew she was probably only asking him so she could get him out of the room.

"My herbal tea." Nina pointed toward the dresser. "The box is right there on the nightstand."

George didn't correct his wife to tell her it was the dresser and not the nightstand. In three short steps, he crossed the little room. Next to her box of assorted herbal teas was her bottle of vitamins. "Which packet of tea do you want?"

"You choose. Let it be a surprise," Nina said.

And so he did. Figuring one was just as good as any other, George pulled the first one his fingers touched. "This tea is pretty good, huh?" he asked.

"Yeah, you should try one." Nina rubbed her eyes.

George pulled out another pack of tea to make for himself. "I think I will try some."

Nina stood and stretched.

George looked back down at the dresser and picked up the bottle of vitamins. Shaking it, he said, "Maybe I should try some of these vitamins also. They do seem to give you energy.

Before he knew it, Nina was standing next to him. "Uh no, you can't take any of these vitamins."

She grabbed the bottle with both hands. The tired sleepiness she'd just been displaying was completely gone. Nina smiled, trying to cover her abruptness. "Honey, these vitamins are made for women, and there's no telling what they might do to your body." She turned to tuck the vitamins in her toiletry bag. Then she placed her arms on George's shoulders. "Now, sweetheart, why don't you just go and make that tea for us."

"I don't see what the big deal is. All it's probably got is a little more calcium or something for osteoporosis," George said.

His wife was probably having another one of her mood swings, and he figured he'd leave before it escalated any further. It was too early in the morning to have to deal with seesawing emotions.

Nina chuckled as if trying to make light of things. "Get your own vitamins, mister."

George shook his head. "Go ahead and wash that hair of yours and get dressed. I'll have some tea for you when you come out."

Nina rolled her eyes as she touched her matted hair again.

He left the room and headed for the kitchen. As he opened the cabinet looking for a couple of mugs, Phillip rounded the corner of the kitchen.

"Good morning," Phillip greeted.

"Good morning. How was your walk last night?" George asked.

"Pretty good; no mosquitoes. What about you all? How did the marshmallows turn out?"

George chuckled. "You all must have thought we were crazy, two grown people outside roasting marshmallows."

"Not really. To tell you the truth, I wouldn't have minded roasting some too," Phillip said. "It reminded me of when I was in the Boy Scouts. We used to roast marshmallows on our camping trips."

George stopped while holding one of the mugs he'd just gotten from the cabinet in mid air. "I knew there was something special about you. So you were in the Boy Scouts too?"

"Yeah, I had some really good times in my troop. Although I never quite learned how to make fire with two sticks," Phillip said and laughed.

"You either? We were finally able to make a fire with a couple pieces of flint," George said. He placed the cup down on the counter. "You want some tea or coffee or something?"

"Nah, I'll get some coffee after Shelby makes it," Phillip said.

George looked at Phillip, thinking he was the type of man to wait for his wife to serve him.

Phillip put his hands up quickly. "I see that look in your eyes. I am not one who wants my wife to wait on me hand and foot, but when I make the coffee it's always either too weak or way too strong. My wife has banned me from coffee making and I can't say I blame her."

George filled a kettle with water and set it on the stove to heat.

After a few moments of silence, Phillip said, "So how's everything going so far for you?"

George looked around, making sure no one was within listening range. His gut told him Phillip had a sincere, concerned spirit. He felt comfortable talking to him. "It is going good for me. Everything you've gone over with us parallels with what I teach. Much of what you've said is in *I Do, I Don't*."

Phillip's gaze turned sheepish. "George, I have to admit that I haven't read that book, or any of your books for that matter."

George nodded his head in understanding. "The sad thing is, my wife hasn't read them either. I've encouraged her, but often times, it's hard to get the ones closest to you to value the gifts God has given."

Phillip nodded.

"When I wrote the letter applying for this retreat, Nina and I had talked extensively about the problems in our marriage at that time. You know, the credit cards, the gambling my wife was doing, and the pending foreclosure."

Again Phillip nodded his head, listening and not interrupting.

"We've worked through those things. I've taken over the finances, and to her dismay, taken her name off our joint accounts. She still has an account, but I felt it wouldn't do any good to still have her connected to the other accounts which might cause her to deplete them," George said. "That didn't go over easy at all. We both went to the bank, and she had to sign stating it was okay to take her name off.

"And I am glad to say we're out of foreclosure status, praise the Lord. The check cashing places have been paid off, and the amounts for the church bank accounts have been restored, using the little bit of funds we had left in our emergency account," George said.

"That's good," Phillip replied. "You've been able to correct most of the damage in a fairly quick amount of time."

"The monetary damage, yes. But the emotional damage is another story. Sometimes she just seems to be going with the flow. At first she was fighting me on the changes I was making with the finances and bills, but now if I say something about them or ask for her input, she's nonchalant. And let me just tell you, my wife, the Nina I know, doesn't have a nonchalant bone in her body. It's like she just doesn't care at all, and even when I find something else dealing with the finances she'd forgotten about hiding from me, and I confront her with it, it doesn't seem to faze her."

"Why do you think that is?" Phillip asked.

"I don't know. It's like she's another person. And the latest thing that you all have been able to witness is her mood swings. They aren't part of my wife's personality either. I bet everyone here probably just thinks she puts on a front with me in public and on television and is a true witch at home, and when the cameras are off. My wife is a diva, but normally, she's a classy diva." George shook his head in confusion. "These displays of irritability and tranquility she's been displaying are totally new to me," George said.

Phillip was about to speak when they both heard a door close, soon followed by Travis shuffling into the kitchen.

Phillip looked at George, signaling with his eyes that they'd talk later. George nodded his head in agreement.

Chapter 20

George Jones

Wednesday: 8:01 A.M.

As George sat down at the breakfast table, he looked toward the hall where their room was situated. Nina still hadn't emerged. As he stood back up to search for her, she rounded the corner of the kitchen bopping up and down like a teenage cheerleader ready for her first pep rally.

"Good morning, everyone," Nina said. She took a seat next to George, picked up her mug of tea, and took a sip. Her hair had been washed and smelled like the shampoo and conditioner he'd been using the last couple of days. She'd pulled it back into a ponytail, which fell to her mid back. George hadn't realized her hair had grown so long since she always chose to wear it in some sort of up-do.

"Mmm, this is good. It's a little cool, but don't worry about it," Nina said.

George wanted to say to her that it had been ready for her thirty minutes ago, but decided to let it go.

"So, Shelby, what's for breakfast this morning?" Nina asked.

Her voice was so full of cheer, George wondered what

had happened to the woman who could hardly speak in more than mumbles just an hour ago. If he hadn't known any better, he'd have thought Nina had gotten a hold of one of those caffeine-laced drinks he often saw on display at the convenience store.

"I'm making Belgian waffles, and you have your choice of topping," Shelby said.

"Do you have any strawberries?" Nina asked.

"I do. And I also have blueberries, cherries, regular syrup, and this new stuff I've never tried with caramel and pecans."

"Oh, that sounds good. I think I'll try some of that too," Nina said. She took another sip of her tea and gave George a firm pat on his leg. "Umm, this tea is good."

"What kind of tea is that?" Travis asked.

George saw the way Travis had been eyeing Nina's ponytail. George figured Travis probably thought Nina's hair wasn't real—either a weave or a wig.

"It's an herbal tea I get from an Asian store," Nina said.

"Beryl, ain't that the same kind of tea you like; that herbal tea?" Travis asked his wife.

"I drink it sometimes," Beryl said. "I mainly like to drink the green tea for its antioxidants." She directed her comment to Nina.

George sat in awe as he watched the exchange between his wife and the other ladies at the table. She'd been so standoffish and snobby toward them the previous days, he was surprised they were even speaking to her at all. But deep down he knew most people had forgiving hearts and was glad these two women had wiped the slate clean, dismissing his wife's former behavior.

He'd sat throughout breakfast enjoying his waffles, topped with warm blueberries and whipped cream, barely saying a word unless spoken to. His wife's behavior continued to puzzle him. George wondered when the current high she was on would drop to an infamous low. Bracing himself, he sat ready for the other shoe to drop.

After breakfast, everyone gathered back in the meeting room at The Round Table. Charlotte hadn't said a word to her husband. Xavier looked as if he'd lost his best friend.

"How's everybody doing this morning?" Phillip asked.

A trio of 'goods,' a couple of 'fines,' and one 'great' was emitted from around the table. One of the 'goods' came from Charlotte while her husband sat looking bleak. The great, which was louder than anyone else's reply, had come from Nina.

"Glad to hear this. I'm doing pretty good myself. I slept like a baby last night," Phillip said.

"I beg to differ," Shelby said. "Babies don't snore as loud as you did."

"I don't snore," Phillip said.

Shelby pointed at the bags under her eyes. "While you slept like a non-snoring baby, I was pulled out of my sleep a few times."

Phillip placed his arm around Shelby's shoulder. "You still like me?"

"Naw, I still love you, silly." Shelby nudged him in the arm.

"Aw, ain't that just lovely," Nina said with visible admiration. "Are the violins going to be piped in here soon?" There wasn't a trace of sarcasm in her voice.

George did a double take.

Phillip cleared his throat and sat up. "Okay, okay, we'll stop with the mushy stuff."

He stood next to the dry erase board and wrote on it as he spoke. "Seven steps to rebuilding your marital house. I couldn't think of an acronym for this one, so we'll just number them one through seven."

"My hopes are that at some time, either during this retreat or soon after, you'll seriously look at keeping your marriages together. And hopefully the tips and notes I am giving you will be parts of the foundation you'll use to assist in rebuilding or renovating your marital house.

"So I urge you to take legible notes. Feel free to reflect on them during your free time here and especially when you return to the hustle and bustle of your daily lives at home, away from these serene surroundings," Phillip said.

Upon hearing the word serene, George saw Xavier shifting uncomfortably in his chair.

Phillip erased the board and wrote two words at the top. "Start over. The first step in trying to rebuild or renovate your marital home is to simply start over. There are many times when people have to start over, like trying to recover from a category five hurricane, for example. The old is gone, and the new has to come. Leave the old ways of the past, cast old thoughts into the sea of forgetfulness, and welcome your new life. Start from today and begin from right now." He clasped his hands together in a large sounding clap. "Later, in your free time, I want you to read 2 Corinthians 5:16-18."

Phillip wrote a second word and continued his lecture. "Forgive. Next, you need to forgive. Seven times if you need to, or even more, if necessary. In Matthew 18:21-35, you'll find the parable of the unmerciful servant. One day Peter went to Jesus asking Him how many times he should forgive his brother when he sins against him. He asked if he should forgive up to seven times. The Lord told him not seven times, but seventy-seven times.

"Then Jesus went on to explain the parable of the unmerciful servant, saying the kingdom of heaven is like a king who wants to settle accounts with his servants. As the settlement began, a man who owed him ten thousand talents was brought to him. The man was not able to pay and the master ordered that he, his wife, his children, as well as all that he had, be sold to repay the debt. The servant fell before the master, begging for patience, promising to pay back everything. And the servant's master took pity on him, and he canceled the debt and let him go."

Phillip shook his head. "Now listen to this part. The servant went back out and found one of his fellow servants who owed him money. He grabbed the man and began to choke him, telling him he'd better pay back what he owed. At this point, the fellow servant fell to his knees and begged for patience and promised to pay what he owed back. But the man refused and had the other servant thrown into prison until he could pay the debt."

Phillip folded and then unfolded his arms. "When the other servants saw what was happening, they were upset and told the master what was going on. The master, in turn, called the servant back in and said the man was evil. He reminded the servant that he had canceled all of his debts because he begged. But he was unmerciful to his fellow servant. So the master turned him over to the jailers to be tortured until he paid all of the original debt he owed."

Phillip looked around the table at everyone. "Now, how would you feel if our Heavenly Father treated us the same way when we don't forgive our brothers and sisters in our hearts?"

This parable happened to be one of George's favorites. He'd long ago lost track of how many times he'd counseled married couples on the need to forgive a spouse, and others who had loved ones, like parents or children, who needed to forgive one another for what they deemed as some wrongdoing.

In George's eyes, many of the disputes were trifling,

but not in the eyes of the persons seeking atonement. The discretions were rocking their world. The most trivial example he could remember was the time he counseled a man who was still holding a grudge against his fourth grade teacher for always making him last when it came to any and everything, like getting in line for lunch or presenting his items for show and tell.

The man's last name was Wilson, or Wilkins, or something like that. He was the last to appear in alphabetical order on the class roster, and for whatever reason, the teacher strictly went alphabetically for any and every event. The man had held a grudge and often had flashbacks.

George helped him realize that the grudge he held was only affecting him. The teacher of over twenty-something odd years earlier had more than likely never given much thought to what she was doing and was probably just a very methodical person. As the man thought about the advice George was giving him, he realized George was probably correct. The teacher did other things in a certain order, in a very methodical way, and always wanted everything precise and neat when it came to her classroom as a whole.

In the end, the man forgave his teacher, thus releasing built up anguish and animosity he'd held for decades. Afterward, the man said he'd felt as if a weight he'd been dragging for years had finally fallen off, and he was grateful.

"Very simply put, you must forgive to be able to rebuild your marital home," Phillip said.

Xavier looked over at Charlotte, but she sat stone-faced, staring at Phillip, giving no indication that she was going to heed to anything Phillip had said so far. Meanwhile, Travis placed his arm lovingly on his wife's arm. Beryl acknowledged the touch by momentarily staring at her husband with an icy gaze. This caused him to slip his hand away.

Nina, who had been so perky and talkative earlier, was now gazing glassily at a nick in the wooden table. George gave her a slight nudge, and after a couple of seconds, she finally came out of her daydream.

"Justify," Phillip said as he added the word to his list. "To be justified by faith. Treating the person just as if they'd never sinned and never sinned against you. Treat them just as if they'd never hurt you. And as it says in Romans 5:1, *Therefore, having been justified by faith, we have peace with God through our Lord Jesus Christ.* The fourth step in building is for you to count the cost. Make sure you have everything you need to finish what you've started. Truly think about how much this thing will cost you. Take a step back and look at what the true cost would be," Phillip said.

Both Charlotte and Beryl's eyebrows rose in question as if they hadn't understood.

Seeing this, Phillip continued. "Think about the problem, the thing. Let's say the problem, the thing, is another person who has tried to come between you and your spouse. You know this person is up to no good. Do you let this other person, a foreign enemy, fester in your marriage to tear the foundation you've put together? Or do you recognize that three is a crowd and annihilate the existence of this foreign enemy in your marriage?

"Either way, you count the cost. Ask yourself how the presence of this enemy will affect your marriage if it continues to be a party of three. Or how are you going to recover after you've decided to give it a go as a duet? And don't forget to ask yourself what the residual will be?

"One way or the other, rest assured, there will be costs involved. And you must count them," Phillip said. Once Phillip saw that both women plainly understood what he was trying to say, he continued. "Use knowledge to your benefit. Remember, you are rebuilding your marital house. You want this house to be bigger, better, and stronger than it was before, and knowledge is key. So by any means necessary, you use things that will help you strengthen your marriage.

"How do you do this? Make it your personal project to remember the things your spouse likes, and feed their ego. There are thousands of books on marriage and relationships. There are books on communication, budgeting, and making romantic meals. You name it, and there's probably a book about it. Even our brother here, Pastor George, has books out there to help marriages in trouble."

As eyes looked upon him, George felt undeserving of the stares of admiration. If he were such a great writer and knew so much, why hadn't he been able to do his own self assessment and fix his and Nina's problems?

Phillip continued. "And if you don't know how to start looking, go on the Internet and search, using various key words of interest to you. You'll find a slew of books you can check into. You don't have to worry about buying a ton of books either. You can go to your local library and find many books in the self-help section. Where there is a will, there is a way.

"This next step might be a little uncomfortable for some of you," Phillip said.

"Honestly, most of what you've said so far is more than a little uncomfortable," Charlotte told him.

"I agree. Except for what you've said about starting over, the rest seems a little farfetched," Beryl said.

Travis looked hopefully at Beryl. "Starting over is a start, right?"

"I mean literally starting over," Beryl said.

"Yeah, that's what I said," Travis said.

Beryl rolled her eyes. "You just don't get it."

"Get what?" Travis said.

"Nothing. Forget it, really," Beryl said.

Travis put his hands out, palms open and again said, "What?"

"Phillip, can you please continue? I'm listening," Beryl told him. Crossing her arms, she ignored Travis.

"As uncomfortable as it might be, you've got to change. Change, be it positive or negative, is always uncomfortable, and many times, hard. But once you adapt, it isn't as bad as you think. So this is yet another step in building this refurbished home. You've got to adapt, stretch, and grow. Cut off the fat, if need be, in this metamorphosing process. This change may mean cutting off people and things that will bog you down or hinder you from nearing a final inspection date of your newly renovated marital home. It will be a sacrifice, but the sacrifice on both fronts can be well worth it."

Blank faces stared at Phillip, none seeming eager to run out and try these steps.

"Nothing in life is ever easy. I've rattled off the first six steps to you all, and I won't lie, it's going to be hard. But you've both got to take part in these steps and incorporate the last step, which is to believe.

"Let me be totally frank with you all. Shelby and I heard these same steps you just heard. Our marriage had been in turmoil. When I talk about letting a foreign enemy fester in your marriage, I am not talking about anything I don't know about.

"We decided to face the enemy together. We didn't let it continue to destroy our marriage. We started over. My wife forgave me, and most importantly, I forgave myself. Shelby treats my deception as if it never happened. We counted the cost, and in some ways, we are still paying for it today.

"We used knowledge to our benefit, enhancing our

marriage and making time for ourselves as a husband and wife. We cut the fat, and most of all, we believed that with guidance from God and His prophets, we would make it. We've prayed and applied the scriptures, believing God would stand behind His Word and He has.

"I implore you to all do the same. If the Lord could do it for Shelby and me, then He can do it for you too. But you both have to work at it and believe." Phillip ended, placing the dry erase pen down flat on the table.

"Let's take a break right here, and afterward, find a spot where you can talk with your spouse about these seven steps. Seriously look at each step and talk about what kinds of bricks, if you will, you'll use to rebuild your marital house," Phillip said.

With a visible lack of enthusiasm about talking with their spouses, Charlotte and Beryl excused themselves from the table. Shelby placed her hand on Phillip's arm, squeezing it. George pushed his chair out to leave the table and saw that Nina wasn't moving. Again, she was staring off in a dazed daydream. George nudged her. Realizing everyone was leaving, Nina pushed back from the table and stumbled toward their room.

Minute by minute, George was becoming more and more concerned with his wife's behavior. With long strides, he tried to catch up with her. As he reached the bedroom, he saw Nina pulling out her bottle of vitamins. She took one out and popped it into her mouth, then walked into the bathroom, closing the door behind her.

He heard the water faucet being turned on for a couple of seconds and then being turned back off. He walked over to the dresser and picked up the bottle of vitamins. He could have sworn Nina said she'd taken one just a few hours earlier, which would explain why she'd been so perky. But then she had gone into another one of her lows. Now she was in the bathroom taking another one of the vitamins. He slipped the bottle into his pants pocket. George didn't know what was going on with his wife, but so help him God, he was going to get to the bottom of it.

Chapter 21

George Jones

Wednesday: 1:13 P.M.

"How are you feeling, baby?" George asked Nina. They were sitting next to each other in the rocking chairs on the wrap around porch.

It was their free session. The couples had been encouraged to further discuss specific steps in which they could strengthen their marriages.

"Fine, why are you asking?" Nina replied.

Nina's roller coaster behavior was really weighing on him. But the way she answered, and the look on her face, reminded him of the Nina he'd first met almost nine years prior. The woman who had stolen his breath at a church conference he'd attended in Raleigh, North Carolina.

That night, he'd preached just as he had the three nights prior in two other cities. George had been exhausted after the sermon and just wanted to get back to his home in Greenville. As a normal custom, the host church fed the ministers after service. Even though his stomach growled for food, the rest of his body longed for his bed even more.

The smell of roast beef and potatoes tickled his nose as

his heaping plate of food was served to him. George knew after he ate he'd immediately have to be ushered to his limousine, where he'd be sure to get some much needed z's.

Once he finished cleaning his plate, George sat back in his chair with an unexpected sweet tooth. Sleepy eyes weighed on him. When a hunk of chocolate was placed before him, his sleepy eyes were jolted open, not by the smell of chocolate, but by the sweet aroma of a fragrance he'd never had the pleasure of smelling before.

He turned abruptly to see who had served him, and was greeted by the radiant smile of a striking and voluptuous, chestnut brown woman. Noticing his abrupt turn, the woman asked if he needed anything else. He shook his head, speechless for the first time in a long time.

She turned and returned to the abyss of the kitchen. Unlike other women who normally fawned over him, this woman turned away, treating him as if he were an everyday Joe Blow.

He cut a piece of the chocolate cake with the edge of his fork. He forked in a piece, and his mouth was filled with what he was sure had to be chocolate from the heavens above. It wasn't the normal Duncan Hines or one of the store bought slices he often received. This hunk of cake was homemade. Somebody had actually cracked some eggs and sifted some flour to make it. And who ever had made the cake had also had the presence of mind to make the frosting from scratch.

He'd devoured the cake and was staring at crumbs before he knew it. And just as he wiped his mouth with the napkin, the same woman from before was floating back toward him. This time he couldn't let her leave again without saying a word. He decided to ask who made the cake. It was the only small talk he could think of.

She'd asked him if he liked it, and when he told her he

did, she told him she'd made it. She then joked, saying that if he hadn't liked it, she would have blamed it on someone else. She laughed an infectious laugh. He'd laughed also, thinking of more small talk. He asked her who taught her how to cook such a mean chocolate cake and wanted to know what other kinds of foods she could burn so well.

They talked and talked, and before George realized it, the rest of the church staff had finished cleaning up. Not wanting the conversation to end there, he asked the woman for her name and number.

George was used to women vying for his attention. He was what most would call a good guy. At thirty-seven years old, he had never been married and was a virgin, although he was sure most people wouldn't believe it. Thus he didn't have any children. He was a gem of a find; financially independent and a highly respected, up and coming pastor. George had to be very careful about who he let into his inner circle. And many times he was lonely in that circle, especially without the companion-ship of a good woman.

Something in his spirit told him this particular woman did have an interest in him, but she also had a classiness about her. She wasn't the type to paw at him and make herself look like a fool. She was okay with giving him her phone number, but also acted like she'd be fine if he never spoke to her again.

He was so used to what he called *skinny women*, trying to talk to him. Since grade school, he'd never had an affinity toward thin girls. As a child he was a little on the heavier side, and at that time, only the heavier girls ever approached him. Now, as an adult, he still appreciated a woman with a little meat on her bones. Not too much meat, but a good, solid, healthy sized woman. And this woman carried herself in a way he could appreciate. She looked like his dream woman.

That night he'd left the church with a number and a name. The woman he'd had the pleasure of meeting was named Nina, and ever since that night, she'd been the only woman he thought about and dreamed of. Once he got to know her better, George knew she was the one for him. Their courtship had been brief, only six months. It was so brief that rumors started flying in the church by jealous women. Rumors that Nina was probably pregnant and they needed to marry quickly in order to escape a possible scandal. But as the months went by without producing a baby, the rumors finally ceased.

Even to date, there were still many jealous women who didn't respect Nina's status as the first lady. George saw firsthand how so many men of the cloth had been tempted, fallen to the desires of the flesh. It was a sad thing in his eyes. George was just glad he'd continued to stand firm in his vows to not forsake his wife.

Nina handled things like a trooper. She knew about the jealously, but didn't entertain any of the women's childish ways. Many people took her actions as being snobbish, like she was better than everyone else. But George knew better. There were many times Nina thought just the opposite about herself. Nina was a good woman; people just took her the wrong way.

"Earth to George," Nina said, pulling George out of his reminiscing.

"Oh, yeah, what were you saying?" George asked.

"Have you seen my bottle of vitamins?"

Without realizing it, George's hands glided toward the bottle in his pants pocket. He hated to lie about it, but said, "No, I haven't seen it."

Nina rummaged through her purse. "I know I had it earlier, and I thought I put it on the dresser."

George felt bad about hiding the bottle from her, but something nagging on the inside wouldn't allow him to give it back. His gut told him something just wasn't right about the whole situation.

"Maybe it just rolled behind the dresser or something," George said.

"You might be right," Nina replied.

And before he knew it, she'd jumped up from her rocker and headed for the doors of the cabin.

George stood to follow. When he reached their bedroom, Nina was peering alongside the dresser, pulling it out from against the wall. Not seeing anything, she then she got down on all fours and crawled toward the twin beds. Flipping the covers up on both beds, she looked under them. She was looking and feeling so closely to the carpet, one would have thought she was looking for a contact lens instead of a bottle of multivitamins.

George sat on his twin bed as he watched. Nina got up off the floor and unzipped her garment bag. After searching the main compartment, she began unzipping the smaller compartments of the bag. From there she pulled out a plastic rectangular pill container with seven compartments, each labeled with the first letter of each day of the week.

Flipping each compartment open, Nina grinned like a Cheshire cat when she opened the last three. Relief swept over her face like the woman in the Calgon commercials George remembered as a child.

"What's that?" George asked.

"I found three vitamins I must have put in this pill case the last time I traveled," Nina said. She headed toward the bathroom and popped one in her mouth. Then she drank a full cup of water.

"Baby, didn't you just take a vitamin this morning?" George asked.

"Yeah, but to get the full affect, I need to take these particular pills, I mean vitamins, three times a day. They've got special herbs in them."

"If I didn't know any better, I'd think you were on drugs or something. You look like you need a fix.

Nina shook her ponytail. "Don't be so silly. It's nothing of the sort. I just don't want to break my routine, that's all." Nina looked back around down toward the floor. "I just hope that bottle turns up soon."

With the nagging feeling still nudging him, George asked, "Nina, do you want to talk about anything?"

"Yes," Nina said.

George was surprised. He didn't think it would be so easy to get Nina to talk about her strange behavior. He sat up, all ears.

Nina picked up her folder and notepad for the retreat. "Why don't we go over these seven steps to improve our home? I don't know about you, but I think we're well on our way to having all these steps taken care of."

George slumped slightly where he sat. Nina wasn't going to shed any light on her strange behavior. He was going to have to figure it out on his own.

Part II

Her Side

Chapter 22

Nina Jones

Wednesday: 6:07 P.M.

"What's for dinner?" Nina asked. She sat down at the table, rubbing her hands in anticipation. "I'm starving."

"Nothing too spectacular," Shelby said. "And not too heavy. I don't want you all trying to dose off right after dinner."

"Sure smells good."

"You have a trio of soups to choose from, as well as grilled cheese sandwiches," Shelby said.

"What kinds of soups?" Nina asked.

"Chicken noodle, vegetable, and clam chowder."

"Umm, that does smell good," Travis said, piping into the conversation. "My wife—"

Travis didn't get a chance to finish before Nina said, "Let me guess. Your wife can make the best soup in the whole world, better than Campbell's I'll bet."

He nodded his head. "And you know it."

Beryl rolled her eyes. "Travis doesn't know if I'm making canned or homemade. Half the time I just add some extra vegetables, meat, and tomato sauce to the canned soup to beef it up a little."

Travis chuckled. "I knew. I just pretended I didn't know." He looked around, acting as if he really knew.

George shook his head.

Nina had a feeling Travis hadn't known. But she'd bet he could recite the whole schedule for the ABC, NBC, and CBS Thursday night television lineups.

Shelby served dinner, and everyone dug in, filling their bowls with heaping amounts of soup. Afterward, the group gathered in the living room area to take part in a game of charades. Phillip and Shelby explained the rules so everyone would know what to do. The couples split into two groups with the men on one side and the women on the other.

Being gentlemen, the men let the ladies go first.

Beryl pulled a slip of paper out of a basket. She looked at it and immediately smiled. "Okay, this one is cute." She folded the piece of paper back up.

"Remember, no talking," Phillip said. "Just pantomime."

"Okay, sorry," Beryl apologized.

"Are you ready?" Shelby asked.

Beryl nodded her head.

Shelby turned over an hourglass timer. "Okay, start."

Beryl made hand movements like she was cranking an old fashion movie camera.

"Is it a movie?" Charlotte asked.

Beryl nodded, then turned both hands over with her palms facing up. She hunched her shoulders while looking around the room like she was perplexed.

"You're confused about something?" Nina asked.

Beryl slowly rolled her hands and nodded her head in a keep guessing motion. She stopped and placed her forefinger on her temple and furrowed her eyebrows as if thinking really hard. Then once again, she turned her palms back up and hunched her shoulders.

"You are wondering about something," Charlotte said.

Beryl again rolled her hands in a keep guessing motion, this time a little more quickly. She placed five fingers on her arm to indicate the phrase had five words in it. Next she put the first finger on her arm, to indicate she was working on the first word.

"What?" Charlotte said.

Beryl shook her head.

"Why?" Nina said.

Beryl nodded her head profusely and grinned, then she pointed to herself with her index finger.

"You?" Nina said.

Beryl shook her head.

"I?" Nina said.

Again Beryl nodded her head to indicate Nina had gotten the word right. Beryl pointed to her wedding ring.

"Married?" Charlotte said.

Beryl nodded her head, and in a fluid motion, acted out all three words again in sequence.

"Oh, oh, I know," Charlotte said. *"Why Did I Get Married?"*

"Time," Shelby called out.

Beryl let out a deep breath. "You got it." She stepped over to Nina and Charlotte, giving them high fives.

"Ah, I knew it. Now that's a great movie," Travis said.

Beryl rolled her eyes at him.

Nina had only known the couple for a couple of days, but she wondered if Travis did anything besides watch movies and television. Most of his comments and conversation circled around some movie he'd seen, commercial he'd watched, or sitcom that was hot on television.

But she did agree with Travis on this point. "It is a good movie. It's actually my favorite of all Tyler Perry's movies," Nina said."

"I've never seen it," Charlotte said.

All heads but Xavier's turned toward her.

"Well, Charlotte; you, my friend, are in luck," Shelby said. She pulled out a brand new copy of the movie from a bag Nina hadn't noticed sitting next to the couch and handed it to Charlotte.

"So, not only do you ladies get a point for your team. Charlotte, you and Xavier have a copy for your library," Phillip said.

"You mean to tell me you've never seen *Why Did I Get Married*?" Travis asked.

"No. When the movie came out, we had our own drama going on, and I couldn't stomach seeing other people's problems being played out on the big screen," Charlotte said. She flipped the movie over in her hand and read the back. "But thank you. I'll finally get a chance to see what everyone has been raving about."

"Sooner than you think," Phillip said. "I want to borrow it later on this week so we can all look at it."

"Xavier, have you seen the movie?" Travis asked.

"No," Xavier said. Then shook his head as if contemplating with himself. "Yes, I've seen the movie."

This time it was Charlotte's head that snapped toward him. She crossed her arms and stared.

"Let me explain," he said, directing his full attention to Charlotte instead of Travis. "I went to the movie one night. I'd asked you if you wanted to go, and you didn't. So I went by myself."

"By yourself, Xavier?" Charlotte asked with disbelief covering her face.

"Yes, by myself."

"And you expect me to believe that?"

"Look, baby, I'm trying to get you to understand that I'm not keeping more secrets from you. I just want you to know I am serious about this. I could have very well kept it from you, but I didn't. If I were still keeping secrets, I would have lied about seeing the movie. I did go by myself so you won't find anything to the contrary," Xavier said.

Charlotte took a deep breath, tightening her folded arms.

Nina didn't know this couple well at all, but she could plainly tell that Charlotte wasn't planning on listening to anything her husband had to say. And in some ways she couldn't really blame the woman for her actions, especially after everything she heard and saw about Xavier's extracurricular activities. But who was she to judge? Xavier looked like he truly wanted to come clean about any and everything he had to hide. Nina figured the blatant coaxing from Charlotte had been the strong determining factor in his decision to do so.

"Look, either you're going to believe me or you aren't. I'm not going to ruin everyone else's night arguing about it," Xavier said. "Is it our turn yet? Let's continue playing."

Xavier stood and picked up the basket with the words folded on the slips of paper. He pulled one out, read it, and nodded his head saying, "So true."

After folding the paper back up and placing it in his pocket, he did just as Beryl had done and held up eight fingers indicating his phrase had eight words. Then he also made hand motions, indicating his phrase was a movie. With various hand gestures, he made an imaginary straight line, drew an imaginary heart in the air and contorted his face into a scowling hateful look.

Travis quickly guessed the movie saying, "*A Thin Line Between Love and Hate*. Now that movie was a trip. Sort of like *Fatal Attraction*, only the black version," Travis said. "I have to say I liked Martin Lawrence and Lynn Whitfield better. Especially the line where Lynn says—"

Nina cut Travis off. "We believe you, Travis. You can probably recite the whole movie."

"Pretty close," Travis said.

Phillip handed Travis a copy of the movie. Nina saw pride in the man's eyes. A pitiful sort of pride, she felt. She didn't mean to be so short with Travis, but he was getting on her nerves—partly because he was annoying, but mainly because he reminded her of Bruno.

She'd been racking her brain trying to remember Bruno's last name. She thought it was Lawson or Latson or something to that affect. She wondered where Bruno was living now. She figured he had to be somewhere on the west coast, especially since she hadn't seen or heard from him since the night they parted Old Lady Crowell's, or Old Lady Crabby as the kids used to call the woman behind her back.

She and Bruno had lived in that particular foster home for almost two years together. At the time she'd been eleven and Bruno had been eight. He'd been placed in the home a few weeks after Nina. And just like Nina, his mother had died, and he didn't know who his father was. The only other family Bruno had was an uncle who wasn't able to take care of himself, much less an orphaned eight-year-old boy.

Nina had taken the scared little boy under her wing. Old Lady Crowell's home had been her third foster home, so she'd seen many a child come and go in the foster care system. So many that she became numb to any feelings for the children, and quickly learned to not get too attached to any of them. But the fear in Bruno's eyes wouldn't allow Nina to look away, letting the little boy fend for himself.

Like Travis, Bruno was the type of kid who liked to talk nonstop. His favorite topic of discussion was about trucks. The boy loved trucks so much that he could tell the make of one just by hearing the engine crank. Bruno had a book with all different types of trucks, which he carried with him all the time. While other foster kids clung to baby dolls and security blankets when snatched from their homes at only a moment's notice, Bruno had clung to his book about trucks.

There were many days when Nina had to tell the kid to shut up and stop talking about the trucks. He would only adhere to her request for short moments, and before she knew it, a truck would pass by on the street or one would flash across the television screen, and he would start spitting out truck facts.

"Nina, it's your turn," Phillip said.

"Oh, all right." Nina stood quickly and immediately felt woozy. She reached out and held the side of the chair for balance. "Ooh."

"You okay?" George asked, standing to assist her.

"Yeah, I'm fine. I think I stood up too quick, that's all," Nina said.

Once she gained her balance, Nina did as her predecessors and pulled a slip of paper out of the basket. Nina held up two fingers to indicate her phrase had two words. Then instead of indicating she had a movie, she acted like she was holding a microphone and singing. She used her fingers to form an imaginary heart in the air, representing love. Then she started pretending she was singing again while holding a note forever."

This time Beryl was the one to guess "Endless Love," a song sung by Diana Ross and Lionel Richie. Afterward, Beryl received a CD with Diana Ross songs. The teams played until they were both tied at three. For the tiebreaker, Phillip pulled the last piece of paper out of the basket and told them that the first person to call out the answer would determine the winner between the men and the women.

Phillip held up three fingers, then pointed to his ring finger. Voices called out in unison, "Married." Then he pretended like he was pushing a stroller while also picking up another child.

Travis screamed out, *"Married with Children,"* correctly guessing the sitcom that ran during the eighties and nineties.

The men gave each other high fives. Travis was elated to have won the game for the men. He received a DVD collection of the first season of *Married With Children.* He looked and acted like he'd just won the Heisman Trophy award in football.

With blurring vision, Nina could have sworn she saw two, and then three identical Travises jumping up and down. It was time to take another one of her so called vitamins.

Chapter 23

Nina Jones

Wednesday: 9:25 P.M.

Nina stared at her face in the mirror of the bathroom. The vitamin she'd taken was starting to kick in. As Travis and the other men celebrated their win in the charades game, Nina slipped away to the bedroom. It had been a daunting task, especially with the multiplying chairs and walls she passed while trying to walk. She'd played it off as best as she could, loud talking and laughing as if the game had been the best recreational activity she'd ever played in her life.

She thought she had seen George looking at her from the corner of his eye, but she didn't have time to wait for a confirmation. Figuring he'd follow her soon enough, she made her way as quick as she could to the little pill container she'd been sure to leave on the dresser in their room.

She had a fear the case might have disappeared like her bottle had, and she prayed it was still where she'd left it. Her fears were unfounded because the case was right where she'd left it and still had two pills in it. She took one pill out and carefully placed the container back on the dresser. She popped the pill in her mouth and followed it with a cup of water from the bathroom.

To her surprise, George hadn't come in right behind her. It had taken him almost thirty minutes before she heard him entering the room. She was relieved because it gave her time to gather herself while letting the medication kick in. She'd also had time to take a long hot shower. Now she could face him with a straight face.

When she opened the door of the bathroom, George was lying across his twin bed, snoring lightly. He was as handsome as the first time she'd seen him in person. He was the popular G.I. Jones, and she had no thoughts or even hopes of speaking to him the night she served after the church service, much less holding a conversation with the man that ended with him asking for her phone number.

Hundreds of women had been swarming throughout the previous church service, lining up for a touch and prayer from G.I. Some of them were supposedly falling out onto the floor in the Spirit. Nina knew most of them were just acting because she'd seen people slain in the Spirit many times before, and when it came to the Holy Ghost, they didn't care how or where they fell. The actresses made sure they fell gracefully, without messing up their fresh hairstyles. At least they had the decency to keep their dresses and skirts down. The spectacle of women shamelessly throwing themselves at the man made her sick. She figured G.I. Jones had some woman he was already courting.

It had thrown her for a loop when he'd decided to hold a long conversation with her. She'd felt like Cinderella, a lowly servant helping to feed the royal court. In her mind, she was still that same little foster child now grown up into a foster woman.

The man had looked lonely sitting at the table, so she

didn't mind talking to him. G.I. was easy to talk to. She asked him questions, trying her best to steer away from anything that had to do with her personal life. If she'd told him about all the foster homes she'd lived in and things she'd seen and done to survive there, he probably would have looked for the nearest door marked with an exit sign.

When the night was over and he asked for her name and number, she made sure to give him her cell phone number. She had a home phone, but depending on her priorities from month to month, that phone often fell low on the list of necessities. She tried her best to keep her cell phone on just in case G.I. ever called.

After not hearing from him for a couple of days, Nina figured he had only talked to her to pass time that night. She abandoned all thoughts about him calling, which wasn't a hard thing for her to do. The foster care system had taught her not to get her hopes up.

But one night, the phone call came. She'd pinched herself a few times during the conversation to make sure she wasn't dreaming. They'd talked until the battery on her cell phone beeped with a low signal. Again, they talked mostly about him. He seemed to need someone to talk to, and Nina didn't mind at all.

G.I told her personal things she was surprised to hear. She hardly knew the man, and he was telling her things a gold-digger would have loved to hear. Lucky for him, she wasn't the type to run to the tabloids for a few quick bucks. She figured there must have been something in his spirit that told him she could be trusted. After a while, Nina felt the same way about G.I.

She'd told him things she'd never even told the social workers she was the closest to as a child. She told him about physical abuse she'd suffered from some of her foster parents and from some of the other foster kids. She had also told him about how she went hungry at night in some of the homes until she got smart and learned how to steal food and money to get by. It was in foster care that she learned how to budget and handle money so well. Nina could stretch a dollar further than anyone she'd ever known, especially when she had no idea where more money might come from or when she might actually get another meal.

She was truly thankful to God that she had never been sexually abused. She'd heard stories from girls and boys alike that had been abused at the hands of their caretakers. Nina didn't know how she would've turned out if that had ever happened to her. She already had enough psychological problems stemming from abandonment issues and control issues, which often caused her self-esteem to be low.

George hadn't turned a deaf ear when she shared her past. He'd done just the opposite, causing them to be drawn closer to each other. He helped her with her issues of low self-esteem. He made her understand that God had not left or forsaken her. He also made her understand that everything in life happened for a reason and that the storms she'd gone through had actually made her stronger, and at some point in her life, her experiences would help others.

Within a few short months, they were married, and she felt like a real life Cinderella. Their wedding had been featured in *Essence* and *Jet* magazines. It had felt surreal then and still sometimes seemed surreal, especially when nightmares of the past crept into her psyche. She had dreams, which often made her wake in cold sweats. For long moments after waking up, she had to acclimate herself to her surroundings, wondering which foster home she might be in. It was only after she focused on the golden angel statue she kept on her nightstand at home and saw the glowing light from her similarly golden hued bathroom, that she realized she wasn't back at Old Lady Crabby's or any of the other houses.

The nightmares had pretty much ceased until George found out about her gambling. Nina had been good with money, but after she got married and saw the seemingly endless supply of money, she'd started enjoying things she'd never been able to enjoy before. The newly acquired money had introduced her to a whole new world of food, travel, and even gambling.

It didn't take her long to find out that with gambling, she could win more money. In the beginning, it had been fun to buy a scratch off ticket here and there, winning five dollars or twenty dollars. One time she'd won a thousand dollars on one of the tickets. Out of her winnings, she'd taken a hundred dollars of the money and bought more scratch off tickets, keeping the hundred dollar pace up on a weekly basis for months.

She'd also bought a few random lottery tickets, but never won anything with them so she abandoned that idea. The thrill of scratching off tickets was more alluring anyway. Her hundred dollar obsession turned into a three hundred, and then five hundred dollar obsession. Before Nina knew it, the amount she was spending was outweighing the winnings.

She'd also wanted to go to a Bingo parlor to see what the big deal about them was. Old Lady Crabby always went on Wednesday nights to play Bingo. Nina often heard her on the phone with friends bragging about her winnings. So Nina found a local place to play and was instantly hooked. And just like with the tickets, before she knew it, the money she was putting into the games was out weighing the winnings. And even though she wanted to stop playing, the possible thrill of being the one to yell Bingo for the jackpot, kept her coming back.

Nina had gotten to the point in which she was spending her entire paycheck and borrowing money from check cashing places. And what had once given her euphoric feelings had ended up being a burden.

She told herself she'd have to stop one day—this was after she started bouncing checks and owing various check cashing places around the city of Greenville. Nina had even sunk so low as to borrow money from one of the church's bank accounts that she had access to, all the while vowing that she'd pay it all back.

Before she had a chance to win back enough money, George had confronted her. She'd been devastated and ashamed. He'd gone and hired a private investigator who'd found out what she'd been doing. When confronted with the proof, Nina realized she had a problem with gambling that was totally out of hand.

George helped her by paying back the check cashing places and replenishing the church bank account. She was ashamed for what she'd done and refused to go to counseling for the gambling. She didn't want her shame to turn into a scandal for her husband, who didn't have any blemishes on his personal record. Nina knew if the information got out, it would make every one of the tabloids.

She told George she would be fine and that her gambling days were over. But each and every time she went to a gas station or the grocery store, the lottery scratch offs beckoned her. Going cold turkey on the gambling turned out to be harder than she thought it would be.

Soon the nightmares about her past returned, and she began experiencing anxiety attacks. At her wits end, one evening, Nina drove to the house of the one and only true friend she'd acquired in the church since marrying

George. The friend listened to Nina's dilemma and told her about a drug that might help her with the anxiety.

The drug was called valium, and this friend knew a doctor who could prescribe a few pills for Nina. Nina took the friend up on the information and obtained some pills.

They'd helped at first, but now it seemed as if the pills weren't working as well as they used to. She needed more of them more often to suppress the anxiety and ward off the dreams. And on the downside, she'd been getting dizzy lately, her vision was often blurry, and she was constipated beyond belief.

Nina eyed the pill container on the dresser. The euphoria of taking the helpful little pill with the 'V' on it had worn off just like the gambling. When she didn't take them, the side effects were too severe, and she couldn't fake the funk, as the phrase went. And even though she wanted to stop taking the valium, she found herself dependent on them.

George had been asking her questions about how she was feeling and if there was anything she wanted to talk about. She couldn't tell him about the pills, especially after he'd already helped her with all the gambling debts she'd incurred. How could she tell him she was hooked on drugs?

She was ashamed and had really felt like some sort of drug fiend, especially when she found herself on all fours searching the floor for a pill. Her cheeks had flushed and felt like they were burning when he made the comment about her needing a fix. She was surprised George hadn't noticed the redness in her cheeks.

Nina sat on the floor beside her twin bed. She stared at her husband as he peacefully dozed on the bed across from hers. She'd have to figure out a way to wean herself off of the drug without him finding out. She originally wanted to do so gradually, but since she'd lost her whole bottle of valium, Nina had a sinking feeling that she was going to have to do it the hard way—cold turkey, just like she'd done with her gambling problem.

Chapter 24

Beryl Highgate

Thursday: 7:15 A.M.

Refreshed from her shower, Beryl stepped out. With her face still wet and eyes closed, she maneuvered her hands along the towel rack, feeling for her towel. Instead of feeling the softness of terrycloth, she felt the roughness of something damp. She couldn't make out at first, but soon realized it was her husband's underwear.

The refreshing invigoration she'd felt from her cozy shower only moments before had been depleted like air being quickly released from a pierced balloon. With jarring dread, Beryl was reminded that her husband wasn't using the brains God gave him. She was so tired of letting him use her brain to think all the time.

To make matters worse, Beryl's reflection stared back at her through the partially steamed bathroom mirror. There were bags and dark circles under her eyes. And even though she'd had what felt like the best night's sleep in months, it was impossible to think that one night of sleep could undo years of the stress and strain that had overtaken her body.

The underwear hanging on the towel rack was only

one of the subtle reminders Beryl knew she would get throughout the day, reinforcing the reason she'd taken a chunk out of her savings and paid for the retreat. This was to be a last ditch effort in hopes to save her marriage. She prayed Travis would get some clues on what she needed out of their marriage. And in the process, also get a clue about what kind of father their kids needed. But so far, it didn't seem like Travis was learning anything.

Sure he was talking a lot, but Beryl knew all about Travis' ramblings. Most of his rambling, which embarrassed her beyond belief, was just so he could find a way to fit into conversations others were having, always trying to bring the conversation back to something he could relate to in the world of television.

While Charlotte was having problems with a husband who was *stepping out* on her with other women, Beryl had a problem too; Travis *staying in* watching the television. She wished he would stay on a job for more than a few months at a time. She figured everyone probably thought her husband was a television addict. And they were probably right.

She didn't really think Travis was addicted to television. She actually thought he was just plain lazy. She hated to think that about her own husband, but as she analyzed things, it was the only solution that made any sense.

Point blank, the man didn't want to work, didn't want to keep a job, or worse yet, *couldn't* keep a job. Meanwhile, she worked full time managing a fast food restaurant and selling makeup on the side, struggling to make ends meet.

Beryl tried to be understanding, especially in the beginning. She knew firsthand what it meant to stand by your man. Her mother had done so when Beryl's father broke his back on the job. Beryl's mother stepped in carrying their entire family by working two jobs day and night. So when Travis lost his jobs, Beryl knew exactly what she needed to do.

But during their relatively short five-year marriage, he'd had eight different jobs. The years had been filled with pink slips and reasons—actually excuses—Travis had given her as to why he was again out of work. One day something finally clicked in Beryl's head. The man just didn't want to work.

And if she had any doubts about his lack of desire to keep a job, Travis made it very clear to her one day when she was pressuring him to find a job. He'd blatantly told her he was waiting for the right kind of job, and he wasn't going to work just anywhere and take just anything. He told her that he wanted an employer who would appreciate his associates degree in general studies. This was during a time when Travis had been dropping her off at work, because their second car had broken down, needing a new alternator. With money as tight as it was, Beryl couldn't spare the money to buy an alternator and have the car fixed. She couldn't believe Travis had the nerve to continue to stand on his soapbox about not taking any kind of job. If it hadn't been for her two children, Beryl knew she would have strangled the man.

As the realization set in that Travis didn't want to work or pull his weight around the house, Beryl realized she couldn't change the man. The only thing she could change was herself and the situation she and her children were enduring.

Before hearing about the marriage retreat, she'd contemplated leaving, but her conscience wouldn't allow her to do that. Plus, she really loved Travis, and deep down just wanted him to do the right thing; act like a man and take care of his family.

So, with hopeful reluctance, she'd pulled two thousand

dollars out of her four thousand dollar savings account, money she'd stashed away for a rainy day, and paid for a spot at the retreat to help save their marriage. It was already Thursday, and Travis hadn't changed one bit.

Beryl didn't let Travis's lack of clarity bother her. She'd done all she could do, as far as they were concerned. Now it was up to her to do what she needed to do to get her life back. She was going to stop taking care of an adult sized kid. If she had to do it by herself, she'd move on and take care of the two children she had given birth to.

There was a phrase that stuck in her head: 'I can do bad by myself.' But Beryl had a better phrase that kept running through her mind: *I can do better by myself.*

Once she located her towel, she dried off and dressed. She picked up her sketchpad and charcoals and headed for the bedroom door. Just as she was about to touch the doorknob, Travis stirred on the bed.

"Baby, what time is it?" Travis asked.

Beryl sighed, looking at the clock. "It's seven fifty-five."

"Ah, man, why didn't you wake me up?" Groggy, Travis sat up with eyes still closed.

Feeling her heartbeat quicken, Beryl took another deep breath, deciding she wouldn't start the morning off with an argument that would put her in a bad mood. Especially knowing it would be a waste of time and breath anyway.

"It's Thursday, Travis," Beryl said.

"Huh? No, I said what time is it," Travis said.

Was the man too lazy to look over at the same clock she was looking at? She shook her head.

"It's Thursday, Travis," Beryl said again.

"Why are you talking crazy? I didn't ask what day it is, I asked what time it was."

"I know what you asked. But I felt it was more important for you to know what day it was," Beryl said with a calm voice. She wasn't going to let Travis ruin the rest of their stay.

"Why you trippin'?" Travis asked, finally opening his eyes.

"Oh, I'm not trippin'," Beryl said. "You can best believe that." Then she left the room, quietly closing the door behind her.

Chapter 25

Beryl Highgate

Thursday: 7:58 A.M.

Beryl sniffed the air as she walked into the kitchen, trying to decipher what Shelby had whipped up for their breakfast. Everyone except Phillip and Travis were already gathered in the kitchen.

She took another sniff. Working in the fast food industry for so many years, her nose was able to hone in on the source of many aromas. The smell of freshly brewed coffee was prevalent, with an undertone of something sweet and toasted.

It was amazing to Beryl how the aroma of food, and music from a good song, could momentarily take her thoughts to another place, making her forget the woes in her life.

On the table, spread out on a platter, were a variety of bagels surrounded by an assortment of cream cheeses and fresh fruit. There were two halves of a cinnamon raisin bagel in a wide mouth toaster sitting on the bar. They were popping up as she walked in.

Normally, Beryl would have frowned about having a continental breakfast, but after the variety of breakfast styles Shelby had already treated them with over the past days, the light breakfast was actually a welcomed site.

Accustomed to eating cinnamon raisin bagels with honey walnut cream cheese, Beryl saw this as an opportunity to try different types of bagels with different types of cream cheese. She wanted to think outside of the box. And even though this kind of thinking would be uncomfortable, she hoped for some pleasant rewards. The old way of thinking was traditional, which equated to boring in her eyes.

Beryl took a seat at the table. "What kinds of cream cheeses are these?"

Shelby looked over and pointed to the containers. "Strawberry, honey and nut, plain, and blueberry."

"I'm going to try the strawberry and blueberry. I've never tried them before," Beryl said.

"Don't get hooked on it," Nina said, "or you might end up with hips like mine."

Beryl didn't know how to take Nina. In the beginning she seemed a bit snobbish. Actually, the word bourgeois-ghetto would be more of an applicable word if the phrase existed. The woman dressed immaculately, but some of the stuff that rolled from her mouth, didn't suggest the culture she tried to display.

Beryl heard the sound of the blow dryer being turned on in their cabin room. She rolled her eyes for what felt like the hundredth time since she'd been there. Travis was drying his damp underwear.

"I don't plan on getting hooked. I'm going to enjoy the rest of my break from the real world, but once I get back, some things are definitely going to change," Beryl said as she picked up a plain bagel and placed it in the toaster. "I've been thinking a lot about what Phillip told us regarding the seven steps to rebuilding."

And what she meant was rebuilding her personal house, not her marital house. First she'd need to start over—without Travis. She would also need to forgive him. In a lot of ways, she didn't think Travis was intentionally trying to hurt her. In a sense, she really felt sorry for him. His mother had babied him, and when she passed away, his sisters did the same thing. Beryl's mistake in the beginning was treating him just like his sisters had, waiting on him hand and foot. Not that she believed her actions were a completely bad thing, because she was taking care of her man. But after a while, she realized she was treating Travis like her king, but instead of a queen, he was treating her more like a maidservant.

She would justify things, and she had already been counting the cost before they stepped foot into the cabin. From her calculations, their whole situation was costing her big time. Her health had deteriorated due to her stress about their bills and Travis's lack of lifting a hand to help her around the house. When she did ask him to do something, nine times out of ten she had to stay on him to finish the task.

Phillip had also said to use knowledge to her benefit, and even though he was talking about it in the sense to help rebuild a marriage, Beryl would tweak this point and find self-help books to assist her in becoming the Beryl she used to know and love. She would also use the Internet to find information about improving the mind, body, and spirit.

She'd come to the retreat hoping her husband would see the error of his ways and do right. But she realized Travis probably thought he was doing right. He didn't think there needed to be any changes. And it was all relative when she thought about it; a person's perception was truly their reality.

"Those are some valuable steps," Nina said. "George and I had already gone through most of those steps before we came here." Nina placed her hand on George's arm while looking at Beryl.

George, who was taking a sip of tea, nodded his head in agreement. He looked directly at Nina. "Now we're just in the belief stage. Believing God will give us further spiritual guidance on how we can strengthen our marriage and stand together so no weapons formed against us will prosper."

Even though Beryl knew George was agreeing with Nina, it looked as if he were also trying to convince her too. After he finished, he kept his eyes on Nina, but for some reason Nina wasn't making eye contact with him.

"Good morning, everyone," Phillip said, entering the kitchen.

Beryl's bagel popped up in the toaster.

"Good morning," George replied, finally taking his gaze off Nina.

Beryl thought she heard a sigh of relief escape from Nina's lips.

"Morning," Xavier mumbled under his breath.

Beryl had almost forgotten he was sitting at the table. From what she could see, he hadn't touched any of the bagel or fruit on his plate.

"Good morning," Charlotte said with only a slight bit more of enthusiasm than her husband.

Travis stepped into the room. "Hey, everybody. Hope I'm not too late for breakfast. Did I miss anything?"

Everything, Beryl thought. Travis wasn't the only one. They were all a haphazard bunch. One couple wasn't speaking to each other, another couple was speaking in private codes, and then there was she and Travis. He was oblivious to the fact that in a few short days, he would find himself out of a place to stay.

The couples all gathered back at The Round Table. Beryl was surprised at how filling the bagels and fruit had been. Whenever she'd eaten a continental breakfast before, she'd had an array of foods, but never felt quite satisfied.

"Again, good morning to you all," Phillip said, "I hope everyone slept well. We've gone over a great deal already, and I pray you've been using your time wisely to review ways to apply some of these teachings in your personal lives."

Beryl nodded, more so to herself than to anyone else in the room. She had slept very well. Much of what Phillip had been saying so far that week was making things crystal clear for her. She felt more and more sure about the path she needed to take once they arrived back home.

Phillip continued to speak. "We talked about loving yourself and the Lord. We also talked about the many love misunderstandings people have and the various love language skills people use to communicate. Hopefully you've been able to talk with your spouses and determine which love language skill you are each more apt to respond to."

At this statement, Travis sat up straight as if in the military and coming to attention.

Phillip smirked, nodding his head up and down in a slow rhythmic motion as he looked at each person around the table. Taking his lead, Shelby did the same. Beryl, Charlotte, Xavier, and George smirked also, nodding their heads in understanding. Nina nodded her head, but it didn't look like a nod of understanding. She was nodding to sleep.

Travis was totally clueless—as usual, but didn't say a word. Beryl was glad he hadn't shown his ignorance and kept his mouth shut.

"Sex, Money, Intangibles, Religion, and Kids," Phillip said, "Need I say more?"

Beryl answered, "No," while others shook their heads.

Travis finally got it and nodded his head. "Ah. No."

Phillip said, "We also talked about steps to help rebuild your marital home. I hope you have been able to come to some sort of agreement in looking at each step carefully."

At this, Beryl couldn't agree. She saw no reason to waste her time talking with a husband who would later forget most of what was said. Hope was out of the window, and Travis had run out of second chances.

"I've given you a great deal to absorb in a short time-frame, but I pray much of it will stick." Phillip tapped the notes in front of him. "Taking notes and talking to your spouses will help bring back to your remembrance what we've said here.

"With that being said, I do have another acronym I'd like for you to commit to memory." Phillip stood, picking up the dry erase pen. He drew what looked like a sail-boat on water, then wrote the acronym S.A.I.L. in capital letters above the boat.

"It won't be smooth sailing when you get home. But here are four more things that will at least help keep you in the boat and hopefully make the trip to strengthening your marriages a little easier," Phillip said. "'S' is for being saved. Being saved can make this trip much easier for you. I am a witness to this fact. When Shelby and I were having marital problems, she was saved and I wasn't. I had to learn the hard way about the love of Christ. One of my very dear friends tried to tell me about Christ's love, but I often changed the subject or avoided talking to him.

"But let me tell you, when I started going through tri-als and tribulations in my marriage, I turned to that same friend who I had often shunned, seeking guidance. That guidance and various other events in my life steered me in the right direction toward Christ. Ever since I accepted Christ as my Lord and Savior, I've had an unbelievable peace on the inside.

"Now, I'm not saying things were smooth sailing after

I got saved, but I can say that putting my trust in God, instead of my own abilities, was the best move I've ever made in my life."

George said, "Amen to that, my brother."

"That move was better than any move I performed on the football field during all of my years in high school and college," Phillip said.

The other men chuckled.

"But on a serious note," Phillip said, "If you aren't saved, then I encourage you to get to know Christ."

Beryl could always tell when Phillip was trying to get a point across. He would quietly look around the table, making eye contact with each person while tapping the eraser of a pencil on his notepad.

The eye contact with Nina hadn't been possible because her head was down, her arms folded and she had fallen asleep. Noticing, George nudged her slightly. She woke up, but her eyes remained droopy.

Beryl wondered how Phillip could have so much patience and keep his composure. He acted as if he hadn't noticed Nina's actions.

"The 'A' is for anniversaries and special dates and times," Phillip continued. "This one is for everyone, but mainly the men. You've got to remember the special days in your marriage. It is not cute or funny to forget your wedding anniversary, birthdays, and other special days your spouse holds dear. You can sail a little smoother if you remember the special times.

The juice Beryl drank at breakfast had hit her bladder. She needed to go to the bathroom, but didn't want to miss anything.

"So, do whatever you think you need to do to keep those dates in mind. Keep a calendar you'll look at regularly. On New Year's Day, before the big game, program your phone with reminders for special dates and times for the upcoming year. Or write a list and make yourself memorize it or at least look at it frequently enough that you'll be ahead of the game."

Beryl nodded. There were countless times when Travis had forgotten about their anniversary and there were a few times she had to remind him of their children's birthdays.

"'I' stands for intimacy. We talked about sex during S.M.I.R.K., but I just thought I'd say it again. Make sure you perpetuate intimacy in your marriage. Intimacy is more than just sex. Intimacy will give you a closeness and a bond that only you and your spouse can share and appreciate. This type of intimacy is reserved for your spouse only.

"Make quality time for each other. Set aside time for yourselves, without children and other distractions. Use this time to connect emotionally with your spouse, talking more than touching. And set aside some time to go out on a date with your spouse," Phillip said.

At this, Xavier's eyebrows raised in question.

Phillip nodded his head in response. "Yes, you and your wife can date. Who says you can't? What is dating anyway? Dating, very simply, is going out with someone. All you are doing is setting up an appointment for a rendezvous. Why is it when people get married, they forget about what they used to do before the marriage?

"Take your spouse out on a date once a week, if you can. And if once a week doesn't work, then twice a month. But talk about it, set the dates, and date. You need one on one time together to have some fun," Phillip said. "And I do mean one on one time. I don't mean going out to a class reunion, a function at church, or with a civic group you might be a part of. It's all great to mingle and mix with your peers, but you and your spouse need some time to make sure you're able to establish and maintain the emotional intimacy your marriages will thrive on."

At this, George nodded his head. It seemed George was actually learning something from Phillip.

"Last, but certainly not least, 'L' stands for lying. Thou shalt not lie. Leviticus 18:22 states, *Thou shalt not lie with mankind, as with womankind: it is abomination.* And likewise, lying can be an abomination in your marriage.

"What I'm talking about is something that's simple to do—don't lie, as in not tell the truth. Believe me when I say that even the littlest of lies can grow and fester into an unrecognizable and uncontrollable monster. Don't lie, be open and honest. It can save you a great deal of heartache in the end."

Phillip smiled. "Thou shat not lie. That sounds like it should be listed along with The Ten Commandments, doesn't it?"

Travis shifted uncomfortably in his seat. Beryl hoped Travis would take Phillip's advice to start telling the truth and to stop embellishing on the smallest of things. It wouldn't necessarily make life easy, but it would make it more bearable.

Phillip stopped looking at his watch. "Any questions?" he asked.

No one said anything.

"Okay then. Why don't we take a short break?"

Beryl was glad he called for a break, she didn't think her bladder could take much more. She stood, taking steps to head toward the bathroom, but had only gone a couple of steps when she heard a crash behind her. It sounded like something or someone hitting the table and floor.

She spun around to see Nina sprawled on the floor.

Chapter 26

Beryl Highgate

Thursday: 10:52 A.M.

"Oh my God, is she okay?" Beryl asked.

"Nina, baby, are you okay?" George was frantic. He knelt next to her, shaking her shoulders. "Nina, baby, wake up. Talk to me. Are you okay?"

Shelby knelt down on the other side of Nina. "Phillip, honey, move this table out of the way."

Phillip and Xavier pushed the table and chairs to the side. "Nina?" Shelby said, "Nina can you hear me?"

Everyone else crowded around, trying to see what was going on.

"Stand back please, so she can get some air," Shelby said. "Nina, can you hear me?" Shelby felt Nina's neck for a pulse, and then checked to see if she were breathing. "She is breathing," Shelby announced. She felt Nina's forehead. "She's burning up."

George grabbed his notepad and began fanning Nina's face.

Beryl's bladder got the best of her. She turned and did a limping skip toward the bathroom to prevent another accident. She relieved her full bladder and washed her hands as quickly as possible, all the while wondering what she could do to help.

Upon returning to the room, she saw that Nina still remained unconscious. George held what looked like a cold cloth on Nina's forehead.

"Let's get her off this floor," Shelby said.

Phillip assisted George in moving Nina out to the couch in the living room.

Shelby tried waking her by squeezing her shoulders and talking to her. "Phillip, grab the first aid kit for me," Shelby said.

Phillip did as he was asked, leaving the room in search of the first aid kit.

Beryl stood motionless, watching at the edge of the living room. Except for Shelby, no one else was saying a word. Beryl felt like she was holding her breath as they waited for signs of life from Nina.

Charlotte, Xavier, and Travis stood stark still. George kneeled again on the floor next to Nina, his face stricken with worry. Kneeling there, Beryl saw a regular guy—not the well known television icon. He was a regular man lovingly trying to see what was wrong with his wife.

"Nina, wake up," George pleaded.

"Nina, Nina, can you hear me?" Shelby continued to ask.

"Dear Lord . . . Jesus, please let my wife be okay," George pleaded looking up toward heaven.

"George, has Nina ever done this before?" Shelby asked.

George shook his head.

"What about medical conditions? Does she have any medical conditions? Is she diabetic? Does she take medications for anything?" Shelby asked question after question, trying to figure out what might be going on.

"No, she's healthy," George said. His face contorted with perplexity.

"I don't know." Shelby shook her head. "She doesn't have diabetes so it doesn't sound like it's low blood sugar. And she isn't on any medication, so it isn't like she's either taken too much or hasn't taken enough. Something's got to be wrong."

"Is she allergic to any foods? Maybe something she ate this morning?" Shelby asked, still trying to figure out what might be going on.

"No, she isn't allergic to anything that I know of," George said.

Phillip returned to the room with the first aid kit and joined the exchange, trying to offer his help. "How was she this morning?"

"She seemed fine enough at breakfast. But she did seem a little tired during the session," George said.

Beryl couldn't keep quiet any longer. She wanted to offer anything she could if it would help Nina. "I noticed how sleepy she looked. She nodded off a couple of times."

"Have you noticed anything different about her other than that?" Shelby asked.

"No. This morning was like most mornings. We got up, and she talked about getting some tea to drink. She was upset about some vitamins she lost yesterday. Then we came into the kitchen—"

"Vitamins, what kind of vitamins?" Shelby cut in.

"Just some kind of vitamins that are supposed to give her energy. Nina has been taking them for a few months now," George said.

"So she didn't take them this morning?" Shelby asked.

"No, she couldn't find them," George said, his face downcast with the kind of guilt Beryl occasionally saw in her children's eyes when they were up to no good.

"What did the vitamins look like?" Shelby asked.

"I don't know. She never showed them to me. I noticed how much energy they gave her. I joked with her the other day, telling her I should take them for all the energy they gave her. She almost had a fit saying I needed to get my own vitamins. And I . . ." George stopped.

"You what?" Shelby asked.

Beryl was in pure suspense. She had stopped breathing again, waiting for the response. She wasn't the only one in pure suspense. Whether she realized it or not, Charlotte was standing at the end of the couch, practically leaning on Xavier for support.

Travis sat on the edge of the loveseat, on the other side of the room, as if watching a made for television movie. All that seemed to be missing from his hands was the bag of popcorn and a jumbo soda.

George buried his head in his hand. "I took the bottle of vitamins from her."

"You did? Where is it?" Shelby asked.

From the pocket of his jeans, George pulled out a small bottle. It didn't look like any kind of vitamin bottle Beryl had ever seen before, but she figured it was some kind of high class vitamin that wasn't sold at the stores she shopped in.

Shelby took the bottle from George and examined it. "Vitality vitamins? I've never heard of these." Then she opened the bottle and looked inside.

From where Beryl was standing, she could see flat little round pills with a hollow shaped heart cut through the middle. But as she tried to look a little closer, she saw that the heart wasn't a heart shape at all, it was really in the shape of a V. It made sense. The V was for vitality.

Shelby's eyes widened, then her eyebrows furrowed. "Where did she get these from?"

"I don't know. I think one of her friends told her about them," George said.

"Phillip, hand me that first aid kit," Shelby said. After taking the kit from Phillip, she rummaged through it, tossing aside bandages, ointments and packets of medica-tion. She finally stopped when she located a little packet that looked like the hand wipe packets Beryl sometimes got from KFC. Shelby tore the top off and ran the open packet under Nina's nose a few times. Upon whiffing the contents, Nina groggily came awake.

Beryl's body relaxed, and she let out a deep breath.

"Nina, baby, are you okay?" George asked again.

Nina moaned as she opened her eyes to slits, trying to focus. After opening and closing her eyes a few times, she finally opened her eyes fully. She looked directly into her husband's eyes. "George?"

"Yes, baby," George said. He wiped her forehead with the damp cloth he was holding.

Nina felt around, patting the couch with her hand. She then looked around and saw Shelby hovering above. "Shelby?" Her eyebrows wrinkled. "What is going on?" Looking over toward the loveseat, Nina continued to focus in order to see who was sitting on the loveseat. Then she tried to sit up and immediately placed her hands on her stomach. "Ouch."

"Hold on a second," Shelby said. She placed her hand on Nina's shoulder. "Just lie back for a moment."

"You fell out of your chair and hit the floor," George said.

"I what?" Nina asked.

"You must have fallen asleep or passed out," Shelby said.

Beryl watched as Shelby took the bottle of vitamins and placed them in her pocket.

"How are you feeling right now?" Shelby asked.

Nina rubbed her stomach with her hand. "I've got sharp pains in my stomach, and I feel like I'm going to throw up."

"Can you see me okay?" Shelby asked.

"Right now I can, but a moment ago I couldn't," Nina replied.

Shelby kneeled down, moving closer to Nina. "Nina, when was the last time you took a—uh—vitamin?"

Shelby sounded as if she were trying to find the right words, and even though she was speaking to Nina, Shelby's eyes often darted around the room as if trying to gauge exactly what she should say.

Something wasn't right; Beryl could feel it in the pit of her own stomach.

Nina's face was perplexed as she looked back and forth from Shelby to George. She remained speechless.

"Nina, it's very important that you tell me the last time you took a *vitamin*." Shelby stressed the last word.

With a visible squirming discomfort, Nina looked into George's eyes again. Tears began welling in her eyes. In a hoarse whisper she said, "George, I didn't want you to find out."

George placed his hands on Nina's cheeks. "Baby, what is it? Don't cry."

Nina tried to speak again, but the words got choked in her throat.

Shelby spoke. "Phillip, help George get Nina to the bedroom, then you can talk in there."

A brief moment of relief appeared on Nina's face, until she tried to sit up again. With a grimace she hollered out in pain. "Oh my Lord."

"We'll take it easy," George said, "Don't try to rush. If it takes all afternoon, we'll get you moved."

Nina attempted a smile. "Don't joke. It just may take all afternoon."

"Let me know if there is anything I can do to help," Charlotte said.

"Yeah, me too," Xavier said.

They both continued to stand out of the way, at the end of the couch.

Beryl moved one of the chairs from the dining room table and placed it along the path heading toward George and Nina's bedroom. "Here's a chair just in case you need to sit down and take a rest."

A few moments later, Nina had to use it. And with gratefulness, she smiled at Beryl mouthing, "Thank you."

With painstaking effort, Nina continued until she reached the bedroom. Beryl wished there was more she could do to help out. So while Phillip and Shelby joined George and Nina in their room, Beryl took it upon herself to look around for food to prepare lunch for the group.

She figured they'd all need something to eat after the morning they'd just had. Beryl was pleasantly surprised when Charlotte joined her in the kitchen and offered a helping hand. They didn't say much to each other while working together, but Beryl was thankful to have the woman there with her.

Just as she found herself lost in the preparation of cold cut sandwiches and chips, Beryl felt a tap on her shoulder. Travis was standing behind her.

He whispered in her ear, "Man, can you believe that? It was like an episode of that show on Discovery Health called *Mystery Diagnoses*." Travis paused, looking conspiratorially to see if anyone else was listening or watching them. "I wonder what's going on with Nina?"

Again, for the umpteenth time, Beryl found herself rolling her eyes. "Travis," Beryl whispered louder than

she intended, "why don't you find something construc-
tive to do?"

"There isn't anything to do," Travis replied.

Beryl could think of quite a few things Travis could be
doing, like reading over the notes they'd been given over
the past few days—starting with examining his own life
and paying attention to the needs of his own wife instead
of someone else's. But obviously, self-improvement wasn't
an appealing enough subject for him.

"There's a lake out there," Beryl offered.

"What am I going to do on the lake? I don't have a boat
or any fishing supplies."

"I was thinking more like what you could do in the
lake."

"In the lake?" Travis asked.

"Yeah. Why don't you just jump in?"

"Funny, Beryl . . . real funny."

Even though she knew it was wrong, she wasn't being
funny. She really did wish he'd just jump in the lake or
find some other method to disappear. Sometimes she
wished they'd never even met, but then she wouldn't
have her two beautiful little boys. So for now, she hoped
they wouldn't find themselves standing along the side of
the lake, alone in the darkness. Because given the opportunity, she just might push him in.

Chapter 27

Shelby Tomlinson

Thursday: 11:43 A.M.

"Nina, are you okay in there?" George asked.

Nina didn't answer immediately. With patience, George, Phillip, and Shelby sat on the twin beds in George and Nina's bedroom. Nina had been in the bathroom for over ten minutes. She'd vomited at least once, but otherwise there wasn't any sound or movement from the other side of the door.

"I'll be out in a minute," Nina said after a few moments.

Shelby's mind was running a mile a minute, trying to remember what she could about various drugs and their side effects. It was times like these she wished she had the Internet at hand or at least one of her pharmacology books handy. She was 99% sure that the pills in Nina's so called vitamin bottle, were actually valium. They definitely weren't vitamins as George had thought.

The bottle didn't even look like a regular vitamin bottle. It was rigged to look like a vitamin bottle and had an almost real enough looking pharmacy label, but it didn't have a patient number or a prescription number. Shelby had had a couple of patients at the hospital where she worked who had gotten addicted to valium. They'd been so hooked that they eventually needed multiple doses each day to prevent heightened withdrawal symptoms. Symptoms much like the ones Nina was currently experiencing: blurred vision, sweating, abdominal pains, and vomiting.

These symptoms were just the tip of the iceberg. Patients who had tried on their own to go cold turkey from the drug often dealt with problems of muscle cramps, tremors, convulsions, diarrhea, and even psychosis. Shelby knew things could deteriorate pretty rapidly if they didn't get to the bottom of what was going on with Nina. She didn't look forward to seeing what the rest of the iceberg was hiding.

Nina emerged from the bathroom, holding her stomach with one hand and the wall with the other. Her skin was pallid, and there were dark circles under her eyes. "Ugh, I feel like a sumo wrestler is twisting my arms and legs from the inside." She made her way to the twin bed on which George was sitting.

"Do you want to lie down?" George asked.

"No, I've had enough of that. Besides, I might have to jump up and run to the bathroom again. My stomach hurts like crazy," Nina said.

"Nina, we need to talk," Shelby said. "I'd really like to give you and George some time to talk alone, but I am afraid time is of the essence."

Nina's eyes flitted to each person in the room.

Phillip sat next to Shelby. She knew he was confused, but also sensed something wasn't right. He'd been supportive by letting Shelby take the lead and not speaking or questioning any of the instructions she had been dishing out like a commander in an army.

Shelby pulled the bottle of pills from her pocket and held it up for Nina to see. "What can you tell me about these?"

Nina's eyes lit up like a child on Christmas morning. "You found my vitamins." She stood so quick she stumbled, almost falling. With outstretched arms she reached for the bottle.

Shelby gave it to her. With triple the speed she'd had only a few minutes before, Nina headed straight for the bathroom and ran water in a cup. Opening the bottle, she popped a pill into her mouth, then followed it with two cups of water.

George and Phillip watched Nina's movements in awe. Shelby wasn't surprised. The actions further confirmed her suspicions. Nina was addicted.

After wiping the water off her mouth, Nina grabbed her stomach again. "Ugh, I wish this pain would just go away." With bottle in hand, Nina walked back over to the bed, gingerly sitting back down next to George.

"I am sure the pain will start to subside soon," Shelby said.

Nina looked down at the bottle in her hand, squeezing it as tight as a child with a security blanket. "I hope so."

"It will, as long as you're taking those pills. If you go cold turkey, the symptoms will get worse before they can get better," Shelby said.

Both George and Phillip watched the exchange between Shelby and Nina, neither speaking a word.

"Nina, do you want to tell us about those pills?" Shelby asked.

Nina's voice rose an octave, "They aren't pills, they're vitamins." As Nina spoke, she looked at George.

George looked over at Shelby, finally speaking, "What's going on here?"

"I have a pretty good idea why Nina's body has been out of whack. But I want to hear it from Nina. And you need to hear it from Nina," Shelby said.

Phillip placed his hand on Shelby's arm, giving it a squeeze.

"Nina, what is going on? Is there something you need to say?" George asked.

Not speaking, Nina looked down toward the floor. Shelby she saw tears streaming down the woman's face.

George placed his arms around Nina and pulled her into his body. "Don't cry, honey, talk to me. You can talk to me. Whatever it is, we'll get through it."

Nina began to sob so loud that Shelby figured the sounds permeated the walls of the tiny room. Shelby knew this wasn't the time for Nina or George, for that matter, to worry about who may or may not hear them. Prayerfully, they'd be able to get to the bottom of what was going on so Nina could get the help she needed.

Nina's sobs continued until finally subsiding into intermittent sniffles. Phillip decided to speak. "George, Nina, please know that Shelby and I are here to help you. We're not here to be nosey or judge you. We just want to be of assistance. I don't want to pry, but from what I am gathering here, something isn't right about those vitamins. With God, all things are possible when two or three are gathered in His name, we can pray and touch and agree. But the flesh can be a tricky thing; oftentimes making us forget rational thinking and allowing us give in to temptation. Shelby seems to have insight on what might be going on, but Nina, we need for you to talk to us, to tell us what's going on. It's the only way we can help this battle your flesh is having."

Nina wiped the tears from her eyes. Shelby realized the darkness under Nina's eyes was mainly from the eyeliner she was wearing. Remnants of the eyeliner streaked hers cheeks and smeared her hands.

"You're right, Shelby, they aren't vitamins. It's actually valium." Once Nina made her confession, Shelby saw visible relief wash over the woman's face.

"Valium?" George asked.

Nina nodded her head. "I've been taking it for a few months now. I started after I stopped gambling. I was having problems with anxiety and needed something to take the edge off." Nina stopped and took a deep breath.

Phillip stood, picking up a box of tissue from the nightstand. He handed it to Nina who pulled a few out and wiped her eyes and cheeks.

"I thought I could just stop gambling cold turkey, as Shelby put it, but the urge to gamble kept nagging at me. I found myself getting anxious during the times I would have normally been setting up at the Bingo halls. I even got to the point where I couldn't stand going into gas stations that sold lottery tickets and scratch offs.

"I talked to one of my friends about anxiety and the nervousness I was experiencing. She told me about the valium. Her doctor prescribed a few pills for me. I felt a calm I hadn't known since before the gambling got so bad," Nina said.

"Who told you about the pills? What friend?" George asked with an accusing voice.

"It doesn't really matter. My friend didn't know anything about me going back to the doctor a few more times, and the doctor didn't know that I altered the prescription he had given me in order to get more and more pills."

Shelby listened as Nina continued recapping her story. She'd wanted to stop being dependent on the drug, but didn't know how. She'd been praying for God to intervene, knowing there was no way she'd be able to do it on her own. Nina continued telling her story until she'd brought them all up to the present moment. When she finished, she hung her head down low in shame.

George slid off the bed and kneeled directly in front of Nina. With hands cupping her cheeks, he said, "Nina, I said we'd get through it. And we will."

Nina shook her head. "How can you say that? And how can you continue to stand by me with all the baggage I brought into this marriage and the baggage I continue to claim?"

"When I said for better or for worse, I meant it. This is only a storm—a storm we'll get through together."

Shelby reached for Phillip's hand. As if knowing what she was about to do, Phillip stood at the same time as she did.

"Nina, George, we're going to leave so you can talk in privacy," Shelby said.

George stood. "Hold on a second before you both go." George placed his hand on Nina's shoulder. "The devil is trying to destroy my wife. He has come this time in the name of valium. Phillip, can you pray with us?"

Phillip nodded his head. Shelby continued to hold his left hand, with his right hand, he reached out to George. Shelby placed her hand on Nina's shoulder as Nina continued to sit on the bed with her head bowed.

Once the circle was formed, Phillip began to pray. "Dear Lord, our Father in heaven. Jesus, we come to you as humbly as we know how, forming this gathering of four, we are touching and agreeing that no weapon, called valium, formed against Nina will prosper. We pray that you, Lord, will guide Nina in the path she will need to travel in order to overcome this drug that has been trying to thrive in her body. We rebuke this drug demon.

"We also pray that you will bless this marriage between George and Nina. And that you will let them
know at a time of your choosing, the exact reasons they
are going through these storms in their lives. Lord, we
pray you'll give Nina strength and that you will continue
to give George wisdom. And together they will come out
stronger than they were before. We pray this in Jesus'
name. Amen."

"Amen," George and Nina said.

"Amen," Shelby said. She'd heard Phillip pray many
times, but was still amazed by some of the powerful
prayers he pulled from his soul. She squeezed his hand.
Then letting go, she gave both Nina and George a hug.

With glassy eyes, George said to Phillip, "Thanks, my
brother." His voice was raspy and strained. He gave
Phillip a solid hug.

"No problem. We're here for you both, and don't you
ever forget it," Phillip said.

Shelby nodded in agreement. "Nina, we'll talk a little
later on about the pills. You aren't going to be able to go
cold turkey right now. Honestly, you'll probably have to
keep taking them just as you have until you can get back
to the doctor. Then you can be weaned off properly."

Nina nodded her head, still clutching the bottle.

"Baby, I am so sorry I hid those pills from you. I didn't
know what they were," George said.

"No, you didn't know what they were, but if you hadn't
hid them, who knows how much longer I would have lived
the lie?" Nina said. "Everything happens for a reason."

"We'll talk later," Shelby said, then Phillip led their
way out of the room.

Upon walking into the kitchen, Shelby saw the other
two couples seated at the table eating sandwiches and
chips. She'd totally forgotten about lunch.

"Oh, who made lunch?" Shelby asked.

"Charlotte and I," Beryl said.

"Thanks, ladies. I hadn't even thought about it," Shelby said.

"No problem. We've all got to help each other out up in these mountains. Besides, you've been slaving over the stove the whole time we've been here. You probably need a break yourself," Charlotte said.

Shelby took a seat at the table. "These sandwiches look good." She picked up a plate and stacked it with three different sandwiches and a pile of chips.

Phillip's eyebrows arched. "Pretty hungry, huh?"

"I am, but these aren't for me. I'm going to take this plate to George and Nina," Shelby said.

Phillip chuckled. "Good, I was getting worried."

"Honey, can you pour some ginger ale for them?" Shelby asked her husband.

Phillip did as requested, and they both took the food and drinks to George and Nina. Afterward, they rejoined the other two couples who were talking quietly amongst themselves at the table.

It had taken over three days, but Shelby finally felt some sense of community she'd experienced just a few short years prior, when she and Phillip first came to the Lake Turner retreat. One couple was well on their way to recovery. With one couple down, there were two more to go.

Chapter 28

Beryl Highgate

Thursday: 4:36 P.M.

Beryl sat alone at The Round Table, tapping her pencil on the memo pad that lay in front of her. At the top of the sheet of paper she had written: THINGS TO DO. Then she numbered the paper from one to ten, leaving two lines between each number. If she were going to be serious about making changes at home and in her life, she'd have to have a plan.

Tried as she might to come up with a list of things to do, the only thing that kept coming to mind was how Nina was doing and what had gone on behind the closed doors in their room a few short hours prior. Beryl couldn't forget the shift in Shelby's demeanor as she opened the bottle of vitamins and peered in. Nor could she mistake the urgency in Shelby's voice as she tried to get Nina back to her bedroom. Beryl had the distinct feeling that if the rest of them hadn't been in the living room, Shelby would have said a whole lot more.

Phillip and Shelby had emerged from the room with poker faces. They weren't giving any clues about what had gone on. Nina's wailing, which had filtered through the walls, let Beryl know they hadn't been socializing. She wondered what the exact issues were with Nina and George. They all had so many different issues coming into that house.

Beryl knew not to judge other people's situations, especially when most didn't know what they would do in someone else's shoes. But with Xavier and Charlotte's situation, she didn't think she would have put up with her husband messing around on her. In her eyes, his actions would have been a cause for immediate dismissal. But then again, another woman may not put up with the problems she was having with Travis.

The things that Travis did weren't so easy to pinpoint. Like his not being able to keep a job or his not helping around the house. There were times, especially when Beryl felt she was at her wits end, that he'd pitch in without her saying a word. She almost felt like he was gauging her to see just how far he could push and wasn't going to do much more than he absolutely had to.

Beryl truly believed Travis wasn't just lazy but also selfish. He had to be selfish. How else could he be so lazy knowing he had a wife and two kids that needed to be cared for and protected?

Beryl looked down at the sheet of paper in front of her. She didn't have any time to dwell on Nina and George's problems. Besides, it looked as if whatever was going on with them was being addressed. And in Xavier's case, at least he acknowledged the accusations Charlotte had hit him with. There wasn't much dialogue between the two of them, but at least there was a little, which was a start. But when it came to her situation with Travis, it seemed like it was a lost cause. He was in avoidance mode—avoiding the issues of work and responsibility.

The first thing Beryl wrote on her list was that Travis would have to move out. There was no reason for her to move since she would be the one taking care of the children. She could see Travis trying to argue this with her, probably telling her that she should move out since she was the one who wanted it so bad. He might even try to say that he could take care of the children. But Beryl knew Travis could barely take care of himself, much less two children. She wasn't just thinking of the children's financial needs, but their safety also.

Beryl shook her head, remembering the time Travis had come in one night after taking the kids to the park. It was late fall, a time when it got dark before seven at night. Both children had fallen asleep in the backseat of their car. Beryl had seen him take her oldest son to the bedroom to lay him down and assumed he had taken the youngest one also. But two hours later, Beryl heard her baby boy crying. When she looked into the bedroom to check on him, he wasn't there.

Frantically, she listened for the baby's screaming. Beryl started yelling, asking Travis, who was sitting in front of the television, if he knew where her baby was. Travis's face was blank as he shook his head.

Beryl had found her little boy still strapped in his car seat, terrified and screaming. Travis had not only left the boy in the garage, he had also left the garage door up and the door leading into the house wide open. She had been horrified.

That very night she could have strangled Travis. He'd tried to apologize, saying that he'd laid their older son down and remembered having to go to the bathroom. He said he figured she'd taken the baby out of the car.

Again, Travis had an excuse to try to explain his actions. But she hadn't wanted to hear a thing he had to say. And she was too tired to go through the whole gamete of checks and balances. She hadn't felt like checking him on the very simple fact that he'd forgotten the boy while focusing on a rerun of some stupid television show.

Beryl shook her head, still upset about the whole matter. She placed a star next to the first item on her things to do list. Yes, Travis had to go.

Next, she wrote that she'd need to get a lawyer. She'd also need to start thinking about who would care for the children while she was at work, especially when there was a school release and the daycare was closed. Travis usually took care of them since he wasn't working anyway, but after she kicked him out, Beryl didn't have any disillusions that it would be a while before he'd be able to find stable housing. More than likely, he'd end up going to one of his sisters' houses, telling them some sort of pitiful story about how Beryl had kicked him out of the house. They would believe the story and welcome him with loving arms.

It burned Beryl up to think about how much his sisters treated him like a baby. It was true that he was their baby brother, and they had taken on the role of surrogate mothers to him when their own mother died. But for God's sake, someone should have taught him that at some point he'd have to man up and take care of himself, and maybe even a family one day.

The grandfather clock in the living room chimed, as if reminding Beryl that she didn't have the time or luxury to reminisce about displeasing thoughts. Kicking Travis out of the house was going to be easier said than done because it wasn't like as soon as he was gone, all would be right with the world.

It was probably going to be a lot harder than she thought. One of her co-workers, Janice, had left her husband and taken their little girl with her. It hadn't been easy for Janice at all. The woman hadn't factored in how the child would be affected by the separation. Janice confided that every night, for almost three months, the little girl cried for her father; especially at bedtime.

The father and daughter had a nightly ritual in which he said prayers with her, tucked her in, and read her a bedtime story. Janice never seemed to say the prayers right, didn't tuck the covers the right way, and didn't read the stories like the child's father had.

There were many days Janice came to Beryl's desk with bags under her eyes and tears trickling down her face. Beryl hadn't pried into the reason Janice had decided to leave her husband, but in all the woman's complaints about sleepless nights, not once had she said anything about considering to go back home.

Beryl would have to think about how it all might affect her boys. They loved their father, who played with them often, acting more like a loving, playful big brother. Wishful thoughts flooded Beryl's mind as she held the pencil in her hands, pressing it with so much tension that she heard it cracking under the pressure. Why couldn't Travis just find and keep a good job with a few benefits? It wasn't like she was asking him to find a job making six-figures; she just wanted a real helpmate. She wasn't asking for much, and what she was asking for was something that most married couples understood as a normal part of being in a functional relationship. Why did is seem so hard for her husband to grasp this concept?

Why couldn't Travis stop watching so much television and help around the house more—do more with her and the kids as a family? Beryl couldn't remember the last time they all went on a family vacation.

Beryl was tired of giving Travis second chances and turning the other cheek. She had turned the other cheek so many times that her neck literally hurt. This retreat felt like her last resort. But deep down she still held hope that he could somehow get it together and do what a man was supposed to do in a marriage.

She believed miracles could happen and held hope that maybe within the next couple of days, Travis would finally get the clues he needed to what their marriage really lacked. Beryl tore the sheet of paper off of the pad and balled it up. It wouldn't be over until it was over, and who was she to call it completely quits now? Travis still had a couple of days to figure things out. That would be Beryl's determining factor.

As if in answer to her hopes, Travis entered the room with two bowls of ice cream in hand. "I brought you something."

Beryl smiled. One thing they did agree on was ice cream. They both loved it, and in the early days of dating, they often went to local ice cream shops, comparing different flavors. One thing that was always a staple in their freezer was ice cream.

"What kind is it?" Beryl asked.

Travis took the seat next to her. "Butter pecan."

"Um, my favorite. You sure do know the way to a girl's heart."

Travis smiled, a look of pride covering his face.

Beryl took a spoonful of ice cream into her mouth. It was sweet and creamy, and chocked full of pecans. "Oh, my goodness. This is some of the best I've tasted in a while."

Travis spooned some into his mouth. "It is, isn't it?"

Beryl took another spoonful, enjoying the buttery taste and the large pieces of pecans.

"And I think I've figured out Shelby's little cooking secret," Travis said.

Beryl's ears perked up. "What is it?"

Travis ate a little more and winked. "The information will cost you."

With all seriousness, Beryl said, "This trip is already costing me."

Travis put his hand up in surrender. "Okay, okay, you're right. I can give you the information gratis." He spooned another bite of ice cream.

Beryl couldn't help it, she did the same.

"This is that Beans ice cream," Travis said.

"Beans?" Beryl asked.

"Yeah, Beans. You know that company with the refrigerated trucks who will deliver food to your house."

Beryl had seen Beans trucks. There was a guy from Beans who came every other Thursday to their job, delivering to some of her co-workers. Every so often he gave them updated catalogues filled with tasty looking prepackaged foods with various entrees and meal ideas.

Beryl had been tempted to buy a few things until she saw the cost of the food. They weren't cheap. She figured the price made up for the time she'd have to spend in the kitchen preparing the same meals. But as she analyzed it, the amounts weren't large enough, and she wouldn't have leftovers to carry over for the next day. With the way she'd had to budget her money, Beryl had to figure out ways to stretch a dollar as far as possible.

"That deep freezer in the back is full of Beans foods and entrees," Travis said.

"Wow, I was wondering why Shelby never seemed to slave over the stove. It was like she'd be in here with us during the sessions, and then within a blink of the eye, she had our meals cooked and ready to serve." Beryl chuckled. "I thought she might be an undercover Iron Chef that no one had heard about in America yet." Beryl said this, thinking about the one cooking show she did like to watch on cable before she had it disconnected.

"Now we know," Travis said.

"I've been eating Beans food all week. Well, I'll be

darned. I can't wait to get back and tell my co-workers. They'll get a kick out of it," Beryl said.

"I'm glad you mentioned us getting back," Travis said.

Beryl stopped eating and held her breath.

"I've been doing a lot of thinking about what you've been saying about me getting a job. There are a few places I'm going to call as soon as I get back to the house. I saw them in the paper and circled the advertisements. I meant to call before I left, but with packing and all, I didn't get a chance to," Travis said.

Slowly, Beryl released her breath.

"I have an idea." Travis held up his hand. "And give me a chance to finish before you stop me."

Beryl sat, not saying a word.

"Okay, while I am looking for a job, maybe I can start taking some classes online. I checked in to a few online colleges. I can work on completing my degree in general studies." His facial expression was serious and to anyone else his voice would have sounded rational.

"Are you serious?" Beryl asked.

"Yeah, with the job market being so shaky, I'm going to need a better education to compete with the other guys."

Beryl couldn't believe her ears. The man couldn't have just said that he wanted suck more money out of her to take some online college courses. Travis must have completely lost his mind. He didn't have the discipline to look for a job in the newspaper, much less to take intense online courses. And what the heck did he think he was going to do with a general studies degree anyway?

She'd been the one who wanted to go to school. She'd applied to various art schools and had been accepted, but their financial situation never allowed her to go. Beryl loved to draw and dreamed of getting a degree in Art. She was the one who one day dreamed of having her name listed as an illustrator in books and magazines.

These were real dreams Beryl didn't see coming true for her anytime soon.

She had also seen the so called newspaper Travis was talking about with the job advertisements he'd circled. She wondered if Travis thought she was a complete fool. The paper he kept referring to was already two weeks old when they left for the retreat. Those jobs were long gone.

And if he had been so busy packing that he couldn't pick up the phone and inquire about the jobs, why hadn't he packed enough underwear for the trip? Travis had the audacity to talk about competing with somebody in the workplace. There was no way he could compete, especially lying in the bed each morning relying on Beryl to wake him up so he could get ready to go to work.

"Wonders never cease," Beryl said as she reached for the balled up piece of paper. Carefully, she opened it to smooth out the wrinkles as best as she could. She stood gathering her things ready to leave.

"What's that?" Travis asked, looking at the paper. "And where are you going?"

"Don't worry about this." Beryl held up the paper. She turned and walked away.

"Hey, I thought we were talking?" Travis said.

Again Beryl held the paper up. "We'll talk more about it when we get home."

Chapter 29

Shelby Tomlinson

Thursday: 9:37 P.M.

Shelby sat up in the beds they'd pushed together in their bedroom. With the twin beds side by side, it gave the illusion that they were actually sleeping on a king sized bed. With his head in Shelby's lap, Phillip shared his feelings about the events of the previous week and earlier in the day.

"Man, this week has been long," he said. "Is it over yet?"

"Over?" Shelby asked.

"Yeah, I just don't feel like I'm being effective with these couples," Phillip said.

"Don't say that. You are."

"Really, I can't tell." Phillip let out a deep breath. "I mean look at Nina and George. I didn't see any of that coming with Nina and her drug problem. And you figured it out pretty quickly."

"Baby, don't say that. George is her husband, and even he didn't know exactly what was going on, and he saw her almost every day."

Phillip sighed.

"I just went into nurse mode, that's all. I remembered working with some patients when I was in nursing school that showed some of the same signs as Nina. Something had been nagging the back of my mind the last couple of days.

"When Nina fell out and George recapped things he'd been noticing, then I knew something was off kilter. But seeing the pills in the bottle sealed it for me, and I had to have you all get her out of that living room."

"Good thinking. I am glad you had the presence of mind to keep things private for Nina," Phillip said.

Shelby stroked the top of Phillip's forehead and head. "It was obvious that George didn't know what was going on. And it wasn't any of the other couples' business," she said.

"So tell me something."

"What?"

"Why did you let her take some more of the medication?"

"Even though valium is a prescribed medication, it is still a medication. And just like any street drug, when you are addicted, there are times when it isn't best to just quit cold turkey."

"Oh." Phillip nodded his head.

"When they get back home, they'll need to see the doctor and explain what happened. Then her doctor will be able to determine what kind of gradual step down process she'll need in order to be weaned off the drug. It wouldn't have helped for me to take the pills and let her continue to suffer while she's here."

Shelby chuckled and added, "To tell you the truth, I am glad she has enough pills to last her the next couple of days until she can make it home. Or else, we would have had to find the nearest hospital to have her admitted."

"God is good," Phillip said.

"He most certainly is," Shelby replied.

"I had a chance to speak with George a little earlier and he thanked us for all we did."

"How did he say Nina was doing?"

"He said they've been talking, and she can't believe he isn't upset with her. George said that their marriage has been through some rough patches the last year and a half, but he holds hope that they will make it through this storm stronger than they were before," Phillip said.

"Well, amen to that." Shelby shook her head. "I don't know how the man does it with all the responsibilities; not only as a husband, but also as a pastor of a mega church. He always seems to be able to keep his cool."

"I don't know how he does it either. Hopefully one day in the future, I'll be able to visit him and gain some nuggets, which will help me in my walk with God."

"I'm sure he won't mind. But if you ask me, I think you're doing a good job."

"Your vote's bias," Phillip said.

"Maybe so, but I'd like to think I'm a good judge of character."

"Okay, if you say so. What about the situation with Beryl and Travis?" Phillip asked.

"What about it?"

"Do you think I am getting through to those two?"

"I think you are probably getting through to Beryl. She seems to be taking in everything, taking notes and asking questions. Much of her conversation, and the points she makes, seem to really be directed at Travis. It's like she is trying to indirectly get him to understand her wants and needs."

"Sometimes she isn't so indirect," Phillip said.

"That's true." Shelby nodded her head.

"Her emotions flip flop from being angry and frustrated, to showing signs of wanting to work with Travis to keep their marriage together."

"Overall, it is sort of hard to read how strongly she feels about calling it quits or really trying to make it work," Shelby said.

"If you ask me, I think her words are speaking louder than her actions. I think if Travis doesn't start to really hone in to what his wife wants, then he just might find his world completely turned upside down."

"Maybe you can pull him to the side and find out where his mind really is."

"I think I will. That one on one talk with George was good. I'll probably talk to Xavier in the same manner," Phillip said.

"If you'd like for me to, I can try to talk to Beryl and Charlotte also. Nina and I have already said that we'll touch bases tomorrow."

"Yeah. Could you do that, please?"

"Of course."

Shelby shifted, lifting Phillip's head a couple of inches in order to readjust her legs, which were starting to feel numb on the thighs.

"Is my head too heavy for your legs?"

"No, big head," Shelby said placing Phillip's head back down comfortably.

"What about Xavier and Charlotte? What are your thoughts now about their situation?"

"I think Charlotte has been harboring a great deal of anger, and I think her being able to finally confront him allowed her to get a huge weight off her chest." Shelby stroked Phillip's eyebrows with her index finger.

"She had a lot to get off her chest."

"And I think she may have more. Like I said before, it didn't exactly look like she was finished with her confrontation the other day," Shelby said.

"Maybe she was able to talk to him in private. But as far as I can see, it doesn't look like she's talking to him very much."

"You never know what goes on behind closed doors." Shelby didn't know why, but her comment about closed doors triggered her mind to think about Phillip's friend, Will.

Will had recently gotten married to a woman named Morgan who he'd met in church. Their courtship had been relatively short, lasting seven months. There was something about Morgan that didn't set well with Shelby.

"Baby?"

Shelby heard the questioning sound in her husband's voice. "Yeah?"

"What'd you do, zone off on me?"

"Oh, no, I'm sorry. I was just thinking about something, that's all. What did you say?"

"You are right, sometimes things aren't what they seem," Phillip said. "And I'm hoping this is also the case with Xavier and Charlotte. Sometimes the brain distorts stuff."

Abruptly, Phillip sat up. Startled, Shelby jumped.

"That's it," Phillip stated.

"That's what?"

"The fun house effect."

"Huh?"

"My next topic. You know how it is when you're in a fun house like the ones at the fair."

"Okay, and?"

"Fun houses are pretty blatant, and you know you're in one, especially when you're looking into those altered mirrors. From the moment you step into one of those places, almost everything is distorted." Phillip looked around for his notepad and pen. When he found it, he sat on the edge of the bed and began writing. "I've got to get these thoughts down while they're fresh in my head."

"The fun house affect," Shelby said. "It has a bit of a ring to it."

Phillip stopped writing for a moment. "Good, because thus far, this cabin has been anything but fun."

Chapter 30

Charlotte Knight

Friday: 4:55 A.M.

In her bed, Charlotte tossed and turned, feeling like something was clinging to her body. Upon waking, she felt the tangled sheets around her. She clawed at the sheets as if trying to tear them off. Ever since going to bed earlier that night, she'd been unable to shake the nightmares she was having. Picking her head up, she looked over at the clock on the dresser. In a little over two hours she'd need to get up and face another tension packed day.

Forcefully, she pushed her head back onto the pillow, and then pulled the sheet over her head. The light from the alarm clock was bothering her. Maybe if she made it a little darker under the covers, she'd be able to at least salvage an hour or so of sleep.

After several more minutes, Charlotte still hadn't been able to fall back asleep, and the darkness hadn't done anything to swipe her memory of the awful dreams. The dreams were more like out-of-control flashbacks of all the detective work she'd done over the months.

When she'd gotten the copies of Xavier's cell phone

records, it was as simple as going online and pulling up past bills, which had the details of each call. She uploaded each file one by one, then pressed print. Within a matter of minutes, she had a neat stack of pages detailing thousands of calls placed to and from her husband.

To her dismay, the dreams were distorting those very simple steps. In her dream, when she pressed the button to print the pages, they'd ended up flying out of the printer, causing pages upon pages to fill the room. It reminded her of one of the old *I Love Lucy* episodes where Lucy was in a chocolate factory and the chocolates kept coming so fast that she couldn't keep up with them. Lucy ended up putting the chocolates any and everywhere to hide them.

Charlotte's dream shifted as she remembered the time when she'd placed a home phone recording device on their home phone. She'd read in a book once about a character who recorded her phone conversations because she was being harassed by a crank caller. During a quick trip to an electronic store, she'd explained to a salesman what she wanted, and he led her to exactly what she needed.

It was a little recording device, unlike a regular answering machine, in that there was no announcement to leave a message. There weren't any beeping or clicking sounds to make anyone aware that the recording was being done. Whenever the phone rang and the call was answered, the device would automatically start recording the conversation between the people talking.

During Charlotte's quest to catch Xavier in as much dirt as she could, she wanted to also catch any actual conversations he might be bold enough to have from their home. The device ended up working like a charm, recording all of his conversations and even all of Charlotte's conversations, since she'd left the machine hooked up at all times. It was hidden behind the couch in her living room, hooked up to a phone jack they never used.

But again, Charlotte's dreams were taking her actions to a whole new level. In the dream, she saw herself back at the electronics store buying an arm full of the recording devices. She'd placed more around her house, and had even put recording devices on the phones in Xavier's office at work and various other offices throughout the car dealership.

In another dream, she remembered the time she'd taken a little handheld voice activated recorder and duct tapped it under Xavier's driver's side seat in his SUV. It turned out this device hadn't been as effective as the home recording device. The sound of Xavier talking to people, whether it was on the phone or to other passengers riding with him, were often muffled. At times, there were also the competing sounds of the engine and the radio.

This last dream was the worst of all in distorting her true life detective actions. Charlotte was in a hardware store buying an Acme sized roll of duct tape. The huge size of the roll reminded her of something the Coyote would have bought to try to catch the Road Runner.

Charlotte used the roll of duct tape not only to put a recording device in Xavier's SUV, but also in her own car, just in case he borrowed it, which he rarely ever did. Then one night she snuck out to the car dealership, picked the locks and broke in to obtain the keys to all the cars on the lot. Charlotte proceeded to duct tape minisized recorders under the driver's side seats.

With sticky fingers and a sweat drenched forehead, Charlotte ran from car to car, installing the devices. After a while the Acme size roll of tape started wrapping around her body like a boa constrictor, trying to squeeze her. She clawed at the tape, trying to tear it off. That's when she woke up realizing the sheets were actually tangled around her body.

She was happy to be awake and glad the nightmares had come to an end. But now she faced the true life living nightmare she was currently in. Charlotte sighed in frustration. She wasn't proud of the things she'd done to try to catch her husband in his lies. Especially since the listening devices hadn't helped her find anything new about his extracurricular activities. Most of the phone calls made to and from their home were the ones she'd made. The phone calls Xavier had made were one hundred percent legitimate—calls regarding bills, telemarketers, and conversations with his kids.

It was when she overheard the conversations Xavier had with his kids that Charlotte felt she had hit her lowest point. She stepped back and re-evaluated things. Even now she shook her head, not wanting to think about the other minute things she had done to gauge whether her husband was telling the truth or not.

All the detective work she'd done had almost driven her crazy. The things she'd been doing were so out of character it was amazing. Charlotte had gone to so many desperate measures trying to keep a twenty-four-seven watch on her husband. She knew if her friends or family ever found out the extent she'd gone, they might actually try to have her committed to an institution.

She hated the person she'd become, always suspicious and harboring anger toward a man she once loved and adored to the utmost. She'd give just about anything to have her old life back again. The life where she could trust her husband without a shadow of doubt, and a life where the women on the commercials with him hadn't fazed her in the least bit because she knew Xavier had a woman at home who wouldn't hesitate to take care of his every need.

A tear trickled down her face as she wished for at least one night of peace. A night in which she might be able to dream of a better time, making her forget the living nightmare she was playing a staring role in.

Charlotte looked back over at the alarm clock. It was now five thirty-eight. Throwing the covers off, she sat up and let her legs hang over the side of the bed.

On the other side of the room, Xavier continued to sleep. She'd heard him tossing and turning during the past few nights also. Neither one of them were getting any sleep. But for now he seemed to be resting pretty well.

If she were a vindictive woman, she would turn on all the lights and start making noise to wake him. If she weren't sleeping well, why should he? But she wasn't a vindictive woman. She hadn't pulled out all that damaging information in front of six other virtual strangers to embarrass him. If she wanted to do that she could have done so in many other ways at home with people they both knew.

No, she was once again just trying to get her husband to come clean about all of his wrongdoings. She had to admit that when she had confronted him with everything, he did come clean as far as she could tell. But Charlotte still couldn't get over the fact that her husband had strayed from home with at least one other woman and the fact that he'd found it so easy to lie to her for months about his extracurricular activities. How in the world was she going to be able to believe him now? Why would he all of a sudden start telling her the truth, especially when she'd caught him in so many lies? She wondered how he would feel if the shoe was on the other foot?

She also wondered what Xavier would do if he really

knew where she had gone those three days when she'd left their home. What would he think if he found out Charlotte had been less than eight miles away on the other side of town, closed up in a house with her co-worker, Shawn— the same co-worker Xavier didn't like because he thought the man was a little too friendly with her.

Deep down, she knew the answer. Xavier would freak out.

Chapter 31

Charlotte Knight

Friday: 9:26 A.M.

Everyone in the house sat in the living room patiently waiting for Phillip. Shelby had asked them to meet in there instead of at The Round Table. Charlotte was glad to see that Nina was looking better than she had the previous evening and had even gotten a little bit of her spunk back.

Breakfast had been over for almost thirty minutes, and Phillip had failed to appear as he normally did during breakfast. And now he was late to start their morning session. The group had already gone through as much small talk as they could take during breakfast and during the first few minutes of their assembling in the living room.

Nina sat on the loveseat, leaning her head and body against George, and Beryl sat on an armchair on one side of the room while her husband sat in a matching chair on the other side of the room. Xavier sat on one end of the couch, while Charlotte had made sure to sit on the other end, as far as she could get away from him. Now all that could be heard was the ticking of the grandfather clock in the corner of the room.

Shelby had pulled two chairs from The Round Table and set them in the front of the living room area, on opposite sides of the fireplace. At first, even Shelby's face had been pleasant, but now her eyebrows furrowed as she looked up at the grandfather clock every other minute to check the time.

When the clock's bell chimed indicating it was half past the hour, Shelby leaned forward and stood up. As she did, Phillip entered the room. A look of relief washed over everyone's face.

"Good morning, everyone," Phillip said. His face and demeanor was calm and refreshed. He walked over toward the seat designated for him. Passing it, he leaned down to give Shelby a kiss on the cheek. He sat, continuing to look at his wife. "Thank you, Shelby, for having everyone gather in here."

"You're welcome," Shelby replied.

Phillip brought his hands together in a single clap. "I guess you're all wondering why we're sitting in here. Very simply, I thought we needed a change of scenery. And I think the chairs," Phillip pointed to the living room chairs, "are a great deal more comfortable. It's Friday, and I don't know about you all, but to me it feels like this week is going by pretty slow. So I want us to have a little fun and kick our feet up a little."

"Sounds good to me," Travis said.

Out of the corner of Charlotte's eye, she saw Beryl roll her eyes.

"I've given you all a great deal of notes and things to consider in your decision to move your marriages forward," Phillip said. I am going to give you a few more things to ponder for the remainder of your time here and once you get back to your homes.

"We won't be spending the whole day working, per se. During this morning's session, we'll go over some things, but this afternoon, I want you all to make a true effort to find somewhere quiet to talk to your spouse about any and everything you want to and need to talk about. Who knows when you'll have the luxury of time to do so again? Especially once you get back to your busy lives at home."

Charlotte didn't mind sitting and listening to more insight from Phillip and didn't care if they did so from sun up to sundown. What she didn't want to do was say two words to her husband, much less spend time alone with him carrying on a whole conversation.

Looking at the scowl on Beryl's face, it seemed like her sentiments were the exact same. The only two people who looked like they were okay with the suggestion were Nina and George. They sat all snuggled up, looking like they were on their second honeymoon or something.

"Do we have to—" Beryl started to say, but was cut off by Phillip's hand. He'd held it up indicating she didn't need to finish the sentence.

"Yes, you have to," Phillip said. "You need to know that you and your spouse have had ample time to hash out any problems and concerns."

Like a child upset about not getting a lollipop, Beryl folded her arms.

"During your conversations with your spouse, you may also realize that sometimes things are not always what they seem. Which brings me to our last main topic of the week: the fun house," Phillip said. "How many of you all have been inside a fun house, like at a state fair or an amusement park?"

Charlotte, along with a couple others, raised her hand. Charlotte had only been inside one fun house and vowed never to enter another. She'd had a hard time navigating the maze of mirrors and ended up walking into so many of them, that she'd bruised her nose. She'd also fallen a couple of times on stairs, which had been moving from side to side.

Then she'd bruised her hip trying to walk through a cylindrical shaped walkway, which continually turned around and around like the mixer on a cement truck. The walkway hadn't been what caused her to bruise her hip. That had happened when just after she'd safely maneuvered out of the cylinder and came face to face with a large, distorted, neon-colored face which seemed to be barreling straight at her.

It was only after she fell back against a wall that she realized the face was hers, reflecting off of a fun house mirror. The neon purple and green lights gave an eerie look to her reflection. A chill came over her body at the memory of it, causing her to shudder involuntarily. She wrapped her arms around her upper body.

"Well, if you've ever been in a fun house," Phillip continued, "you know sometimes you can find things that aren't so fun, and things that can often be a little scary; especially with the weird music and the sound of a laughing clown. At night, when they've got all the neon lights flashing, it can add to the overall goal of trying to deceive you. Now, let me ask you another question. Have any of you been inside a fun house during the day? Especially when the amusement park is closed?"

No one raised their hand this time.

"Here's the funny thing." Phillip chuckled. "During the day when everything is turned off, you can see the true facets of the house. The illusions are just that."

Shelby nodded her head in agreement.

"Sometimes there are things in our life which might be having the same affect as the fun house does. Sometimes we mistake something for something else, or we have a misunderstanding about something that can be resolved, especially when a little light is shed on to it. Believe me, I know," Phillip said. "But that's another story."

Shelby nodded her head a little more adamantly this time, making Charlotte wonder what kinds of problems she and Phillip could have had in their marriage.

"Now my example of the fun house is a little on the extreme side. But to put it very simply, the brain often distorts stuff. In many cases, a person's perception will turn into their reality. And no matter what you say to that person, they will stand firm in their belief.

"There are many reasons the brain distorts stuff. One reason the brain might distort something may depend on a person's value system. Or even references a person may think about, which apply to a certain situation."

Phillip sat on the edge of his seat. "For instance, I remember one time when I was a little boy, I was visiting my grandparents. For some reason, my mom and dad had come to pick me up a few days early. My grandmother wasn't home at the time, so I wanted to leave her a little note, to let her know I had to go.

"Well, the only pen I could find had red ink. I wrote the note and left it on the refrigerator under one of her favorite magnets."

Phillip took in a deep breath and sighed. "Long story short, my grandmother ended up calling my mom, crying. She was upset because I had written her a nasty note. When my mom got on me about leaving a mean note to my grandmother, I was absolutely dumbfounded. My mother ended up getting to the bottom of it. It turns out my grandmother felt that because I had written the note with red ink, I was mad at her."

Phillip laughed. "I laugh now, but believe me; it wasn't funny at the time. It took months to convince my grandmother that I wasn't mad. She had been taught that you only use the color red to write to someone if you were angry at them. And my leaving early supported the fact that I must have been angry with her—in her mind at least.

"To this day, I hesitate before using red ink to write anything. And to this day, if I receive something written in red ink, I think about how my grandmother would have interpreted it," Phillip said. "You all may be able to think of some examples. So again, different value systems can cause our brains to distort stuff. There are times when we only hear what we want to hear. Like when a person says one thing but you hear another thing."

"And times when a person's emotions will cause them to misinterpret information, especially times when the person is experiencing anger or grief."

Phillip sat back slightly in his chair. "With communication being so key in marriages, we must try to eliminate as much brain distortion as possible. So that's why it is often important to listen to what the other person is saying, and for clarification, repeat what they've said to make sure you are getting a full understanding of what they actually meant."

As Phillip continued talking about how the brain often distorts things, and how people can be mistaken, Charlotte, thought about her own situation, reflecting on each of the things she'd accused Xavier of doing and the concrete facts she had to prove his wrongdoings. In her mind, there was absolutely no way she had misconstrued anything.

Her thoughts were interrupted when she heard George's voice interjecting.

"May I say something?" George asked.

"Sure, go right ahead," Phillip said.

George addressed the group. "I often encourage couples to do just as Phillip is saying. And you'll be surprised how much people do and don't hear." George directed his attention back to Phillip. "The other thing you'll be surprised about is how much of their communication isn't verbal."

"Bingo," Phillip said. He stood and gave George a high five. "You see, I love it when things fall into place. Like minds do think alike." Phillip took his seat again. "Communication isn't just about what you say, but also how you say it. The inflection in your voice can be a form of communication, as well as your tone and body language. So what you actually say is only a small percentage of effective communication."

"Amen to that," Beryl said. She looked directly at Travis. "Can you repeat that last part again?"

Phillip smiled as if feeling Beryl's pain. Heck, Charlotte figured by now that everyone, except Travis, felt Beryl's pain.

"It's very important to make sure you know without a shadow of doubt what your spouse means. And it is also important to figure out what might be an actual brain distortion. Make sure you are communicating effectively via verbal communication, voice inflection, the tone of your voice, and body language," Phillip said.

"And if the other person has done all of what you've said and is pretty sure the other person is telling the truth, what happens when they don't deliver?" Beryl asked.

Phillip's eyebrows rose in question. "I'm not sure what you mean."

"Okay, I'll use Travis and me as an example. What if we have talked and supposedly have an understanding. Like for instance, he knows he needs to look for a job and he says he is going to look for a job. His body language and tone are screaming that he will follow through on what he says he is going to do. But then days and weeks turn into months and he hasn't looked for a job. What happens then? Am I supposed to sit back and continue to let him lie to me like I am Boo Boo the fool?" Beryl asked.

Travis sat up. "Beryl, that's not fair." Travis looked around at everyone in the room. Charlotte saw his cheeks flush. "I have been looking for a job. It's just hard out here for a black man," Travis said.

"Oh really? What I hear you saying is that you've been looking for work," Beryl said. "Is that true?"

"Yeah, you know I have."

Beryl held up her hand and started ticking off fingers. "And I see you are sitting upright, looking directly at me, so your body language is suggesting that you are telling the truth."

"I am, Beryl." As Travis spoke to Beryl, he continued to glance at the others around the room. His embarrassed face continued to flush.

"Okay then maybe it is me. Maybe it's my fault. Maybe my background and value system is a little different from yours. Now if it were me looking for a job, I'd be doing something on a daily basis to find one. I'd put in applications on a daily basis at various places. I'd also be scowling the Internet and talking to friends and family to find out if they knew of anyone hiring." Beryl shrugged her shoulders. "But I guess your value system is a little different."

"I have put in applications, and I looked on the Internet for jobs. I even asked my sister if anyone was hiring where she worked," Travis said. This time his face took on a smugness, as if trying to save face.

"Ha," Beryl said so loud that Charlotte almost jumped out of her seat. "In the last six months you've only put in about five applications. And you've been on the Internet even less times than that looking for anything, much less jobs. And I can't believe you are sitting there looking at me with that little smug face of yours."

Charlotte wished Xavier had only been on the Internet less than five times in the last six months. She was lucky if Xavier only got on to the Internet once a day.

Beryl continued. "Don't think you've been fooling me for a moment circling the ads in the newspaper and conveniently leaving it out for me to see. You were too cheap to even buy a daily paper. Didn't you think I'd notice the date on the paper hadn't changed? I mean if you are going to pretend, then do it right, Travis."

Ouch, Charlotte thought to herself. Why did men think they were so sneaky?

Phillip interrupted, directing his attention between Beryl and Travis. "Okay, okay. That is a good start. Why don't you continue along those same lines when we break?" Changing his direction to the whole group, Phillip said, "I want you all to talk to your spouses, leaving no stone unturned. Use the notes I've given you during this week." Talking directly to Charlotte, he said, "And any evidence you've gathered over the months, talk about it, ask questions, communicate.

"You all need to talk over the who, what, where, when, how, and even whys. Especially if there are things you think your spouse needs to know about. Be honest with one another so you can process the information and move on with your lives—prayerfully as a couple in a united front."

Phillip looked at his watch. "It's almost lunch time. Let's take a break while Shelby finishes getting our lunch ready. After lunch you can spend the afternoon with your significant other, talking about whatever most concerns you.

"This evening we'll gather back here in the living room to watch the movie *Why Did I Get Married*," Phillip said. "Hopefully, by that time, you'll be able to stop focusing on your own lives for a moment. You might even realize your problems are nothing compared to the couples in the movie." Phillip smiled. "Any questions?"

Charlotte figured watching the movie must have been what Phillip had referred to as the fun part of the evening, and she truly hoped the movie was a comedy, because she didn't anticipate any fun during the next few hours.

Chapter 32

Charlotte Knight

Friday: 1:34 P.M.

With each step Charlotte took, her legs felt as if they were laced with lead. She longed for the day to be over. Beside her, Xavier walked as they ventured on a narrow path just outside of the cabin. George and Nina had found seats on the wraparound porch to have their talk. Charlotte had seen Beryl and Travis heading in the other direction, walking alongside the lake.

Not wanting to stay in the cabin and possibly be heard by Phillip and Shelby, they'd gone in the only other direction in which they might have the privacy Phillip urged them to seek for their ultimate marriage saving discussion.

Charlotte viewed it as a waste of time. There was no doubt in her mind that her husband was up to no good. Just as Phillip had suggested, she brought along the folder with all the hard facts tucked within, even though she knew most of the information like the back of her hand. Just in case Xavier tried to dispute something, she'd whip it out and stop him dead in his tracks.

She'd been avoiding this discussion for months, scared to hear what the ugly truth really might be. Now somewhere deep inside she was actually glad they were going to finally talk. It was now or never. If they didn't discuss their problems, then she'd just return home to continue the living nightmare. Once they talked, she could make some decisions.

"At some point we're going to have to talk," Xavier said.

They'd been walking along the path for almost five minutes without saying a word to each other. Charlotte didn't say anything.

"Did you hear me?"

She could hear the frustration in Xavier's voice. "I heard you," she said and continued on without offering anything else.

They walked a few more steps, then Xavier stopped abruptly. Charlotte stopped also once she realized he wasn't moving anymore.

Looking around, Xavier pointed to a tree, which had fallen. He walked toward it and sat down. "I am not walking another step. We're going to talk. Now."

Charlotte was surprised by the command in his voice. He spoke in a business like tone as if he were talking to one of his trainees. With only a slight moment of hesitation, she sat down next to him on the trunk.

Without hesitation, Xavier spoke. "I understand you're upset and you've been harboring some appropriately warranted anger toward me, but at some point this has all got to stop."

"I—" Charlotte started to speak.

Putting his hand up, Xavier cut her off. "You, you, you. I've heard from you, Charlotte. Now, you need to listen to me.

Charlotte folded her arms and looked away from him at the trees in front of her.

"I know you've gone to a great extent to find out as

much as you could about what I was doing behind your back. You asked me time and time again to come clean with you, and I didn't. I understand I should have." He paused, tapping the folder on Charlotte's lap. "I am sorry you had to pull all this stuff out in front of strangers to get me to fess up. So what's done is done. I apologize for everything. And believe it or not, I have nothing else to hide. You were completely on point with the information you discovered. I honestly hadn't realized I was talking to those women so much," Xavier said.

"Did you realize how many times you slept with those women?" Charlotte asked, trying to catch him in a lie.

"I only slept with Yasmine—twice. That is the God's honest truth."

"Oh, now you want to bring God into this. And you expect me to believe you?"

"Yes, I do. Because I am telling the truth, and I'm so sorry this all happened."

"Why, Xavier? Why did you do this to me? To us?"

"I don't know. I really don't know. Most of it, like the Internet stuff, was just so . . ." He looked around as if searching for the right word. "Addictive. It was like all I could think about was getting on the Internet, and once I was on there, time flew by. But I promise you, ever since you confronted me with the STD results, I've given it all up. I'm scared to even get on the Internet and check what the week's weather forecast is anymore."

"So what was it? What wasn't I doing? What did those women have that I didn't have?"

"Nothing, absolutely nothing. Like I said, I don't know what was so addictive about all of it. I really thought I had conquered that part of my life during my first marriage." Xavier looked down at his feet. "I am pretty sure I've conquered it this time."

"Pretty sure?" Charlotte asked. "How am I supposed

to live with pretty sure? Do you know what you've put me through? How in the heck do you think I felt getting a venereal disease from my husband, like some common street hooker or something?"

Xavier winced, but didn't say anything. Charlotte was glad, she needed to let him know exactly what he'd put her through.

The volume of Charlotte's voice increased. "And then to find out my husband has been soliciting women on the Internet. And talking to other women more than he talks to me. How do you think I felt?"

Xavier continued to look at the ground.

Charlotte took her hand and hit Xavier's shoulder as hard as she could. He barely flinched. "Well, I'll tell you how it made me feel. I felt sick to my stomach, and I almost turned into a mad woman going around like I was some sort of detective. I almost drove myself crazy. And if it weren't for a good friend of mine, I probably would have gone completely mad. It took that friend to remind me that my actions were not what God could be pleased with. And that was the last thing I wanted to hear. But the more they talked to me and the more I thought about it, I realized, I couldn't handle the situation in an eye for an eye manner.

"Just because you had done some ungodly things to defile our marriage, I didn't have to reciprocate or continue to sneak around finding out about your dirt. This person encouraged me to talk with you about the things I'd found and get it all out into the open. He was the one who gave me the information about this marriage retreat, hoping it might help us."

Xavier's eyebrows rose finally turning his attention to Charlotte in order to look squarely at her face. "He?"

"Yes, he," Charlotte said.

"I know most of your friends, and what male friend do

you have close enough to give you advice about our marriage?"

Charlotte could hear the defensiveness in Xavier's voice.

"Shawn," she said. She braced herself for his reaction.

"Shawn? You've got to be kidding me. That guy has been trying to talk to you ever since you two started working together." Xavier paused, shaking his head. His male ego had been bruised. "So he's been talking to you, huh? Probably filling your head with nonsense. He's probably really trying to make it look like he's the good guy and I am the bad guy so he can finally get a chance to be with you."

"You have some nerve. For your information, Shawn is a true friend. And I really don't know where you get the idea that he wants to be with me. He has a girlfriend. A very nice and understanding girlfriend, I might add."

"Oh sure, have you ever seen this girlfriend? She's probably just a figment of his imagination, just a part of his story to make you believe his nice guy routine. And how do you know she is so nice and understanding?"

"I met her once. She lives in New Jersey. She was *very* understanding when she found out I was staying at Shawn's house," Charlotte said, again waiting for Xavier's reaction.

Xavier snapped his whole body around to her. "What do you mean when you stayed at Shawn's house? When did you . . ." His voice trailed off.

"You know when. And for your information, Shawn was nothing but a gentleman the entire time I was there. He gave up his bed for me and slept on the couch. And the only thing he tried to do the whole time I was there was convince me that I needed to go back home and talk to you about everything. So you can get all the crazy ideas out of your head that the man is trying to get with me."

Xavier shook his head. "Do you expect me to believe you were in some man's house for three days and he didn't try anything?" Xavier took a deep breath. "Am I supposed to believe you two didn't do anything?"

"You have some nerve. First of all, I don't have the proclivity you have with talking to and sleeping with other people," Charlotte said. "And let's not forget, you are the one who drove me to go to that other man's house in the first place."

Xavier recoiled as if Charlotte had slapped him in the face.

Several moments passed without either saying a word. Finally, Xavier broke the silence. "Okay, you are right, and I guess I deserved your last comment."

"You're doggone right you deserve it. You've done all this dirt and you sit here trying to turn the tide on me? Then you want me to believe you are a changed man and you'll never do this to me again? You did it to your first wife and now to me. When will it ever stop?"

"Baby, I am sorry. Sorry for accusing you of doing anything with Shawn. I was wrong. It's just that I've always had it in my mind that that guy likes you."

"He does like me, but only as a friend. So can we please stop wasting time and get off the subject of Shawn? Because if it weren't for Shawn, we wouldn't be sitting here right now."

"Okay, you're right. I don't want to waste anymore time either. Bottom line is I love you, and I'll do whatever it takes to earn your love and trust back."

Charlotte shook her head. It wasn't that she didn't love her husband, she had always loved him. She was extremely hurt by what he had done and didn't know if she'd ever be able to trust him again.

Xavier continued. "I know you have all that evidence, but if you look at the dates closely, you won't find anything damaging, on my part, since I found out about having gonorrhea."

Charlotte reached for the accordion file again.

"Stop. I don't have to look at those papers to know that. I haven't contacted any of those women since before the day you confronted me in the dining room. It is true that Yasmine continued to call me for a while after I broke it off with her, but I told her time and time again to stop calling me. So you go ahead and look at all that so called evidence and check the time stamps and dates. I haven't called anyone I wasn't supposed to," Xavier said.

From what she could remember about the timeline of the phone calls and the calls Xavier had made to all three women, what he was saying was true. And the recording devices she'd put in their home and in his car hadn't even remotely suggested that he'd wanted contact with another woman.

"Is there anything else you need to come clean about?" Charlotte asked.

"No, and if you do have something else you've been waiting to spring on me, I can honestly say that I have no idea what it could be. As far as I can recollect, you've done some really good detective work."

Charlotte listened to what her husband was saying, hearing the sincerity in his voice. His tone and body language didn't suggest he was lying, and if she hadn't been pretty much monitoring his every move, she might still have doubts. But deep in her heart she believed her husband was telling the truth. She didn't know if it was because she wanted to believe him or because she needed to believe him. But deep in her heart she did.

"You've got to believe me, Charlotte," Xavier said.

With a sigh, Charlotte said, "I do believe you."

"I promise you, baby, I'll never hurt you like that again. You've got to believe that too."

"I believe what you say. But, honey, I think you have an unnatural problem with your appetite for women. You are going to need to seek professional help for this. I really don't think it is something you can control on your own."

"I can. I just had a brief moment of weakness. But I know I can do this by myself."

"Look, I still love you. I never stopped loving you, but it will take some time for me to work through all of this. And after all you've put me through, I don't think I'm asking too much for you to seek some professional help."

"I really don't think I need any help, but if you want me to, I'll see someone. I am willing to do anything it takes to get us back to the way we used to be."

"I hope you have patience because the road to the way we used to be will be pretty long," Charlotte said.

"Well, I'll pray to God that the road will not be too long," Xavier said.

"Good, because the Father, Son, and Holy Spirit are really the only hope you have." She meant this.

Chapter 33

Charlotte Knight

Friday: 7:07 P.M.

"So, Shelby, when do we get to find out what the secrets for all of these great meals you've been preparing us?" Charlotte asked. She was going to miss the wonderful meals they'd eaten at the cabin once she returned home.

"Do you want me to put you all out of your misery?" Shelby asked.

The couples had just finished eating a dinner of Shrimp Scampi with Linguini and red peppers. Now they found themselves migrating from the dining room into the living room to get ready for the movie Phillip had promised they were going to see.

"I know the secret," Travis said with an unbelievably smug look on his face.

"Oh, really?" Shelby asked.

"Yep," Travis said.

There was something about Travis that Charlotte just didn't like. She wondered, not for the first time, how Beryl could put up with him on a daily basis. But she figured that everyone had a soul mate and Travis must have been Beryl's.

"So what's my secret?" Shelby asked.

"You've been using those frozen meals and snacks from Beans," Travis said as if his cow had won first prize at the state fair.

"Ah, very good. You must have some really good taste buds," Shelby said.

"Yeah, my taste buds are pretty good," Travis said.

"Don't listen to him. He saw some of the boxes in the deep freezer the other night when he was looking for the ice cream. If not for that, he wouldn't have known," Beryl said.

"Now, Travis, it sounds like you did a little cheating to find out," Phillip said.

Travis hunched his shoulders. "Yeah, I was going to say so, but Beryl beat me to it."

If Charlotte was a betting person, she'd say Travis would have never come clean on his own.

"Beans, what is Beans?" Nina asked.

"Have you ever seen the refrigerated trucks driving around Greenville with the cute little animated beans dancing on the side?" Shelby asked.

"No, I don't think I have."

"Well, they have catalogs and you can order a variety of foods, many of them already prepared and frozen. When I found out we'd be coming up here for this retreat, and I knew I'd probably be the one doing most of the cooking, I immediately thought of Beans. There was no way I was going to spend my whole week in the kitchen slaving over a hot stove," Shelby said.

"Amen to that, my sister," Beryl said.

"I used to buy things from Beans a few years back, but I stopped for some reason. I forgot about the company.

I'll have to look them up when I get back home," Charlotte said.

"Don't worry, I've got the catalogue here, and I can
give you the toll free number before we leave," Shelby
offered.

"Oh, I know the number. They have commercials that
come on late at night," Travis said, still looking like he
had a prize winning cow.

Charlotte looked over at Beryl who was rolling her
eyes, and then at Xavier who rolled his also.

"Okay thanks, Travis. I don't have anything to write
with right now, but I'll get the number a little later."
Charlotte took a seat on the couch right next to Xavier.
While everyone else found comfortable seats in preparation for the movie, Charlotte whispered to Xavier, "Can
you believe that guy?"

"No, not really," Xavier replied.

"Poor Beryl, she's got to put up with him all the time. I
don't see how she does it," Charlotte said.

"I don't know either. He's a snoop who can remember
almost anything from television, but can't remember to
look for a job or how to keep one." Xavier shook his
head.

"He puts more work into not trying to work than he
does in trying to find a job."

"Yeah, and he also puts a lot of work into trying to impress everybody," Xavier said.

"Everybody but Beryl."

"True, very true."

Once everyone was settled in their respective places,
Phillip stood in front of the television before starting the
movie.

"Okay, you all know the teacher in me can't just push
play on the DVD player and sit down. Before I do, is

there anyone who would like to share with the group how the conversation with your spouse went?"

Charlotte felt okay with how she and Xavier's conversation went. It had definitely gone better than she'd anticipated. But she didn't feel good enough about it to talk to the entire group. She and Xavier would still have a long way to go. And she really wasn't joking about needing the Trinity to help not only Xavier with his problem, but also to help them get through the next rough patches she was sure they had ahead of them. She could only pray that the Lord would provide miraculous intervention as far as their marriage was concerned.

"I'd like to say something," George said. "That is if no one else wants to go first."

Charlotte looked around. Xavier must have felt the same way she did because he hadn't volunteered to say anything. Surprisingly, Travis had kept his mouth shut, and for the first time, Beryl looked completely relieved.

George addressed Phillip. "First of all, I'd like to thank Phillip for stepping in to help marriages in need of spiritual advice. You stepped up to the plate, my brother, and God will reward you for doing so. He has great plans for you, you just wait and see."

Phillip and Shelby shared a knowing look between one another, then Phillip replied to George. "Thanks, George. I'm just stepping in and doing the little bit that I can do to continue to help build God's kingdom." Phillip chuckled. "And the last time someone told me God had special plans for me, I was unsaved and scrambling to get my wife back. I wasn't the man you see before you today. And I wasn't the type of man to say I'd help plan a retreat, much less be a teacher and moderator."

"God is good," George said.

"Yes, He is," Phillip agreed.

George nodded. "What I wanted to say to the rest of you is to be encouraged. We all need encouragement. I know I needed it before coming to this retreat. And I am so glad I didn't let my pride and ego get the best of me and not come. I didn't want anyone to know I had problems in my marriage. Heck, I counsel hundreds of couples on a yearly basis. How was it going to look for me to be having problems?" George shook his head.

Nina stroked his arm as he continued. "Nina and I have been truly blessed during this retreat. I know you all noticed my wife's behavior in the beginning of the week. And I am sure you probably thought my wife was very clumsy and a little on the irritable side. Some of you might even say she was acting like a diva to the utmost."

George smiled at Nina. "My wife is a diva, but in a good way. And she isn't usually clumsy and as irritable as you saw her this week. Because of this retreat, my wife was able to come clean about a prescription drug she's been taking—a drug which she'd gotten addicted to."

Charlotte looked at Nina who had tears welling in her eyes. George patted Nina's hand. "I'm sharing this with you because Nina and I discussed it, and agreed for me to do so.

Nina nodded her head.

"The drug she was addicted to had her acting completely out of character. I couldn't put my finger on it, but I knew something wasn't right with my wife. She'd been taking the drug to squelch some anxiety problems she was having. Nina knew she was addicted to the drug, but didn't know what to do, and she was scared to tell me about it.

"Shelby was able to see the symptoms and recognize what was going on. Now that everything is out in the open, Nina feels as if a huge weight has been lifted off of her, and we were able to talk openly and honestly about the problem. It has done us a world of good.

"So I encourage you all, if you have not done so already, to be open and honest with your spouse. It is the first step in getting your marriages back on track," George stressed.

Charlotte felt tears welling up into her own eyes. She felt pretty sure she and Xavier had taken that first step. She hoped and prayed this was the case. Now all she could do was wait and see what God had in store for their marriage.

Shelby handed Nina a couple of tissues to wipe her face. When she handed Charlotte the box of tissues, it was then that she realized her tears were falling. She cried not only for George and Nina, but for her and Xavier also.

"Thank you again, George and Nina, for sharing." Phillip looked around at everyone in the group. "Would anyone else like to share?"

No one else volunteered.

"Okay, as promised, we'll watch *Why Did I Get Married.*" He turned to activate the DVD player. "Hopefully this movie will also give you some inspiration and show you that there are three sides to every story. His side, her side, and the truth.

Charlotte didn't have any doubt about why she got married, but she did have doubts about why she should stay married. She wondered if the movie would give her any insight about that.

Part III

The Truth

Chapter 34

Phillip Tomlinson

Saturday: 3:14 P.M.

"Does Bean's sell ribs and chicken like this?" Xavier asked.

"Nah," Phillip said as he set the pan of raw beef ribs on the side of the grill. "Shelby purchased most of what we've eaten this week from Bean's, but not everything. Those omelets, waffles, and pancakes were the real thing, believe me. And I was the one to purchase the meat for the cookout today."

Phillip checked the charcoals to see if they were hot enough yet. He hoped to get the meat on the grill before the women returned from their paddle boat ride on the lake. Deciding the coals needed a little longer, he pulled a bottled water out of the cooler and took a seat in one of the lawn chairs next to the other guys sitting lakeside.

"Man, I wish I'd brought my fishing pole," George said.

"You like to fish?" Travis asked.

"I sure do. I am a fisher of fish and of men." George laughed at his own joke.

"A fisher of men, like Jesus, huh?" Phillip asked.

"That's the way I like to think of it," George said.

"You know you remind me a lot of my pastor back at home. He was the one who told me that God had special plans for me and great works for me to do," Phillip said.

"What did you think about that when he said it?" George asked.

"To tell you all the truth, I was clueless. Like I said, I was unsaved at the time, and my wife had left me. I was confused as I don't know what. I wanted answers that could help me get my wife back, not a prophecy from a preacher man." Phillip shook his head and laughed to himself.

"If you don't mind me asking," Xavier said, "how did you go from that man to the man you are today?"

"Yeah, I was wondering the same thing," Travis said.

"Nah, I don't mind. It's part of my testimony," Phillip told the men.

All three men turned their full attention to Phillip.

"Shelby and I had some problems in our marriage. Problems I caused. My deceit caused my wife to be banged up so bad that she had to be put in a hospital, during the time she was pregnant. For a little while, we didn't know if our unborn baby was going to be okay. She blamed me for it and rightly so. She kicked me out of the house, and I had to really re-evaluate my life.

"I found that the great job I had, beautiful home, and the vintage automobile meant nothing without my wife and daughter. Something else was missing in my life, and it took almost losing my family to realize it.

"A very good friend of mine, Will, often tried to tell me about the goodness of the Lord. He tried to get me to understand that there was more to life than just material things. But all the while, I didn't want to listen. I knew I was the king of my own destiny. Little did I know, I wasn't.

"Thankfully, Will was my friend. When my wife kicked me out, my very good friend took me in and gently guided me in understanding about the love of Christ," Phillip said.

"Did your friend lead you to Christ?" George asked.

"No, I was actually led to Christ—" Phillip broke off his own sentence and looked around them. "I was led to Christ right here at this cabin." He pointed to an area just beyond them next to the water's edge. "Right over there."

"When you say you were led to Christ, what exactly does that mean?" Xavier asked.

"It means that I accepted Christ as my Lord and Savior. When I professed that Christ was my Lord and Savior and stated that I believe He died on the cross for my sins, I became saved," Phillip said.

"Is that all there is to becoming saved? That's all I would have to do?" Xavier asked. "Don't you have to be in a church and have a ceremony to become saved?"

"No, sir," Phillip said. "I used to think that way also. I used to think that being in the church and being a part of the church meant there were all these stringent rules you had to follow, and to be a Christian, you had to be just downright perfect. But with the help of my friend, I learned better.

"One morning, out here by this very lake, the minister who was running the retreat led me in what they call the sinner's prayer. You can say the sinner's prayer anywhere, by a lake, in a church, or even sitting in your car in a parking lot. It doesn't matter where you say the prayer. What matters is that you say it in earnest, with all sincerity, believing without a shadow of doubt that Jesus Christ is your Lord and Savior," Phillip said.

Xavier nodded his head.

Phillip could tell that Xavier was in deep thought. He

took in every word, as if in a desert thirsting for water. In some ways Xavier reminded him of himself when he first started learning about Christ.

"So you got everything back, huh? Your wife and kids?" Travis asked.

"Yeah," Phillip said.

"So God really did bless you," Travis said.

"God had been blessing me all the while. Shelby and I were already back together before we even came to this retreat, so my family had been physically restored well before we ever came." Phillip opened the bottle of water and took a couple of sips.

"But I still felt like something was missing in my life, and it was here that I found what it was. I got saved and haven't looked back since." Phillip laughed. "Now I am not saying there haven't been ups and downs since I got saved. But I know I've got the Lord on my side, so that lets me know I don't have to do it all by myself."

Xavier hung his head and took in deep breaths. He clasped his hands together and started nodding his head. "That's it. That's what I want . . . what I need. Will you lead me to Christ? I want to say the sinner's prayer."

Placing the bottle of water in the cup holder on the chair, Phillip said, "Yes, my brother. I'd be honored to lead you in the sinner's prayer."

All four men stood and held hands. As Phillip led the prayer, Xavier repeated. In the end, Xavier accepted Jesus as his Lord and Savior. Afterward, Phillip prayed for Xavier as a new brother in Christ and also prayed for the prosperity of each of the couples attending the retreat.

Once Phillip was done, he hugged Xavier, congratulating him. George did the same, and then began clapping his hands, shouting, "Hallelujah."

Travis also gave Xavier a hug. The men were so enthralled in celebration, they hadn't noticed the women return from their boat ride.

"What is going on here?" Shelby asked.

"Xavier just got saved," Travis said.

"What?" Charlotte asked.

"I just got saved, baby." Xavier made his way toward Charlotte. Once they reached each other, he repeated his words. "I just got saved."

"Are you serious?" Charlotte said, looking around at the other men.

Phillip nodded his head.

Charlotte gave Xavier a warm embrace. Overjoyed, Xavier held on to her as if for dear life.

"I'd say this calls for a celebration," Shelby said. "I have just the thing."

Shelby excused herself and entered the cabin. Xavier recapped his conversation with the men earlier and told Charlotte that he'd felt like something wasn't right in his life. He also said he realized he would need not just professional help for his problem, but God's help also.

He reassured her that he was going to be a changed man and he'd never hurt her again the way he had in the past.

Returning from the cabin, Shelby held plastic cups and a bottle of sparkling white grape juice. She handed everyone a cup as Phillip twisted the cap off of the bottle.

After being handed the bottle, Shelby poured juice into each person's cup. "Let's toast," Shelby said.

"To Xavier, may you continue to learn more about the love of Christ," Phillip said.

Everyone toasted the plastic cups.

"Xavier, may you grow and prosper with God's guidance," George said.

Again, they toasted the plastic cups and took sips of the juice.

"Xavier, congratulations on the first day of eternal life with Christ," Phillip said.

With each toast, Xavier's eyes welled with tears. Phillip could tell the man was trying his best to keep the tears in; trying to be a man, he guessed. Phillip remembered the morning he'd gotten saved. He'd cried and hadn't cared who saw it. The other couples congratulated him although there hadn't been any sparkling grape juice to commemorate the event, but he hadn't needed any. He had been fine knowing he was a true child of God.

"Hey, guys, what's up with the meat?" Shelby asked. "I thought we were trying to have a cookout sometime this evening."

Phillip turned and walked to the grill. "Oh, we are. I was just waiting for the coals to get hot enough. Then we got a little sidetracked," Phillip said.

"Okay, you're forgiven, but let's go ahead and get this show rolling. We need to continue this celebration," Shelby said.

"I've got the meats, young lady. Will you just make sure the salads and baked beans are ready?" Phillip asked her.

Shelby saluted Phillip as if she were in the military. "Yes, sir." Then she ascended the steps of the porch.

"Man, this is going to be our last dinner together," Travis said. "It will be the last supper."

"Yeah, like the last supper. Cleaver, Travis," Phillip said.

Travis nudged Beryl. "Did you hear that joke I just made? It will be the last supper." He laughed at his own joke.

"Yeah, I heard you, Travis," Beryl said. "The last supper, real funny." Phillip hadn't seen any semblance of a laugh on Beryl's face. What he saw was despondence.

And Travis hadn't seemed to notice or care as he continued to repeat his joke, making sure everyone heard it.

As Phillip placed the ribs and chicken on the grill, he thought about all three couples. Two of the couples seemed to be getting back on track. But Beryl and Travis still seemed to be at a standstill. It was as if they hadn't benefited from any of the sessions the entire week.

This bothered him. He wondered if Shelby had gotten a chance to talk with Beryl yet. He'd have to ask her later. But he'd make sure at some point before the couples left the retreat to pull Travis aside and have a talk.

Chapter 35

Phillip Tomlinson

Sunday: 6:00 A.M.

Phillip took his time rising from bed, trying his best not to wake Shelby. At the end of the bed he kneeled to say a silent morning prayer. *Dear Lord in heaven. Thank you for this another day you've blessed me to see; thank you again for eternal life. And thank you, Lord, for my new brother in Christ. Lord, I pray that you put Godly teachers and people in his path, especially during this, the infancy of his salvation.*

Dear Lord, I pray that you watch over each of these couples as they make their way back home. Please bring back to their remembrance most, if not all, of what I've tried to impart to them this past week. Lord, you are all knowing, and only you know the beginning as well as the end.

Lord, I have a heaviness in my heart where the Highgates are concerned. I pray that you will guide them in the direction they should go—and that your will shall be done. My hope is that they'll be able to work through any problems they are having. And that if there are any other words of impartation you have for me to tell them, you will let me know so that I can do so.

I also pray that you will continue the work that has been

started here at this retreat in regard to the Joneses and the Knights. Thank you so very much for using me as your vessel in these two couples' lives.

And last, but most certainly not least, Lord please continue to bless Shelby and me as we do our part in assisting with the growth and development of your kingdom.

I praise you, Lord, and I thank you, Lord, in your Son Jesus' name. In a whisper, Phillip then said, "Amen."

Upon standing, he heard movement coming from the kitchen area. It sounded like the refrigerator closing. He slipped on his robe to see who was there. He hoped it was Travis, though he doubted it because he was always known to be late for breakfast each morning. Phillip guessed he was sleeping until the last possible minute, pushing to get as much sleep as possible.

Stepping into the kitchen, Phillip saw Travis standing in front of the sink, drinking the last of the sparkling white grape juice.

Phillip said a silent thanks to God and greeted the man. "Good morning."

"Morning," Travis mumbled.

"You're up a little early," Phillip said.

"Yeah, I couldn't sleep last night, and I was thirsty." Travis downed the remaining juice in the glass, rinsed it and placed it in the sink. "I'm going to try and get a few more z's. I'll see you in a couple of hours."

"Hey, Travis, hold up," Phillip said. "Can I have a word with you for a moment? I wanted to talk without anyone else around."

Phillip saw a dread like dismay cover Travis's face.

"Right now? Can it wait until after breakfast? I'm still a little tired," Travis complained.

Phillip wondered what reason Travis had to be tired. He hadn't lifted a hand to help with the cookout the day before. As he thought about it even more, the man hadn't offered a helping hand with anything that didn't benefit him.

"Yes, right now." Phillip wasn't going to be able to act like this was just a casual conversation. He felt like he was talking to his teenage son—like someone who needed to be guided and told what to do. "Why don't we have a seat in the living room?" Phillip said.

Travis looked toward his bedroom with longing in his eyes, but Phillip wasn't budging. This man needed straight talk. He didn't need innuendos or someone being passive aggressive in order to try to get him to do the right thing.

Once they were seated, Phillip said, "Look, I'm not going to beat around the bush and waste my time or yours."

Travis yawned, slumping back in his seat. "Okay, so what did you want to talk about?"

"Travis, you have got to wake up to what your wife is trying to tell you. I don't know what you are hearing when you talk with her. But I hear her silent cry loud and clear. She's screaming that if you don't get it together, or at least even act like you've got it together before you leave this retreat, she's probably going to leave you," Phillip said. He hoped he wasn't reading Beryl wrong, and he also hoped he hadn't stepped completely out of line, but deep down his gut told him he was right about what he was saying and doing.

"Aw man. Is that all you wanted to talk about?" Travis said. He waved his hand as if swatting a fly.

"Is that all?"

"Yeah, you don't know Beryl like I know her. She complains about stuff I do and don't do sometimes, but she is all bark and no bite. She ain't going to leave me. She loves me. And she ain't the type of woman who wants to be without a man. Besides, she wouldn't be able to take care of those kids by herself. So don't you even worry about my wife leaving me, because she ain't. She's said it before, and we are still together. She keeps nagging me about getting a job, and I'll get something when I get home to make her happy."

"Do you hear yourself? You'll get a job if it will make her happy? How do you feel having your wife take care of you?" Phillip asked.

"She ain't taking care of me. I work sometimes, but things happen, you know. And I know how the system works, so I normally collect unemployment, so she ain't footing the whole bill. I do contribute."

"Oh, really? Do you even know how much it cost to attend this retreat?"

"Nah, she said she wanted me to come so I told her I would, but I wasn't going to pay for it. She paid for it, just like she pays for other things when she's claiming she doesn't have any money. I know she's got a secret bank account somewhere. I just haven't figured out where it is yet.

"But it's all good. Don't sweat it, man. I got this," Travis said.

Phillip shook his head. He couldn't believe this man's audacity. And if he weren't sitting there live and in person, hearing the nonsense that was falling out of his mouth like the water at Niagara Falls, he wouldn't have believed it.

"Are you done?" Travis asked.

"Yeah, go ahead and get some rest." Phillip wasn't going to waste anymore time or words with him.

Travis stood. "Thanks for all your concern, and this vacation was pretty nice. I've always wanted to visit the mountains."

Phillip wanted to literally take the man and shake

some sense into him. He'd heard of people getting book sense and other people getting common sense, but he hadn't been aware of the group of people that got neither. Phillip figured he'd met the first person in that other line.

Chapter 36

Phillip Tomlinson

Sunday: 10:20 A.M.

"Thanks again for everything. Are you sure I can't help you pack up some of this stuff in the kitchen?" Charlotte asked.

"No, but thanks for offering. We aren't leaving until tomorrow, so Phillip and I will take care of it."

"Thanks, man, for your help. And thank you for helping me start my walk with Christ," Xavier said.

Phillip gave Xavier a firm handshake and hug. "It was a pleasure, my brother. Make sure you seek Godly advice when you get back home. My email address is in the back of your packet. Feel free to email me. I'm no expert, but I'd be glad to offer any advice I can."

"Thanks, I appreciate that," Xavier said.

Phillip helped the couple take their bags to their SUV. Upon ascending the front porch steps, George and Nina walked out of the front door.

"Hey, you need some help with your bags?" Phillip asked.

"You know we do," Nina said. "You know I'm traveling like Eddie Murphy in *Coming to America*."

Phillip laughed. "You said it, I didn't."

"Shoot, I said it too," George said. "Thanks, I could use the help."

Phillip stepped onto the front door and picked up two of the suitcases. Once George and Nina's SUV was packed, Phillip and Shelby said their goodbyes to them also.

"Nina, you let me know how everything goes with your doctor, and if you need to talk, I'm a phone call away," Shelby said.

Nina patted her purse. "I've got your number, and thank you. I don't know what I would have done the last couple of days without your help."

Shelby gave Nina a firm hug. "Don't worry about that. Everything will be fine, and you are both going to get through this." Shelby gave George a hug also.

"Phillip, if you need anything, don't hesitate to call me. God does have great things in store for you, my brother; just get ready," George said.

"Thanks, man." Phillip gave George a brawny hug.

With that, George and Nina, left to head back to Greenville.

Almost ten minutes passed before Beryl and Travis emerged from their room.

"Hey, where is everybody?" Travis asked.

"The other two couples left about ten minutes ago," Phillip said.

"Ah, I wanted to say goodbye to them. And I wanted to get both George and Xavier's autograph. Oh well." Travis hunched his shoulders.

"Thank you, Phillip and Shelby, for all your work this week. I really appreciate all you did," Beryl said. She gave Phillip and Shelby hugs as if not wanting to let go. "Well, I guess we'd better get on the road."

"Hey, Beryl," Shelby said. She looked around for a pen and piece of paper. "Here is my cell phone number and my email address. Call me sometime and let me know how you all are doing. We can swap tips on raising kids."

Beryl smiled for what seemed like the first time in days. "Sure, Shelby, I'll do that. Thank you." With downcast eyes, she picked up her suitcase and purse and headed for the front door.

"Beryl, let me get that for you," Phillip offered, taking the suitcase into his hand.

Suddenly Travis spoke up. "Ah, no; I got it, man." He took the case from Phillip. "Thanks anyway."

Phillip took a deep breath.

"Have a safe trip," Shelby said.

"Thanks, we will," Travis said.

Phillip and Shelby stood on the front porch as they watched Travis and Beryl's car pull off. With no surprise to Phillip, Beryl was in the driver's seat.

"Is the door locked?" Shelby asked.

"Yep."

"And are you sure Reverend and Mrs. Nelson are not due to come back until tomorrow?" Shelby asked.

"Yes, honey. It's just me and you here, and God willing, we won't be interrupted."

"Okay then." Shelby pulled out an armful of blankets and comforters and placed them on the floor in front of the fireplace. Then she pulled out a tray she'd made with cheese, crackers, cantaloupe, honeydew, and pineapple chunks.

After setting the tray on the floor next to the blankets, Shelby pulled two glasses out of the cabinet and poured a bottle of chilled sparkling grape juice. "Now where were we seven days ago?" she asked.

Understanding exactly what Shelby meant, Phillip said, "I believe we were..." He placed his hands on Shelby's cheeks and began to kiss her. "Right here," he whispered.

Shelby smiled. "So that's where we'll take it from."

Epilogue

Phillip Tomlinson

8 months later

"Just a minute," Phillip called out toward his front door. Upon opening it, he saw his best friend. "Will, what's up, man?" Phillip greeted the man with a firm handshake and hug. Will stepped into their foyer.

Seeing the mailman pull up, Phillip asked Will to hold on for a second and left to retrieve the mail. Upon returning, Phillip again asked his friend what was up.

"Nothing much. I just had a question for you." Will paused. "I tried to call but your cell phone keeps going straight to voicemail and so does your home phone."

"Kids, man," Phillip said. "Phillip Jr. has put my cell phone in a secret hiding place and we've been looking for it a couple of days. If I can't find it soon, I'll have to just get another one."

Phillip noticed his friend was acting a little strange. "Come on in and have a seat." He turned to lead his friend toward the family room.

"No, I can't stay long. I just wanted to ask you something real quick. I've got to get back home. Morgan needs me to do some things for her."

"Oh, okay. What did you need?"

Will paused for a moment, visually struggling to make the words form in his mouth. "You know when you and Shelby were having problems a few years ago and you went to that couple's retreat?"

"Yeah. The retreat was wonderful. You know I was able to lead one of the retreats a few months back. It did wonders for Shelby and me, and it also did wonders for some of the couples I taught. I'm thinking about going up there again to lead another retreat within the next few months."

Phillip wondered why his friend was asking. "Why do you ask? Do you know someone who is thinking about marriage counseling?"

A far off look formed in Will's eyes, like he was concentrating hard on something. Then he said, "Yes, I do know of someone who would like more information about the retreat." Will paused again, "Me."

"You?" Phillip asked in bewilderment. "You and your wife are having problems?"

Will nodded his head. "I don't really want to get into it right now. I'm still trying to sort some things out. But I know the retreat worked wonders for you and Shelby, and I was thinking maybe it will work for our marriage."

Phillip didn't know what to say. It did make sense now though. Will hadn't been acting like himself in recent months. He wondered what kinds of problems they could be having. From the outside looking in, Will and his wife, Morgan, had what seemed like the perfect marriage. He didn't think his friend had been stepping out on his wife; the man had been a virgin until he got married. He wondered if it were the opposite, and Will's wife was stepping out on him. Then Phillip cut his thoughts off. He shouldn't be thinking anything bad about his friend's marriage.

"Will, I'm here for you if you need me, not only as a friend and fraternity brother, but also as a man of God and your brother in Christ."

"I know," Will said. Looking at his watch and with urgency, he said, "Can I get that information from you? I really need to be getting back to my house."

"Oh, yeah. Just a second." Phillip left his friend standing by the front door to retrieve a sheet of paper to write down the information.

After he handed it to over, Phillip reiterated, "I'm here if you need me."

Will looked at the piece of paper and held it as if it were gold. "Thanks. If I need to talk, I know exactly who to call." He turned toward the door.

Reaching for the doorknob, Phillip gave his friend a hearty pat on the back. "Hang in there."

"I'm trying," Will said. "Talk with you later." Then he left.

Closing the door behind him, Phillip looked upward. "Dear Lord, if it ain't one thing, then it's another."

"Found it," he heard Shelby exclaim from upstairs.

"Found what?" Phillip asked, calling back upstairs to her.

"Your cell phone."

"Great," Phillip said his voice void of enthusiasm.

A few moments later, Shelby descended the stairs. Phillip hadn't moved from the spot he was standing in deep in thought about his friend.

"The mail came?" Shelby asked.

As if coming out of a trance, Phillip said, "Yeah. I put it on the kitchen counter."

"Oh, look," Shelby said with excitement in her voice.

Phillip joined his wife in the kitchen.

"It's a letter from Charlotte and Xavier. The retreat forwarded the postcard."

"What does it say?" Phillip's ears perked up.

Shelby read the letter, *"Dear Phillip and Shelby, we hope this card finds you doing well. We just wanted to thank you again for being a part of our life changing moment and helping mend our broken family. Xavier and I are doing well. We took all you taught us at the retreat to heart and have studied the scriptures you gave us.*

We communicate throughout the day about big and small things. We strive for agreement between us, but when we don't agree on something, we pray about it and find a middle ground.

And Xavier has been getting professional help for his problems.

We have some good news to share. Xavier and I are expecting a baby! I am about three months pregnant and as ecstatic I don't know what. And if it's possible, Xavier is even more ecstatic!

I encourage you to keep on doing what you are doing to help marriages and families. Stay blessed always, Charlotte and Xavier Knight"

Shelby closed the letter. "That is wonderful. See, I told you the retreat was successful. Now we know the status of all three couples."

Phillip shook his head. "That is wonderful news."

"Then why are you shaking your head?"

"I am glad Nina has been totally weaned off the valium. She and George are on that second honeymoon as we speak, right?" Phillip asked.

Shelby nodded her head. "Yeah, they are. They were supposed to have left yesterday for St. Lucia."

"Two out of three ain't bad, I guess," Phillip said again shaking his head as he remembered the email Shelby had received from Beryl a month before.

"No, it isn't bad. So stop shaking your head like that."

"I just wish all the couples could have been helped by

this retreat. It is a sad thing that Beryl and Travis weren't able to stay together," Phillip said.

"Remember the email she sent me said the retreat had been a blessing to her. The retreat helped her to evaluate many aspects of her life, including the problems in her marriage. So even though they didn't stay together, you still helped her." Shelby placed her hand on Phillip's forearm.

"She said even before the retreat that she'd done all she could do to try and keep the family together. The retreat helped her to be more at peace with her decision."

"No word about Travis, huh?"

"Nope. She didn't mention how he was doing," Shelby said.

"I haven't heard anything from him either."

"Maybe no news is good news," Shelby said with optimism.

"Maybe no news is just that; no news. I don't want to judge the man, but I don't think Travis gave it his all. He was a fast talker and seemed like the type who just liked to take the easy road. There are some strongholds where he is concerned. And at some point, he is going to have to have a come to Jesus meeting with himself," Phillip said.

"Amen to that," Shelby said as she nodded her head in agreement.

Redemption Lake

Discussion Questions

1. Do you think Charlotte went to the extreme to gather information about Xavier?

2. What would you have done if you found out your spouse/significant other was cheating on you?

3. Do you think Beryl stayed with Travis or not?

4. How effective do you think Phillip and Shelby were in helping these couples?

5. Do you think Travis was justified in his reasons for not being able to find a job? (A) It being so hard for a black man? (B) Companies not appreciating his educational background?

6. Do you know anyone as loving and forgiving as George Jones?

7. Do you believe couples should stay together for better or for worse, no matter the circumstance?

8. If you answered no to the question above, then under what circumstances would you say it is okay to end a marriage?

9. Would you have stayed with Travis?

10. Would you have stayed with Xavier?

11. Would you have stayed with Nina?

12. Do you know of any couples coping with some of the same issues these couples coped with?

13. Have you ever accused someone of doing something wrong based on circumstantial evidence?

14. Do you agree with the statements Phillip made about the brain distorting things?

15. Do you ever find yourself asking yourself—Why did I got married?

16. Do you ever find yourself asking why you continue to stay married?

17. Would you consider going to a marriage counselor if you and your spouse were having marital problems?

18. Do you think any of the information Phillip gave the couples during the sessions would help you in your marriage—either to help rebuild your marriage or just to strengthen your marriage?

19. If you are unmarried, do you plan to have some type of spiritual and/or professional premarital counseling?

20. If you knew of someone going through marital problems, would you tell them about this novel?

About The Author

Monique Miller is a native of North Carolina. She currently lives in the Raleigh Durham, North Carolina area with her family, where she is working on her fourth novel. For more information about the author, you can log onto *www.authormoniquemiller.com* or contact her at *authormoniquemiller@yahoo.com*.

Urban Christian His Glory Book Club!

Established January 2007, *UC His Glory Book Club* is another way by which to introduce to the literary world, Urban Book's much-anticipated new imprint, *Urban Christian* and its authors. We are an online book club supporting Urban Christian authors by purchasing, reading and providing written reviews of the authors' books that are read. *UC His Glory* welcomes both men and women of the literary world who have a passion for reading Christian based fiction.

UC His Glory is the brainchild of Joylynn Jossel, Author and Executive Editor of Urban Christian and Kendra Norman-Bellamy, Copy Editor for Urban Christian. The book club will provide support, positive feedback, encouragement and a forum whereby members can openly discuss and review the literary works of Urban Christian authors. In the future, we anticipate broadening our spectrum of services to include: online author chats, author spotlights, interviews with your favorite Urban Christian author(s), special online groups for *UC Book Club* members, ability to post reviews on the website and amazon.com, membership ID cards, *UC His Glory* Yahoo Group and much more.

Even though there will be no membership fees attached to becoming a member of *UC His Glory Book Club,* we do expect our members to be active, committed and to follow the guidelines of the Book Club.

UC His Glory members pledge to:

- Follow the guidelines of *UC His Glory Book Club*.
- Provide input, opinions, and reviews that build up, rather than tear down.
- Commit to purchasing, reading and discussing featured book(s) of the month.
- Respect the Christian beliefs of *UC His Glory Book Club*.
- Believe that Jesus is the Christ, Son of the Living God

We look forward to the online fellowship.

Many Blessings to You!

Shelia E Lipsey
President
UC His Glory Book Club

**Visit the official Urban Christian Book Club website at *www.uchisglorybookclub.net*

MILLE   HVINW
Miller, Monique.
Redemption Lake /

VINSON
05/10